DO YOU KNOW
WHAT DAY
TOMORROW IS?

DO YOU KNOW WHAT DAY TOMORROW IS?

A Teacher's Almanac
Revised Edition

By Lee Bennett Hopkins and Misha Arenstein

Scholastic Inc.

New York   Toronto   London   Auckland   Sydney

ACKNOWLEDGMENTS

Curtis Brown, Ltd., for "Good Books, Good Times!" by Lee Bennett
Hopkins. Copyright © 1985 by Lee Bennett Hopkins; "Last Laugh" by
Lee Bennett Hopkins. Copyright © 1974 by Lee Bennett Hopkins;
"No Matter" by Lee Bennett Hopkins. Copyright © 1973 by Lee Bennett
Hopkins; "Valentine Feelings" by Lee Bennett Hopkins.
Copyright © 1975 by Lee Bennett Hopkins. All reprinted by permission
of Curtis Brown, Ltd.

Prince Redcloud for "Now" and "Spring." Both used by permission
of the author, who controls all rights.

ISBN 0-590-42617-6
Copyright © 1990 by Lee Bennett Hopkins and Misha Arenstein
All rights reserved. Published by Scholastic Inc.

12 11 10 9 8 7 6 5 4 3 2 1   0 1 2 3 4 5/9

Printed in the U.S.A.
First Scholastic printing, January 1990

To Mac and Mollie Aarons
&
Charles J. Egita
for many happy tomorrows.

Lee Bennett Hopkins
Misha Arenstein

Scarborough, New York, 1990

CONTENTS

Introduction............................... ix

January.................................... 1

February 28

March..................................... 54

April...................................... 80

May.......................................102

June 122

July 138

August 155

September 165

October 185

November 210

December 233

Index 251

INTRODUCTION

This revised and expanded edition of *Do You Know What Day Tomorrow Is?* was completed 15 years after its first publication in 1975. We have reedited, reorganized, enlarged, and updated each of the entries in terms of important happenings and events that have occurred since the mid-1970s.

Do You Know What Day Tomorrow Is? is a compendium of concise information about people, places, events, and funfacts selected to tie in with every area of the elementary school curriculum. The text grew out of actual experiences we have shared with children and many events that children have helped us develop. Girls and boys eagerly celebrate happenings; in the process they gain insight into historical and contemporary affairs and develop appreciation of people and events.

We firmly believe that children are more responsive when they are called upon to participate in a plan. Therefore, numerous opportunities are suggested for involving students with the book's content. You and your students can use the almanac as a constant reminder of what is coming or what is here.

Each month contains information on birthdays of famous people from a variety of professions and cultures — historical figures, scientists, artists, musicians, writers, religious leaders, and sports personalities. Major holidays and some minor ones are described, as well as how they came to be celebrated and how they are observed both in the United States and around the world today. To round out the year, we have included unusual events and interesting facts about taken-for-granted things that children will enjoy learning about. Each chapter begins with a brief account of the origin of the month's name, the flower and birthstone associated with the month, as well as a poem of the month.

Many a day can be enlivened when children celebrate something. Youngsters delight in real ceremonies, especially when the celebration helps bring joy into the classroom. Students from first through sixth grade can use the book on their own for planning things to come. It is hoped that the entries will encourage them to supplement the facts presented by flavoring them with their own additional findings.

Another way to use this book is to encourage a group of students to become current event historians; they can write a supplement of contemporary dates and events to add to this volume's daily records.

All the reference books and nonprint media cited have been carefully reviewed and chosen with children in mind; they provide many opportunities for multilevel reading and learning about the same event. School or public librarians can direct children to these sources, most of which are works by popular writers for children.

This volume was planned to dip in and dip out of. Use it when you can and when you want to — weekly, monthly, or every day. Individual entries contain practical, tried-and-tested ideas for activities that children can and have engaged in.

We hope these accounts of people and events will prompt students to want to learn more and to explore further the subjects included in this book.

Happy reading, happy teaching, and happy every day!

Lee Bennett Hopkins
Misha Arenstein

◆

January

FLOWER   ◆   BIRTHSTONE
Carnation   Garnet

The first month receives its name from the Latin, *Januarius*, which was derived from *janua* meaning "door." The word came from the name of the god Janus, who ancient Romans believed opened the gates of heaven to release daylight and closed them when dusk arrived. The god also looked both to the past and to the future.

JANUARY POEM OF THE MONTH

TURTLE SOUP

"Beautiful Soup, so rich and green,
Waiting in a hot tureen!
Who for such dainties would not stoop?
Soup of the evening, beautiful Soup!
Soup of the evening, beautiful Soup!
     Beau — ootiful Soo — oop!
     Beau — ootiful Soo — oop!
Soo — oop of the e — e — evening,
     Beautiful, beautiful Soup!

Beautiful Soup! Who cares for fish,
Game, or any other dish?
Who would not give all else for two p
ennyworth only of beautiful Soup?
     Beau — ootiful Soo — oop!
     Beau — ootiful Soo — oop!
Soo — oop of the e — e — evening,
     Beautiful, beauti — FUL SOUP!"

                 — Lewis Carroll

JANUARY
New Year's Day

Happy New Year!
   No one really knows when the custom of celebrating the New Year began, but New Year's Day is a holiday that is celebrated all over the world — often at different times. In the United States, of course, the annual celebration takes place on January 1 and usually starts well before midnight on December 31. (*See* January/February, Chinese New Year; March

21, Iranian New Year; September/October, Jewish New Year.)

When the children return to school from winter recess, discuss New Year's resolutions with them. Each child can write out one or several resolutions that she or he would like to keep during the new year. Place them on a bulletin board display entitled "Our New Year's Resolutions." Decorate the board with balloons and leftover New Year's Eve paraphernalia — party hats, streamers, and the like.

A good volume to share with students to aid in the celebration is the collection of poetry, New Year's Poems, selected by Myra Cohn Livingston, illustrated by Margot Tomes (Holiday House, 1987). The collection features 16 selections.

JANUARY 1, 1735
Birth Date of Paul Revere

Paul Revere helped to establish colonial independence from Great Britain. He took part in the Boston Tea Party and made his famous ride to warn the patriots that the British troops were coming on April 18, 1775.

Although best remembered for his patriotism, Revere was also an engraver and a master silversmith. He designed the first Continental money and official seal of the Colonies, and his Revere bowl designs are still in demand today.

Read to your students Henry Wadsworth Longfellow's famous poem "Paul Revere's Ride." Explain to younger girls and boys how brave and persistent the patriots were in their fight for independence. Older students can read about the American Revolution in Robert Lawson's Mr. Revere and I (Little, Brown, 1953), a humorous account told from the viewpoint of Revere's horse, Scheherazade. Students will also reap a great deal of information by reading And Then What Happened Paul Revere? by Jean Fritz, illustrated by Margot Tomes (Coward, 1973; also in paperback).

Revere died on May 10, 1818, at the age of 83. (*See also* April 18–19, 1775.)

JANUARY 1, 1752
Birth Date of Betsy Ross

It is said that Betsy Ross made the first hand-sewn flag for the Continental Congress in 1777, at her home in Philadelphia, Pennsylvania. The flag was formally adopted by the Congress on June 14, 1777, which became Flag Day. Except for the addition of several stars and the rearrangement of stars and stripes, today's American flag remains essentially the same as the original. (*See also* June 14, 1777.)

JANUARY 1, 1863

The Emancipation Proclamation was signed. This document was conceived as a military expedient rather than as a moral declaration ending slavery. Six months prior to issuing the Proclamation, President Abraham Lincoln warned the rebelling states that such an act was forthcoming; as commander in chief, the president was fearful of the military use the South could make of its slave manpower. The Emancipation Proclamation freed only slaves held in seceded states. Nevertheless, it set the stage for the Thirteenth Amendment to the Constitution, which outlawed slavery in the entire United States. (*See* December 18, 1865.) Abolitionists, including the black leader Frederick Douglass, hailed the Proclamation as a historic step in the fight for freedom.

Older girls and boys might discuss President Lincoln's attitude toward slavery.

JANUARY 2, 1788

Georgia became the fourth state to ratify the Constitution.

Flower: Cherokee Rose
Tree: Live Oak
Bird: Brown Thrasher

JANUARY 2, 1893

The first commemorative postage stamp was issued by the U.S. Post Office Department. It was called the Columbia issue in honor of the four-hundredth anniversary of the discovery of America. Student stamp collectors might bring in some commemorative stamps to show and discuss with the class.

JANUARY 3, 1892
Birth Date of John Ronald Reuel Tolkien

J.R.R. Tolkien was born in Bloemfontein, South Africa, and brought to England at the age of four years old. He acquired fame with his epic trilogy, *The Lord of the Rings* (Houghton, 1945–1955).

While working on the trilogy, he wrote *The Hobbit*, which serves as an introduction to the works. The character Bilbo Baggins is synonymous with fantasy.

The author died in February 1973 in England. Your better readers will enjoy Tolkien's work.

JANUARY 3, 1959

Alaska became the forty-ninth state.

Flower: Forget-Me-Not
Tree: Sitka Spruce
Bird: Willow Ptarmigan

JANUARY 4, 1785
Birth Date of Jakob Grimm

Both Jakob (1785–1863) and his brother Wilhelm Karl (1786–1859) were born in Hanau, Germany. Following in their father's footsteps, both boys began to study law, but they had tremendous interest in German poetry and folklore. They are best known for their collections of German fairy tales and for producing the *German Dictionary*, a pioneer effort that served as a model for later lexicographers. The first volume of *Grimm's Fairy Tales* (1812) contained 86 stories; the second, published in 1815, contained 70.

Single editions of the Grimm stories abound in library collections. Several to look for are the 1973 Caldecott Honor Book *Snow-White and the Seven Dwarfs*, lavishly illustrated with full-color paintings by Nancy Ekholm Burkert (Farrar, Straus & Giroux, 1972; also in paperback); *King Grisly Beard*, translated by Edgar Taylor with illustrations by Caldecott Award winner Maurice Sendak (Farrar, Straus & Giroux, 1973); *The Devil with the Three Golden Hairs*, illustrated by Caldecott Award winner Nonny Hogrogian (Alfred A. Knopf, 1983); and *The Bremen Town Musician* translated by Anthea Bell, illustrated by Joseph Palecek (Picture Book Studio, 1988). For teacher reference and for older readers, the two-volume set of 27 stories entitled *The Juniper Tree and Other Tales from Grimm*, selected by Lore Segal and Maurice Sendak with pictures by Maurice Sendak, is not to be missed (Farrar, Straus & Giroux, 1973).

In 1983, the discovery of an unknown tale by Wilhelm Grimm made headlines around the world, and in 1988, *Dear*

Mili, translated by Ralph Manheim with illustrations by Maurice Sendak, was brought to publication (Farrar, Straus & Giroux).

JANUARY 4, 1809
Birth Date of Louis Braille

Louis Braille was born in a village near Paris, France. At the age of three, due to an accident in his father's workshop, he was blinded. Seventeen years later he published a system of printing and writing for the blind, which he had adapted from the night writing system used by Charles Barbier, a French army captain. Soldiers sent messages at night by punching coded dots on thick paper. The Braille system employs raised dots representing letters, signs, and numbers. It is still used by the visually impaired today.

Braille died on January 16, 1852. On the door of the house where he was born are these words: "He opened the doors of knowledge to all those who cannot see."

Middle-grade readers can learn more about him in Louis Braille: The Boy Who Invented Books for the Blind by Margaret Davidson (Scholastic, 1971).

JANUARY 4, 1896

Utah became the forty-fifth state.

Flower: Sego Lily
Tree: Blue Spruce
Bird: Sea Gull

JANUARY 5, 1864
Birth Date of George Washington Carver

George Washington Carver, born a slave in Diamond Grove, Missouri, became one of America's leading scientists. In his experiments with the peanut he found more than three hundred products that could be made from it, including wood dyes, soap, linoleum, plastic, flour, paint, ink, and many different types of oil. Dr. Carver worked to bolster the economy and agriculture of the South by introducing by-products for sweet potatoes, soybeans, and cotton stalks as well.

After his death in 1943, many of his personal belongings and scientific papers were placed in the Carver Museum on the campus of Tuskegee Institute in Alabama where he had worked for more than 60 years. In New York State, Carver Day is celebrated on January 5.

An interesting story is told of how the name of America's first president became part of Carver's name. While he was in college another George Carver there often received his mail. He decided to add a middle name — Washington!

Two books about Carver are *A Weed Is a Flower: The Life of George Washington Carver*, written and illustrated by Aliki (Prentice-Hall, 1965) for elementary grades, and *A Pocketful of Goobers: A Story About George Washington Carver* by Barbara Mitchell (Carolrhoda, 1986) for middle-grade readers.

JANUARY 5, 1925

Nellie Taylor Ross became the first woman governor of a state — Wyoming. Do your students know the name of the governor of their state?

JANUARY 6, 1878
Birth Date of Carl Sandburg

> If poems could be explained, then poets would have to
> leave out roses, sunsets, faces from their poems.

— From Carl Sandburg
"Short Talk on Poetry"
in *Early Moon* (Harcourt, 1930)

Carl Sandburg, the son of Swedish immigrants, was born in
Galesburg, Illinois. His birthplace at 331 East 3rd Street is now
a memorial that attracts thousands of visitors each year. During
his 89 years, Sandburg worked at a potpourri of jobs, including journalist, political organizer, historian, folk singer, and
poet. He spent years researching and writing a six-volume
biography of Abraham Lincoln; in 1940, he was awarded the
Pulitzer Prize in History for the last four volumes, *Abraham
Lincoln: The War Years* (Harcourt, 1939). In 1950, he received a
second Pulitzer Prize, this time for *Complete Poems* (Harcourt,
1949).

Mr. Sandburg wrote two books of poetry for children, *Early
Moon* (1930) and *Wind Song* (1960; both Harcourt Brace Jovanovich; both in paperback). In 1982, the award-winning *Rain-
bows Are Made: Poems by Carl Sandburg*, collected by Lee Bennett
Hopkins, illustrated by Fritz Eichenberg, appeared, featuring
70 selections grouped into six sections (Harcourt Brace Jovanovich; also in paperback). Students can hear the poet read
from his work on the recording *Poems for Children and Carl
Sandburg Reading Fog and Other Poems* (Caedmon).

In 1988, a newly illustrated volume of his *Rootabaga Stories*
appeared, illustrated by Michael Hague (Harcourt Brace Jovanovich). In 1989, a biography was published for middle-grade
readers, *Good Morning, Mr. President: A Story about Carl Sandburg*
by Barbara Mitchell, illustrated with black-and-white pictures
by Dane Collins (Carolrhoda).

Sandburg died on July 22, 1967, at the age of 89, in Connemara, North Carolina.

JANUARY 6, 1912

New Mexico became the forty-seventh state.

Flower: Yucca
Tree: Piñon
Bird: Roadrunner

JANUARY 7, 1800
Birth Date of Millard Fillmore, Thirteenth President

Born in:	Summer Hill, New York
Occupation:	Farmer, lawyer
President:	1850–1853, Whig
Died:	March 8, 1874
	Buffalo, New York

About Fillmore
★ Youth spent in poverty.
★ Enacted a law against debtors' prisons, jails for those who owed money.
★ Became president upon Zachary Taylor's death, July 9, 1850.

During His Term
★ Compromise of 1850 was passed with the help of Daniel Webster and Henry Clay. It provided a ten-year respite in the North-South clash over slavery.
★ Created first White House library by bringing books into the executive mansion.
★ Dispatched Commodore Matthew Perry's fleet to Japan in

1853, opening up that nation to trade and diplomatic relations.
★ Approved the Fugitive Slave Bill.

JANUARY 9, 1788

Connecticut became the fifth state to ratify the Constitution.

Flower: Mountain Laurel
Tree: White Oak
Bird: American Robin

JANUARY 9, 1913
Birth Date of Richard Milhous Nixon, Thirty-seventh President

Born in: Yorba Linda, California
Occupation: Congressman, senator, lawyer, author
President: 1969–1974, Republican

About Nixon
★ Early anticommunist; leading member of House Committee on Un-American Activities.
★ Twice Eisenhower's vice president.
★ Lost 1960 presidential election to Kennedy.

During His Terms
★ Elected in 1968 and 1972 with Vice President Spiro T. Agnew.
★ Reelected to second term by landslide majority.
★ Vice President Agnew forced to resign because of criminal charges.
★ Gerald R. Ford chosen vice president in October 1973.
★ Initiated progress in foreign affairs: Communist China admitted to the United Nations, détente with U.S.S.R. began,

diplomatic relations with China reestablished, American troops withdrawn from Viet Nam, Henry Kissinger endeavored to mediate Middle Eastern peace.

★ Resigned rather than face certain impeachment for Watergate scandal of June 17, 1972, and other abuses of presidential power.

JANUARY 11, 1878

A milkman in Brooklyn, New York, delivered milk in glass bottles to his customers for the first time. Encourage children to find out how milk was delivered prior to this. How is it delivered today? What are the advantages of cardboard and plastic containers over glass bottles? What are the disadvantages?

The Milk Makers by Gail Gibbons (Macmillan, 1985; Alladin paperback) easily explains how cows produce milk and how it is processed before being delivered to stores. A reference for better readers is Milk: The Fight for Purity by James C. Giblin (T.Y. Crowell, 1986).

JANUARY 12, 1628
Birth Date of Charles Perrault

Fairy tales such as "Sleeping Beauty," "Little Red Riding Hood," "Cinderella," and "Puss in Boots" have been around for hundreds of years. These tales were passed down for generations by word of mouth; it was either Charles Perrault, a member of the French Academy, or his eldest son, Pierre Perrault d'Armancour, who first wrote them down, preserving them for generations to come.

There have been countless retellings of these tales; in the future there will undoubtedly be many more. Today is a good day to share one of the stories with a group of children. Younger boys and girls will enjoy listening to one. Older children might make comparisons of two or three published versions. Better students might try their hand at writing parodies of the tales set in contemporary times. Another reading-writing project is to have children rewrite the tales or provide new endings to favorite versions.

JANUARY 12, 1812

The first steamboat chugged down the Mississippi River to New Orleans. The Mississippi River, the longest in the United States, is sometimes called Father of the Waters. It flows for about 2,350 miles from near the Canadian border to the Gulf of Mexico. Hernando de Soto discovered the Mississippi in 1541, and it was explored in the 1670s by the Frenchman Robert La Salle.

JANUARY 12, 1933

Hattie Caraway became the first woman elected to the U.S. Senate on this date. After the death of her husband, Caraway was appointed to fill his vacant Senate seat. Everyone expected her to retire from politics, but she surprised one and all by announcing, "I am going to fight for my place in the sun." At the end of this term, she was elected to two full terms of her own, from 1933–1945.

She was also the first woman senator to preside over the Senate. On October 19, 1943, she opened the Senate proceedings and presided as president pro tempore in the absence of Vice President Henry Agard Wallace.

JANUARY 14, 1875
Birth Date of Albert Schweitzer

Albert Schweitzer, born in Alsace, was one of those rare geniuses who was involved in a multitude of activities. He was a theologian, a philosopher, a writer, a medical doctor, an organist acclaimed for his interpretations of Johann Sebastian Bach's works, and a mission director in equatorial Africa. In 1899, he received a doctoral degree in philosophy; in 1900, another for theology, and in 1913, an M.D. degree. After receiving the latter, he and his wife Hélène ventured to Lambaréné in Gabon, a province of French Equatorial Africa (after 1960, the Republic of Gabon) where, with the help of natives, he built a hospital. Later he established a leper colony. In 1952, he was awarded the Nobel Peace Prize for his efforts on behalf of "The Brotherhood of Nations." Schweitzer died on September 4, 1965. For more information on him, steer better readers to *Albert Schweitzer: Genius in the Jungle* by Joseph Gollomb (Vangard Press, 1949).

JANUARY 14, 1886
Birth Date of Hugh Lofting

Born in England, Hugh Lofting wrote many books during his lifetime but is acclaimed for his *Doctor Dolittle* series, the first of which, *The Story of Doctor Dolittle*, appeared in 1920. The novel was an immediate success. He continued writing one *Doctor Dolittle* volume per year until 1927.

The *Voyages of Doctor Dolittle* (Lothrop, 1922) won the Newbery Medal; it was also made into a movie starring Rex Harrison.

The author died on September 26, 1947, in Santa Monica, California.

This is a good day to read parts of Lofting's work or sing the song "I Talk to the Animals," from the film.

JANUARY 15, 1929
Birth Date of Dr. Martin Luther King, Jr.

Martin Lewis King, Jr., was born in Atlanta, Georgia. When he grew up he changed his middle name to Luther in honor of the Protestant leader, Martin Luther. After graduating from Morehouse College, King entered the ministry, and then Boston University where he received a PhD. He received many awards for his nonviolent, direct-action approach in seeking equal civil rights for all Americans. Time magazine chose him Man of the Year in 1963 for his leadership in the protests against segregation in Birmingham, Alabama. On August 28, 1963, Dr. King addressed more than 200,000 Americans who gathered at a march in Washington, D.C., to protest racial inequality in the United States. It was there that he made his famous "I Have a Dream" speech. (See August 28, 1963.) The following year he became the second black American to receive the Nobel Peace Prize. On April 4, 1968, Dr. King was assassinated in Memphis, Tennessee, while fighting for the rights of that city's sanitation workers. The United States observed a national mourning period of six days in memory of this great civil rights leader. In 1983, the U.S. Congress designated the third Monday in January as a federal holiday to honor his life and ideals.

The following children's books will help students understand the important role Dr. King played in contemporary history: Martin Luther King: The Peaceful Warrior by Ed Clayton, illustrated by David Hodges (Archway paperback, 1988); Marching to Freedom: The Story of Martin Luther King, Jr. by Joyce Milton (Dell paperback, 1987); Martin Luther King Day by Linda

Lowery, illustrated by Hetty Mitchell (Carolrhoda, 1987); *I Have a Dream: The Story of Martin Luther King* by Margaret Davidson (Scholastic, 1986); and *Martin Luther King, Jr., Free at Last* by David A. Adler, illustrated by Robert Casella (Holiday House, 1984).

JANUARY 16, 1978

On this date the U.S. National Aeronautics and Space Administration (NASA) accepted its first women candidates for astronauts. Sally Kirsten Ride, one of the six women chosen, became the first American woman in space in June 1983, when she traveled as a crew member on the space shuttle, *Challenger*. (See May 26, 1951.)

JANUARY 17, 1706
Birth Date of Benjamin Franklin

Benjamin Franklin was the fifteenth child and youngest son in a Boston family of 17 children. His parents were shop owners who made soap and candles. Young Franklin attended school for two years; he was excellent in reading, fair in writing, and poor in arithmetic. At age 10 he left school to help in his parents' shop. Learning on his own, Franklin became a jack-of-all-trades and master of many! As a publisher, he developed the *Pennsylvania Gazette* into one of the most successful newspapers in the colonies from 1729–1766; from 1733 to 1758 he both wrote and published *Poor Richard's Almanac*, which contains his wise and witty sayings such as "Early to bed and early to rise, makes a man healthy, wealthy and wise." He was also a civic leader, serving as Philadelphia's postmaster in 1737 and deputy postmaster general for all the colonies in 1753.

Throughout his life he displayed inventive talent. He was one of the first men in the world to experiment with electricity; he invented the lightning rod (see June 15, 1752), the Franklin stove, and bifocal eyeglasses. He was also the first scientist to study the movement of the Gulf Stream in the Atlantic Ocean. Besides all this, Franklin established an academy in Philadelphia that became the University of Pennsylvania. Franklin's political efforts centered around the then evolving United States. He was one of the guiding hands in drawing up the Declaration of Independence and played an important role in the nation's formative years. He died on April 17, 1790, at the age of 84.

An account of his life and times is detailed in *What's the Big Idea, Ben Franklin?* by Jean Fritz, illustrated by Margot Tomes (Coward, 1976; also in paperback). All children will enjoy reading or hearing selected parts of Robert Lawson's fictionalized biography, *Ben and Me* (Little, Brown, 1939; Dell paperback), a tale about the man as told by his good friend Amos the mouse, who lived in Franklin's fur cap.

JANUARY 17, 1942
Birth Date of Muhammad Ali (Cassius Clay)

Muhammad Ali, born Cassius Marcellus Clay in Louisville, Kentucky, was taught to box by a policeman, Joe Martin. When he was 17, he won the national Golden Gloves light heavyweight championship. The next year, in Rome, Italy, he was acclaimed the amateur light heavyweight champion of the world. Ali's colorful statements such as "I'm the greatest!" and his poetry made him a natural crowd pleaser who revitalized the boxing world. When he turned professional, he became the heavyweight champion of the world by defeating Sonny Liston.

The name Muhammad Ali was given him by Elijah Muhammad, leader of the Nation of Islam, a deeply religious group of Black Muslims. Ali lost his heavyweight title in 1967 when he refused to enter the armed forces; the Supreme Court later upheld his right to refuse induction because of his religious convictions. In 1971, he was defeated by Joe Frazier, who became the new world heavyweight champion. In 1974, he won his title back from George Foreman in a match held in Zaire. He lost his title to Leon Spinks in February 1978 but regained it in September 1978, becoming the only man to regain the heavyweight title twice. On December 9, 1974, New York City honored the champ by celebrating Muhammad Ali Day when he was given the city's Bronze Medallion. He retired from boxing in 1980, but returned to the ring twice, only to be defeated.

JANUARY 18, 1882
Birth Date of A.A. Milne

For over half a century, children and adults have selected *Winnie-the-Pooh* stories from library shelves. Younger children love to hear the stories read aloud; older girls and boys reread them; college students study the whimsy of Pooh's adventures along with the writings of Shakespeare and Salinger.

The author of the Pooh stories was London-born Alan Alexander Milne. His first book for children, *When We Were Very Young* (E.P. Dutton, 1924), was a classic collection of poems written for his three-year-old son. This was followed by *Now We Are Six* (E.P. Dutton, 1927). *Winnie-the-Pooh* (E.P. Dutton, 1926) and *The House at Pooh Corner* (E.P. Dutton, 1928; both in paperback) are stories about Milne's son's stuffed animals. Illustrated by Ernest Shepard, they are among the most successful books ever created for children.

There are countless editions of Milne's work available in

hardcover and paperback volumes as well as The-World-of-Pooh dolls, toys, calendars, and films.

A.A. Milne died on January 31, 1956.

JANUARY 19, 1807
Birth Date of Robert Edward Lee

> Who does not love General Lee, who would not barter life for his smile?

The above quotation was written by a Confederate foot soldier during the Gettysburg campaign. In just one sentence it tells how much General Robert E. Lee was loved. Lee commanded the largest Confederate field force, the Army of Northern Virginia, during most of the Civil War. His leadership earned him a place in history as one of the world's greatest military commanders.

A native Virginian, he graduated from West Point, ranking first in his class, and years later he became its superintendent. Lee fought with valor in the Mexican War and was offered the command of the Union Army by President Lincoln on the eve of the Civil War. In 1859, he led the detachment of the U.S. Marines that captured John Brown and his anti-slavery raiders at Harpers Ferry, Virginia. (*See* May 9, 1800.) He did not believe in slavery or breaking up the Union, but when the Civil War came, he felt greater loyalty to Virginia than to the Union.

After organizing and training Virginia's forces, he took over the command of all the Confederate armies. Although he won many important victories, the tide began to turn in 1863 when he lost his ablest general, Stonewall Jackson, at Chancellorsville and suffered defeat at the Battle of Gettysburg. (*See* July 1, 1863.) In April 1865, after a long and bitter retreat through Virginia, he surrendered to General Ulysses S. Grant at the Appomattox courthouse, ending the War between the States.

After the Civil War, General Lee urged the North and South to reconcile their differences, and in the years since, he has been admired in both the North as well as the South. In 1900, he was elected to the Hall of Fame. His estate is now Arlington National Cemetery, and the Curtis-Lee Mansion that overlooks the cemetery is a national monument. In many southern states, such as Arkansas, Florida, Georgia, Kentucky, Louisiana, and South Carolina, January 19 is a legal holiday honoring Lee.

JANUARY 20

The zodiac sign, Aquarius the Water Bearer, begins today and ends February 18. How many of your students were born under this sign?

JANUARY 20
Presidential Inauguration Day

Every four years on this date a president of the United States is inaugurated. Until 1933, American presidents took their oath of office on March 4. When the Twentieth Amendment was passed, January 20 became the official date for taking office. President James Monroe was first to take the oath and deliver his address at the Capitol Building in Washington, D.C. James Madison gave the first inaugural ball, a celebration now part of today's tradition.

JANUARY 23, 1737
Birth Date of John Hancock

"There! King George can read that without his spectacles," declared John Hancock in 1776 when he became the first man to sign the Declaration of Independence. He wrote his name on the document in large, bold letters. Hancock, a Boston merchant, was an early advocate of independence. He served as president of the Continental Congress and was an outstanding rebel. To this day a signature is often referred to as a "John Hancock."

A biography middle-grade readers will enjoy is *Will You Sign Here, John Hancock?* by Jean Fritz, illustrated by Trina Schart Hyman (Coward, 1976; also in paperback).

JANUARY 23, 1849

Elizabeth Blackwell became the first American woman to receive a degree as a medical doctor. (*See* February 3, 1821.)

JANUARY 24, 1848

John Sutter found gold near his mill in the Sacramento Valley, California. His discovery attracted thousands of people to the area near San Francisco in what is now known as the Gold Rush of 1848. Gold is a much sought out metal that has been used for jewelry and artwork since primitive times. Modern nations once used it to back up paper currency. Students can observe the anniversary of Sutter's discovery by reporting on the importance of gold in past and present societies.

JANUARY 24, 1925
Birth Date of Maria Tallchief

Maria Tallchief, an American ballerina, has been hailed internationally for her graceful dancing. One of the first American ballerinas to gain international fame, she proved that American ballet could equal the quality of European dancing. In 1942, Tallchief made her debut with the Ballet Russe de Monte Carlo and five years later joined the New York City Ballet — the year the corps was founded. She was born in Oklahoma, the daughter of an Osage Native American father and Scotch-Irish mother.

JANUARY 26, 1788

Australia, the world's only country-continent, was first settled by colonists on this day. It is best known for its great coral reef, kangaroos, and eucalyptus trees. The nineteenth-century Australian folk song "Waltzing Matilda" became a World War II favorite. Sing or listen to this catchy tune as part of an Australian classroom experience.

JANUARY 26, 1831
Birth Date of Mary Elizabeth Mapes Dodge

Born in New York City, Mary Mapes Dodge is best known for her classic novel *Hans Brinker, or the Silver Skates*, published in 1865. She was also a prominent editor of *Saint Nicholas* magazine and published several short stories for children. She died in upstate New York on September 21, 1905. Share a part of *Hans Brinker* with your middle-graders. Perhaps it will encourage some to read the complete novel.

JANUARY 26, 1837

Michigan became the twenty-sixth state.

Flower: Apple Blossom
Tree: White Pine
Bird: Robin

JANUARY 27, 1736
Birth Date of Wolfgang Amadeus Mozart

Austrian-born Mozart began his musical career by playing the harpsichord at the age of three. By the time he was six, he had learned to play the violin and organ and could compose music of his own. He gave his first public performance when he was five, and he and his older sister played throughout Germany, France, and England for kings, queens, and other nobility. Needless to say, people everywhere were astounded at this musical prodigy. When he turned 13, his father took him to Italy where he wrote music and was honored by musicians and audiences everywhere he played.

Mozart's later years were not as happy as his youth. He had an attack of rheumatic fever, and his health began to fail. He died in poverty at age 35. During his lifetime he created more than six hundred works of music — 41 symphonies, concertos, masses, church music, quartets, and 20 famous operas including *The Magic Flute* and *Don Giovanni*.

JANUARY 27, 1832
Birth Date of Lewis Carroll

Lewis Carroll's real name was Charles Lutwidge Dodgson. He taught mathematics at Oxford University. He used the pen name Lewis Carroll when he wrote *Alice's Adventures in Wonderland* (1865) and *Through the Looking Glass* (1872). The adventures of Alice evolved from his telling stories to a real Alice, Alice Liddell, a daughter of a devoted friend. One Christmas he wrote and illustrated the story as a gift to her. Years later, the story was issued in book form with Sir John Tenniel's famous illustrations. Today such characters as the White Rabbit, the Cheshire Cat, and the Mad Hatter are as fresh as when they first appeared.

◆

Alice's Adventures in Wonderland is certainly a great book for middle-graders; it is filled with adventure, rhyme, and fantasy! The story has been abridged in countless editions, including the Walt Disney film version.

Children will enjoy listening to selected chapters and/or several of the nonsense rhymes such as "Turtle Soup." (*See* the January Poem of the Month.) Encourage better readers to read the complete *Alice* books and report on them to the entire class. This might interest slower readers.

Two recent editions, which students might compare to the original, are those illustrated by Anthony Browne (Alfred A. Knopf, 1988) and Michael Hague (Henry Holt, 1985). A lavishly illustrated book for adults is *Beyond the Looking Glass: Reflections of Alice and Her Family* by Colin Gordon (Harcourt Brace Jovanovich, 1982).

JANUARY 28, 1986

One of the worst and most tragic accidents in space history took place on this date when the *Challenger 2* spacecraft exploded just after takeoff. The seven astronauts who perished were: Francis R. Scobee, Michael J. Smith, Robert E. McNair, Ellison S. Onizuka, Judith A. Resnik, Gregory B. Jarvis, and Sharon Christa McAuliffe, the first teacher to go into space.

McAuliffe, a high school social studies teacher from Concord, New Hampshire, was chosen from 10,463 applicants to be the first private citizen to go into space.

President Ronald W. Reagan's announcement on August 27, 1984, that a school teacher would be selected for this honor galvanized McAuliffe into action. She stated her reasons for applying in her application essay: ". . . this opportunity to connect my abilities as an educator with my interest in history and space is a unique opportunity to fulfill my early fantasies."

◆

JANUARY 29, 1843

Birth Date of William McKinley, Twenty-fifth President

Born in: Niles, Ohio
Occupation: Lawyer, congressman
President: 1897–1901, Republican
Died: September 14, 1901
              Buffalo, New York
              Buried in Canton, Ohio

About McKinley
- ★ Working-class background; son of a foundryman.
- ★ Served in the Civil War as a private, rising to the rank of major under his friend General Rutherford B. Hayes, who became the nineteenth president.
- ★ Advocate of tariffs.
- ★ Governor of Ohio.
- ★ Campaigns made use of telephone for the first time.

During His Term
- ★ U.S. battleship *Maine* blown up in Havana Harbor, setting off the Spanish-American War.
- ★ Assassinated by an anarchist on September 6, 1901, while visiting the Pan American Exposition in Buffalo, New York.
- ★ Acquired the Philippine Islands from Spain and annexed Hawaii.

JANUARY 29, 1861

Kansas became the thirty-fourth state.

Flower: Native Sunflower
Tree: Cottonwood
Bird: Western Meadowlark

JANUARY 30, 1882
Birth Date of Franklin Delano Roosevelt, Thirty-second President

Born in: Hyde Park, New York
Occupation: Public official, lawyer
President: 1933–1945, Democrat
Died: April 12, 1945
              Warm Springs, Georgia
              Buried in Hyde Park, New York

About Roosevelt
★ An only child.
★ Crippled by polio in 1921, he thereafter wore leg braces.
★ Woodrow Wilson's assistant secretary of the navy and later governor of New York.

During His Terms
★ Helped the nation survive the Depression with the "alphabet soup" agencies of the New Deal and his optimistic spirit.
★ Appointed first woman cabinet member — Frances Perkins, secretary of labor.
★ First president to seek more than two terms of office: he was elected four times.
★ His wife, Eleanor, became a world-famous leader and humanitarian.
★ Under his leadership the United States became a world power. He encouraged the creation of the United Nations, which was organized at the end of World War II.
★ Died in office.

JANUARY 31, 1797
Birth Date of Franz Peter Schubert

Born in Vienna, Austria, Franz Schubert was part of a large

music-loving family. He received his music education from his father and elder brothers. He played the piano as soon as he could reach the keys and composed tunes as soon as he could write notes. During his short life he produced over six hundred art songs, or *lieder*, sometimes as many as eight a day. Besides *lieder*, he wrote music for the orchestra, chorus, chamber groups, and piano. His Symphony No. 8 in B Minor ("Unfinished") is one of his finest orchestral works.

In 1822, Schubert made the acquaintance of Ludwig van Beethoven, who later acclaimed his work. Schubert was elected to the Musical Society of Vienna and despite ill health managed to give his first public concert, which was a great success. Despite his productivity as a composer, Schubert received very little recognition. When publishers finally began to request his work — and his future seemed assured — it was too late. On November 19, 1828, Schubert died at the age of 31.

JANUARY/FEBRUARY
Chinese New Year

Asians begin their New Year in late January and early February. The event takes place with the first new moon after the sun enters Aquarius and is celebrated for 15 days. Each new year is named for one of 12 animals: the mouse, ox, tiger, rabbit, dragon, snake, horse, sheep, monkey, rooster, dog, or boar. People spend time visiting relatives and friends. Traditional gifts of fruit and red envelopes containing money are given to children. New Year parades are led by the Golden Dragon, the Chinese symbol of strength.

A collection of 22 traditional Chinese nursery rhymes can be found in *Dragon Kites and Dragonflies*, adapted and illustrated by Demi (Harcourt Brace Jovanovich, 1986).

FEBRUARY

FLOWER   ◆   BIRTHSTONE
Violet   Amethyst

The second month's name is derived from the Latin word *Februarius*, which stems from the verb *februare* meaning to "expiate" or "purify."

The month was not included in the original Roman calendar. About 700 B.C., Numo Pompilius, Rome's king, added two new months: January and February. February became the second month in 452 B.C. Augustus Caesar, a later emperor of Rome, made February the shortest month when he took a day from its 29 to lengthen August, the month bearing his name.

FEBRUARY POEM OF THE MONTH

VALENTINE FEELINGS

I feel flippy,
I feel fizzy,
I feel whoopy,
I feel whizzy.

I'm feeling wonderful.
I'm feeling just fine.
Because you just gave me
A valentine.

— Lee Bennett Hopkins

FEBRUARY
Black History Month

Black History Month was first celebrated as Black History Week, the week that includes the dates of both Abraham Lincoln's birth and Frederick Douglass's death. It was initiated in 1926 by Carter G. Woodson, a black historian, and the Association of the Study of Negro Life and History in Washington, D.C.

You might tie poetry into the celebration of Black History Month by using some poems by Langston Hughes, Gwendolyn Brooks, or Nikki Giovanni. Middle-grade children can research important but little known roles played by blacks in the development of the United States. They can either report orally or plan a bulletin board display featuring black Americans and their contributions.

FEBRUARY 1, 1902
Birth Date of Langston Hughes

> For a whole race of people freed from slavery without
> nothing — without money, without work, without ed-
> ucation — it has not always been easy to hold fast to
> dreams. But the Negro people believed in the American
> dream. Now, since almost a hundred years of freedom,
> we've come a long way. But there is still a way for [us]—
> and democracy to go.
>> — From text of recording
>> The Dream Keeper and Other Poems (Folkway Records)

Langston Hughes was born in Joplin, Missouri. During his
childhood, he moved from one place to another and from
one relative to another.

Hughes's first published poem, "The Negro Speaks of Riv-
ers," appeared in 1919 in The Crisis, the official magazine of
the National Association for the Advancement of Colored People. From that date on until his death on May 22, 1967, his
work was widely published. In addition to poetry, Hughes
wrote plays, nonfiction books for children and adults, novels,
short stories, operettas, and newspaper columns. It was his
poetry, however, that earned him the title of Black Poet Laureate.

Hughes's life is detailed in two excellent biographies for
young readers, including Langston Hughes: A Biography by Milton
Meltzer (T.Y. Crowell, 1968) and Langston Hughes: American Poet
(T.Y. Crowell, 1974). For adult readers an excellent study of
Hughes's life and work appears in The Life of Langston Hughes,
Volume I, 1902–1941: I, Too, Sing America (Oxford University
Press, 1986; also in paperback) and The Life of Langston Hughes,
Volume II: I Dream a World (Oxford University Press, 1988), both
by Arnold Rampersad.

A perfect way to begin February, or any month, is to share
with your students the beautiful words of this great poet.

FEBRUARY 2
Groundhog Day

According to a German legend passed on from the Middle Ages, the groundhog is said to come out of hibernation on this day. If it sees its shadow because the day is sunny, it will return to its burrow beneath the ground for another six weeks of winter sleep. If it does not see its shadow because the skies are overcast, winter will be shorter, and an earlier spring is anticipated.

Every year in a small town in northern Pennsylvania, named Punxsutawney, a groundhog called Punxsutawney Phil predicts when spring will come. Local residents claim that Phil is almost one hundred years old and that he has never been wrong!

Have someone in the class check the newspaper tonight to see if the groundhog saw its shadow.

FEBRUARY 3, 1821
Birth Date of Elizabeth Blackwell

Elizabeth Blackwell, the first American woman doctor, was granted her medical degree from Geneva Medical College in Geneva, New York, on January 23, 1849. Born in Bristol, England, her family came to the United States in 1832. After her father's death, she taught school for several years to help support her family. In 1844, she decided to become a physician but was refused admittance to medical schools in Philadelphia and New York City. For three years she studied privately, until she gained entrance to Geneva Medical College. In 1853, she opened a dispensary in New York City staffed entirely by women; this later became the New York Infirmary. After the Civil War she founded the Women's Medical College, associated with the Infirmary. Middle-graders can find more information about her in *The First Woman Doctor* by Rachel Baker (Scholastic, 1987).

FEBRUARY 4, 1902
Birth Date of Charles Lindbergh

Born in Detroit, Michigan, Charles Lindbergh is remembered for his first nonstop solo flight across the Atlantic, from New York to Paris. (*See* May 20–21, 1927.) He died on August 26, 1974, in Maui, Hawaii.

FEBRUARY 6, 1788

Massachusetts was the sixth state to ratify the Constitution.

Flower: Mayflower
Tree: American Elm
Bird: Chickadee

FEBRUARY 6, 1895
Birth Date of George Herman Ruth

Born in Baltimore, Maryland, George Herman Ruth, better known as Babe Ruth, led a solitary, sordid childhood. Before he turned eight, his parents placed him in St. Mary's Industrial School for Boys — partly a reform school and partly an orphanage.

He began to play baseball as a child at St. Mary's. His skill attracted the attention of the Baltimore Orioles, then a minor league team, who signed him as a pitcher.

When he joined the New York Yankees he became famous

around the world. When he retired he had been at bat 8,399 times and had hit 714 home runs.

He held the title of "Home Run King" until April 8, 1974, when Henry L. Aaron — Hank Aaron — hit his 715th home run playing with the Atlanta Braves. Ruth died on August 17, 1948.

A biography for better readers is *Babe Ruth* by Art Berke (Franklin Watts, 1988).

FEBRUARY 6, 1911
Birth Date of Ronald Wilson Reagan, Fortieth President

Born in:	Tampico, Illinois
Occupation:	Movie actor, president of Screen Actors Guild, sports announcer, governor
President:	1981–1989, Republican

About Reagan
★ Early interest in acting fostered by his mother, led to his being in more than 50 films.
★ Elected president in his sixty-ninth year, becoming the oldest person to ever win the presidency.
★ Reversed the trend toward one-term presidents by winning a second term with a record number of Electoral College votes.

During His Terms
★ Conservative policies led to a reduction in taxes while bolstering the Armed Forces budget and cutting welfare spending.
★ Participated in a summit meeting with Soviet leader Mikhail S. Gorbachev in Moscow, which dealt with nuclear disarmament.

★ Sandra Day O'Connor became the first female justice of the U.S. Supreme Court.

FEBRUARY 7, 1812
Birth Date of Charles Dickens

Charles Dickens was born in Portsmouth, England. A bright youngster, he learned to read and write at an early age, but when he was 11 years old, his education was held back because his father was imprisoned for owing money. Young Dickens had to work in a factory to help support his family. The cruel treatment and harsh living conditions he endured were vividly remembered and recreated in his writings. Later when his father inherited money, he was sent to a boarding school. In his late teens he became a newspaper reporter in Parliament and soon rose to the top of his profession.

His fame as a writer began with the publication of *Pickwick Papers* (1837) and continued with such works as *A Tale of Two Cities*, *Oliver Twist*, *David Copperfield*, and *Great Expectations*, many of which are thought to contain incidents based on his early life experiences. *A Christmas Carol*, first published in 1843, featuring the greatest people-hater of all times — Scrooge — has become a favorite Christmas story. An edition of this classic has been illustrated by Caldecott Award winner Trina Schart Hyman (Holiday House, 1983).

FEBRUARY 7, 1867
Birth Date of Laura Ingalls Wilder

Laura Ingalls Wilder wrote the popular "Little House" books — pioneer stories for middle-grade readers based on her own life growing up on the American frontier in the late nineteenth century. She began the series when she was 65.

The first title, *Little House in the Big Woods* (1932), was followed by *Farmer Boy* (1933), *Little House on the Prairie* (1935), *On the Banks of Plum Creek* (1937), *By the Shores of Silver Lake* (1939), *The Long Winter* (1940), *Little Town on the Prairie* (1941), and *These Happy Golden Years* (1943) — all published by Harper & Row and available in paperback, the last four being Newbery Honor Books. The manuscript for the ninth "Little House" book, entitled *The First Four Years* (Harper & Row), was discovered among her papers and published in 1971, exactly as she wrote it. All of the stories in the series are written in the third person. They are told with humor and warmth and give readers a realistic account of American pioneer life. Wilder lived on her farm in Mansfield, Missouri, until her death, at the age of 90. Her farm is now a museum.

Of interest for both student and teacher reference are *West from Home: Letters of Laura Ingalls Wilder, San Francisco 1915*, edited by Roger Lea MacBride (Harper, 1974); *Laura: The Life of Laura Ingalls Wilder* by Donald Zochert (Avon, 1977); and *Laura Ingalls Wilder: Growing Up in the Little House* by Patricia Reilly Giff, illustrated by Eileen McEating (Puffin Books paperback, 1988).

In 1954, the Laura Ingalls Wilder Award for lasting contributions to children's literature was established by the American Library Association. It is given every three years to an author or artist whose body of work is outstanding.

FEBRUARY 8, 1823
Birth Date of Jules Verne

Ships that could travel underwater? Vehicles that could fly to the moon? These are things that astounded nineteenth-century readers when Jules Verne wrote about them.

Born in France, he became a writer who laid much of the foundation for modern science fiction. A prolific author, he was popular around the world for his fantasies. He died on March 24, 1905.

Mature readers will enjoy Verne's *Twenty Thousand Leagues under the Sea, Around the World in Eighty Days* (both published in 1873), and *Journey to the Center of the Earth* (1874). A number of his books became successful motion pictures.

What futuristic ideas do your students have? Perhaps they can write a short piece on a discovery they see for the twenty-first century.

FEBRUARY 9, 1870
U.S. *Weather Service Founded*

The first public weather prediction is thought to have appeared in 1692 in an English newspaper. The phrase "weather forecast" was first used by Admiral Robert Fitzroy in the 1860s in the London *Times*. Weather prediction soon became a concern of the United States government. As a result, an act of Congress authorized the U.S. Weather Service. Weather reports were gathered by telegraph from approximately 24 sources, and forecasts were distributed around the nation by telegraph.

Study weather with your students. Collect forecasts and compare the accuracy of long-term forecasts with daily predictions. Compare both print and nonprint forecasts garnered from newspapers, radio, and television.

An informative book for younger readers is *Weather Forecasting* by Gail Gibbons (Four Winds, 1987). Also, *Questions and Answers about Weather* by Jean M. Craig provides clear explanations to questions concerning the weather (Scholastic, 1969). For older students, look for *It's Raining Cats and Dogs: All Kinds of Weather and Why We Have It* by Franklin M. Branley, illustrated by True Kelley (Houghton Mifflin, 1987).

FEBRUARY 9, 1773
Birth Date of William Henry Harrison, Ninth President

Born in: Charles County, Virginia
Occupation: Soldier
President: 1841, Whig
Died: April 4, 1841
                Washington, D.C.
                Buried in North Bend, Ohio

About Harrison
★ Only president who studied to be a doctor — he withdrew from medical school to enter the army.
★ Negotiator and Indian fighter. Defeated Tecumseh, Shawnee Chief, at Battle of Tippecanoe in 1811.

During His Term
★ Called "Granny" by Democrats because of his age, 68.
★ Died one month after taking office.

FEBRUARY 10, 1950
Birth Date of Mark Spitz

Born in Modesto, California, Mark Spitz began splashing in the Pacific Ocean off Honolulu, Hawaii, when he was two years old. By the time he was 10, he was swimming 90 minutes a day, seven days a week. Spitz set a world record at the 1972 Olympic Games in Munich by winning seven gold medals, the first athlete to win more than five gold medals in one Olympiad.

FEBRUARY 11, 1751

The first hospital in America opened in Philadelphia. The Pennsylvania Hospital was established with the assistance of Benjamin Franklin and Dr. Thomas Hood. It still functions today! The word *hospital* comes from the Latin word *hospitium* meaning "house" or "institution for guests." Younger readers will find more information in *The Hospital Book* by James Howe (Crown, 1981), and in *Going to the Hospital* by Fred Rogers, with full-color illustrations by Jim Judkis (Putnam's, 1988).

FEBRUARY 11, 1847
Birth Date of Thomas Alva Edison

Thomas Alva Edison's inventions are all around us — the light bulb, phonograph, copying machine, storage battery, and ticker tape machine are just a few. From his youth in Milan, Ohio, until he headed a great laboratory in Menlo Park, New Jersey, Edison was always tinkering. Despite having received only three months of formal education, the great inventor patented 1,100 devices in 60 years, which earned him the title "The Wizard of Menlo Park." At the age of 84, Edison became so ill that he had to use a wheelchair. This did not stop him from going to work every day. The motto he preached to friends was, "The brain that isn't used rusts." He died on October 18, 1931.

FEBRUARY 12, 1809
Birth Date of Charles Darwin

Born in Shrewsbury, England, Charles Darwin developed an early passion for collecting pebbles and minerals. He was less interested in his schoolwork — as a student at the Shrewsbury School, he was such a poor student that his father once told him, "You care for nothing but dogs, shooting, and net-catching, and you will be a disgrace to yourself and all your family."

Darwin later attempted to follow his father and grandfather, who were physicians, by studying medicine at Edinburgh University, but this failed to interest him. He transferred to Cambridge University in 1828 to study theology, where he met several distinguished scientists who reawakened his interest in natural history. In December 1831, after graduating, he obtained a position as a naturalist on the ship *Beagle* and sailed on a scientific cruise around the world for five years. One of the most significant stops was the Galápagos Islands, an archipelago of volcanic rock some six hundred miles off the Pacific coast of Ecuador. Darwin noted the unique nature of the reptiles, plants, and fish native to this isolated site. He studied thousands of specimens of animal and plant life and developed a new concept of evolution. This voyage gave him much of the material for his first book, *The Origin of Species*, published in 1859. The entire first edition of 1,250 copies sold out the first day it appeared.

Darwin's theory of evolution caused great debate in England and all over the world. In 1871, he aroused more unfriendly criticism with the publication of *The Descent of Man*. Although Darwin's theory of evolution is still debated, its fundamental principles prevail throughout the scientific world. He died on April 19, 1882, at the age of 73.

FEBRUARY 12, 1809
Birth Date of Abraham Lincoln, Sixteenth President

Born in: Hardin County, Kentucky
Occupation: Lawyer

President:	1861–1865, Republican
Died:	April 15, 1865
	Washington, D.C.
	Buried in Springfield, Illinois

About Lincoln

★ Frontier background in Kentucky, Indiana, and Illinois.
★ Grew his beard at the request of an eleven-year-old supporter, Grade Bedell, who felt it would help his image.
★ Unsuccessful in his bid for Senate seat from Illinois.
★ His 1858 debates with Stephen A. Douglas, a Democrat, made him famous.

During His Terms

★ Eleven southern states seceded from the Union.
★ Civil War began when Confederate troops fired on Fort Sumter.
★ He directed Union Army at first because of lack of trustworthy generals.
★ Emancipation Proclamation issued. (*See* January 1, 1863.)
★ General Lee and his army surrendered on April 9, 1863.
★ Assassinated on April 14, 1865, at Ford's Theatre, Washington, D.C., after starting second term.

Readers can journey through Lincoln's life with the 1988 Newbery Award winner, *Lincoln: A Photobiography* by Russell Freedman (Clarion Books, 1987).

FEBRUARY 13, 1741

On this day the first magazine published in America, *The American Magazine*, was issued in Philadelphia, Pennsylvania. The editors, Andrew Brafford and John Webbe, thought the idea would catch on rapidly with readers. The magazine, however, had little to offer beyond what newspapers were already carrying and, after three issues, folded!

FEBRUARY 14
Valentine's Day

The origins of Valentine's Day are unknown. Some historians say the celebration goes back to ancient Rome. William Shakespeare wrote about the day in the sixteenth century in *Hamlet*, Act IV, Scene V:

> To-morrow is Saint Valentine's day,
> All in the morning betime,
> And I a maid at your window,
> To be your Valentine.

Most people believe that the day received its name from a man named Valentine who lived over seventeen hundred years ago. He was a priest in Rome when Christianity was a new religion, and he was put to death for teaching Christianity and later named a saint.

Valentine greetings were popular as early as the Middle Ages when lovers said or sang their valentine greetings to their sweethearts, since few could read or write. Written valentines began about the year 1400. The oldest one on record was made in 1415 by Charles, duke of Orleans, a Frenchman who was captured by the English and imprisoned in the Tower of London. There he wrote valentine poems, some of which are in the British Museum.

In the United States, Valentine's Day became popular through the efforts of Esther Howland, whose father owned a store in Worcester, Massachusetts. After receiving a lacy valentine from England in 1847, she decided to make her own to sell in her father's shop. Demands for her original cards became so great that she started a business that earned her close to $100,000 a year. Today, approximately 900 million valentines are sent in the United States and Canada every year.

Children will enjoy making their own valentines to send to family and friends. Why not post the phrase "I Love You" on a bulletin board in English and a variety of other languages? Here is the phrase in several languages:

		Pronunciation
French:	*Je t'aime*	jeh TE-mm
Spanish:	*Yo te amo*	yoh te A-moh
Italian:	*Io ti amo*	e-o tee A-moh
German:	*Ich liebe dich*	eeksh Lee-beh deeksh
Hebrew:	*Ani ohev otach*	ah-Nee o-HEV O-tach
Japanese:	*Watakushi-wa*	WA-ta-SHE-wa
	anato-wo	an-A-ta-o-ah-
	aishimasu	e-she-MA-sue

Several resources to share with students are *Valentine's Day* by Gail Gibbons (Holiday House, 1986), which depicts the lore and customs of the holiday for younger readers, and *Hearts, Cupids and Red Roses: The Story of Valentine Symbols* by Edna Barth, illustrated by Ursula Arndt (Clarion Books, 1974), a volume for middle-grade readers.

Share some poetry, too. (See the February Poem of the Month.) A collection of 20 *Valentine Poems* selected by Myra Cohn Livingston, illustrated by Patience Brewster (Holiday House, 1987), is a delight for all ages.

FEBRUARY 14, 1473
Birth Date of Nicolaus Copernicus

Nicolaus Copernicus was an astronomer of Polish descent who founded modern astronomy around 1543 with his discovery that the earth is a moving planet and that the sun is

◆

the center of the solar system. Prior to this, astronomers accepted the geocentric (earth-center) theory of Ptolemy, an astronomer who lived about 100–170 A.D.

FEBRUARY 14, 1859

Oregon became the thirty-third state.

Flower: Oregon Grape
Tree: Douglas Fir
Bird: Western Meadowlark

FEBRUARY 14, 1912

Arizona became the forty-eighth state.

Flower: Blossom of the Seguaro Cactus
Tree: Paloverde
Bird: Cactus Wren

FEBRUARY 15, 1564
Birth Date of Galileo Galilei

Because Galileo Galilei was steadfast in his support of Copernicus's theory that the earth revolved around the sun, this pioneer astronomer and physicist was brought to trial by Italian authorities. Today he stands vindicated for his discovery of four of Jupiter's moons in January 1610, using a telescope he designed, and for his work in physics regarding the speed of falling bodies.

FEBRUARY 15, 1820

Birth Date of Susan B. Anthony

> I am a firm and full believer in the revelation that it is
> through women that the race is to be redeemed.
>
> — Susan B. Anthony

Susan B. Anthony was a reformer and leader in the American
women's suffrage movement. Among the things she worked
for were women's right to vote, women's property rights,
higher wages for teachers, and the abolition of slavery. When
the Fourteenth and Fifteenth Amendments to the Constitution were proposed to extend civil rights and grant the vote
to male blacks, Anthony demanded the provisions also apply
to women. Failing to achieve this, she voted as a citizen and
person but was arrested, tried, and fined. In 1869, she organized the Woman Suffrage Association. Throughout the rest
of her life she continued the struggle to attain women's rights,
blazing the trail for the adoption of the Nineteenth Amendment (woman suffrage), which was finally ratified 14 years
after her death in 1906. In 1979, the United States government
minted one-dollar coins bearing Anthony's image, making her
the first woman to be pictured on a United States coin in
general circulation.

Have the class discuss women's liberation. Start by having
some children share what their mothers do for a living. Invite
working mothers to class who would be willing to share what
they do at their jobs. *Mommies at Work* by Eve Merriam, illustrated by Eugine Fernandes (Simon & Schuster, 1989) exam-
ines many different jobs performed by working mothers.

FEBRUARY 16, 1796

Yonge Street in Toronto, Canada, the world's longest street,
was opened on this date. Yonge Street runs through the busy

downtown area of Toronto into the outskirts. The street is 1,117 miles long. Traveling this distance would be like taking an automobile trip from Washington, D.C., to New Orleans, Louisiana. Show students this vast distance on a map of the United States. It would also be interesting to compare Yonge Street's length to the longest street in your town or city.

FEBRUARY 17, 1902
Birth Date of Marian Anderson

> I have a great belief in the future of my people and my country.
>
> — Marian Anderson

Marian Anderson was born in Philadelphia, Pennsylvania, and began singing in choirs when she was six years old. At 17 she was chosen from among three hundred contestants to sing with the New York Philharmonic Orchestra. Her first recital in Carnegie Hall in 1935 was an enormous success and was followed by many concert tours throughout the world. She was the first black to perform with the Metropolitan Opera Company in New York. In 1958, President Dwight D. Eisenhower appointed her to the United States Delegation to the United Nations. She retired in 1965. In 1978, President Jimmy Carter presented her with a Congressional Gold Medal, bearing her profile.

Her autobiography, *My Lord, What a Morning* (Viking, 1956), is a good reference.

FEBRUARY 18, 1930

While watching the heavens from an observatory in Arizona, Clyde Tombaugh, an astronomer, discovered Pluto, the outermost of the nine planets in our solar system. Pluto is smaller than earth, 50 times more distant from the sun, and has no moons. It takes 248 years for Pluto to go around the sun and it can only be seen with the aid of powerful telescopes.

Encourage a group of children to construct a model of the solar system showing the relationship of the sun to the nine planets. The positions of the planets outward from the sun are: Mercury, Venus, Earth, Mars, Jupiter, Saturn, Uranus, Neptune, and Pluto. Middle-graders will be challenged to make scale models of each planet. This will reinforce their knowledge of the planets' relative sizes. (See February 15, 1564, and September 23, 1846. They are both astronomical!)

FEBRUARY 19

The zodiac sign, Pisces the Fish, begins today and ends March 20. How many of your students were born under this sign?

FEBRUARY 20, 1872

The Metropolitan Museum of Art opened in New York City. It is the largest art museum in the United States and contains more than three million items. Older girls and boys can "visit" the museum via the delightful Newbery Award-winning book, *From the Mixed-Up Files of Mrs. Basil E. Frankweiler* by Elaine L. Konigsburg (Atheneum, 1968; also in paperback). This is a story about two suburban children who run away from their Connecticut home and live hidden in the museum.

Sharing information about the museum might spark a visit to a local art museum. Perhaps the class can make their own museum corner where their paintings, drawings, and sculpture can be placed.

Visiting the Art Museum by Laurene Krasny Brown and Marc

Brown (E.P. Dutton, 1986) depicts examples of various art styles from primitive through twentieth-century pop art for younger readers. Older students will enjoy *The Natural History Museum of Art Activity Book* by Osa Brown (The Metropolitan Museum of Art/Random House, 1983; also in paperback), which provides instructions for crafts, toys, games, puzzles, etc., inspired by the treasures in the museum's collection.

FEBRUARY 20, 1895
Death of Frederick Douglass

Frederick Augustus Washington Bailey, born a slave in Tuckahoe, Maryland, in 1817 (his actual birth date is unknown), was a journalist, a statesman, and an important figure in the movement to abolish slavery in the United States. When he was 21, he escaped from his master, changed his last name, and fled to New Bedford, Massachusetts. Shortly afterward, Douglass lectured before antislavery societies in Massachusetts, Great Britain, and Ireland. Upon his return to the United States, he bought his freedom and founded and edited the *North Star*, a famous antislavery newspaper. At the beginning of the Civil War, he urged President Lincoln to recruit black soldiers. The first two black men to join the Union Army were Douglass's own sons.

At the close of the war, he became involved in education, the rights of freed people, women's rights, and world peace. He held several positions with the federal government and was finally appointed Minister to Haiti. Douglass died in 1895. In 1965, the U.S. Post Office issued a 25-cent stamp commemorating him. In *Frederick Douglass Fights for Freedom* by Margaret Davidson (Scholastic, 1968), middle-grade readers can discover more about this remarkable man.

FEBRUARY 20, 1962

John Glenn made history on this date by orbiting the earth. Glenn's service as a combat pilot in World War II and the Korean War, and his breaking of the sound barrier in a three-hour, 22-minute flight from New York to Los Angeles helped prepare him for his three-orbit flight around the earth. He became the first astronaut to accomplish this feat aboard Friendship 7.

After leaving the space program, Glenn entered politics and was elected senator from Ohio in 1974.

FEBRUARY 21, 1878

On this date the first telephone directory was issued in New Haven, Connecticut, then one of the largest telephone centers in the United States, consisting of 50 subscribers! Someone had suggested that a list of subscribers' numbers be compiled.

Have your students create a telephone directory listing telephone numbers of class members and/or other important telephone numbers they might need. This can serve as a handy reference to keep at home for special needs.

FEBRUARY 22, 1732
Birth Date of George Washington, First President

Born in:	Pope's Creek, Virginia
Occupation:	Planter, soldier
President:	1789–1797, Federalist
Died:	December 14, 1799
	Mount Vernon, Virginia

About Washington
★ Soldier in the French and Indian War.
★ Served as commander of the American army without pay throughout the Revolutionary War against Britain.
★ Only he and James Monroe ran for the presidency unopposed.

During His Terms
★ Lived in New York but supervised the building of the President's Mansion in the District of Columbia, which later presidents used.
★ Bill of Rights became law.
★ Started departments of State, Treasury, and War.

FEBRUARY 23, 1685
Birth Date of George Frideric Handel

Considered one of the greatest musicians of all times, George Frideric Handel had a strange career. He was trained in German music, became a master of Italian opera, and wound up as an Englishman and one of the most important English composers. Handel was a child prodigy born in Halle, Germany. He started learning music at the age of seven. When he was 12, he performed in Berlin at court, making such an impression that the prince offered to send him to Italy to study music. His father refused to let him go, wanting him to pursue a career in law. Later Handel became a church organist. At 20, his first opera, *Almira*, was produced in Hamburg. He then went to Italy where he achieved fame as a composer and performer, then on to further success in England. In 1741, he turned from opera to writing oratorios — religious operas usually based on Bible stories. His first, and most successful, oratorio, *The Messiah*, is performed at Christmastime and Easter in churches and concert halls throughout the world. Perhaps you can play a recording of the familiar "Hallelujah" chorus from this work today to help the class celebrate Handel's birthday.

FEBRUARY 25, 1913

The Sixteenth Amendment to the United States Constitution, passed by Congress on July 12, 1909, became law. It provided that Congress had the authority to tax the incomes of citizens. Every April 15, Americans file tax returns with the federal government. Older students might examine copies of the federal budget to see how tax dollars are spent.

FEBRUARY 26, 1846
Birth Date of William Frederick Cody — Buffalo Bill

Pony express rider, Union army scout, Indian fighter, buffalo meat salesman, and international showman are several of the jobs Buffalo Bill worked at during his lifetime. Born in Iowa, Cody was orphaned at 11 and attended school briefly. At an early age he moved to Kansas where he began his multifaceted career as a westerner. In his declining years, after the Indian nations of the West were decimated, Cody organized a Wild West Show that toured the United States and Europe, entertaining people who were fascinated with this era of American history.

FEBRUARY 26, 1919

Congress established the Grand Canyon in Arizona as a national park. The park contains 1,052 square miles, parts of which are one mile deep and 18 miles wide. It is noted for its scenic beauty and wildlife, including 300 species of birds and 120 other kinds of animals such as mountain lions, big-horn sheep, elk, and snakes. Ask students to find the names and locations of other national parks. Then put together a bulletin board display using a map of the United States to pinpoint these locations. List important information on each park. Children interested in geology might research the reasons why the Grand Canyon is as deep and colorful as it is.

FEBRUARY 27, 1807
Birth Date of Henry Wadsworth Longfellow

> Listen my children, and you shall hear
> Of the midnight ride of Paul Revere,
> On the eighteenth of April, in Seventy-five;
> Hardly a man is now alive
> Who remembers that famous day and year. . . .
> — Henry Wadsworth Longfellow

"Paul Revere's Ride" is just one of the many popular poems composed by Henry Wadsworth Longfellow. Above is the first stanza of the verse. Other popular poems by Longfellow include "The Song of Hiawatha," "Evangeline," "The Courtship of Miles Standish," and "The Village Blacksmith." Much of his poetry is written in narrative form and recreates colorful events and figures that shaped American history. A New Englander, the poet taught at Harvard University for almost 20 years. His death in 1882 was mourned throughout America and England. He became the first American poet to achieve a memorial in the Poets' Corner in London's Westminster Abbey.

A fine tie-in is *Hiawatha's Childhood*, illustrated by Errol Le Cain (Farrar, Straus & Giroux, 1984), and the sound filmstrip of the same title produced by Random House, narrated by Jamake Highwater. Look for the lavish picture book, *Hiawatha*, illustrated in full-color by Susan Jeffers (Dial Books for Young Readers, 1983).

FEBRUARY 28, 1890
Birth Date of Vaslov Nijinsky

Born in Kiev, Russia, Vaslov Nijinsky became a ballet dancer of legendary fame. At the age of nine his extraordinary talent was discovered. At 16 he was heralded as "the eighth wonder of the world." He danced leading roles in *Swan Lake*, *Giselle*, and *The Sleeping Beauty*. He died in London, England, on April 8, 1950.

Young readers interested in ballet can read *If You Were a Ballet Dancer* by Ruth Belov Gross (Scholastic, 1979) or Rachel Isadora's *My Ballet Class* (Greenwillow, 1980). A fiction series that younger readers will delight in is the *Angelina Ballerina* books published by Crown, about a small mouse and her dancing adventures.

For older readers, *Reaching for Dreams: A Ballet from Rehearsal to Opening Night* by Susan Kuklin (Lothrop, Lee & Shepard, 1987) is a fascinating chronicle of seven weeks in the life of the Alvin Ailey American Dance Theatre — one of the world's most acclaimed ballet corps. The volume is illustrated with black-and-white photographs.

FEBRUARY 29
Leap Year Day

A calendar was introduced by Julius Caesar whose astonomers calculated the year to be 365 days and six hours long. To achieve balance, they added an extra day every fourth year—

a slight overestimation! Their error was corrected in 1582. Leap year still occurs every fourth year except in "century years" not divisible by 400. Thus, 1700 and 1900 were not leap years but 2000 will be! Have students find other century years that will not be leap years. An unusual leap year custom to tell the class about is a rather odd and old Scottish practice. Since 1288 A.D. the Scottish Parliament has permitted women to collect one hundred pounds in cash from any man refusing their proposal of marriage on February 29! France and Italy copied the practice for some years afterward.

MARCH

FLOWER   ◆   **BIRTHSTONE**
Daffodil   Bloodstone

Ancient Rome's god of war, Mars, received the honor of opening the Roman new year. March, named after him, was the first month of the Roman calendar until the adoption of the Julian calendar in 46 B.C. The practice of beginning the year with March continued in England and her possessions until the mid-eighteenth century.

MARCH POEM OF THE MONTH

SPRING

How pleasing —
not
to be
freezing.

    — Prince Redcloud

MARCH 1, 1803

Ohio became the seventeenth state to enter the Union.

Flower: Scarlet Carnation
Tree: Buckeye
Bird: Cardinal

MARCH 1, 1841
Birth Date of Blanche Kelso Bruce

Blanche Kelso Bruce was born a slave in Prince Edward
County, Virginia, and escaped to the North. He attended Ober-
lin College in Ohio. After the Civil War, he returned to the
South and settled in Mississippi. On March 5, 1875, he took
the oath of office as United States senator from Mississippi,
becoming the second black man to hold this position and the
first to serve a full term. (*See also* October 26, 1919.)

MARCH 1, 1867

Nebraska became the thirty-seventh state.

Flower: Goldenrod
Tree: Cottonwood
Bird: Western Meadowlark

MARCH 1, 1872

Yellowstone National Park was established on this date. Yellowstone, the oldest United States national park, covers more than two million acres of land in Wyoming, Idaho, and Montana. Established by an act of Congress, Yellowstone is the world's largest wildlife preserve and has more geysers and hot springs than anywhere else in the world.

Have any of your students visited Yellowstone? Have them discuss their experiences.

MARCH 1, 1961

The Peace Corps was established on this date by President John Fitzgerald Kennedy. In 1971, it became part of Action, a new agency that consolidated several volunteer programs. The chief functions of the Peace Corps are to provide skilled workers and teachers to help developing nations and to promote friendship and better understanding between Americans and peoples of other countries. The corps is staffed by volunteers. Any United States citizen over the age of 18 may apply to serve after passing a physical examination and entrance test. Volunteers are trained while studying the culture and language of the country in which they will serve.

One hundred thousand volunteers, from 18 to 80 years of age, have served, including several hearing and visually impaired individuals. The corps has proved a lasting institution that has transcended partisan politics. Under President Ronald Reagan more emphasis was placed upon private-sector projects and people-to-people contact.

MARCH 2, 1793
Birth Date of Sam Houston

Sam Houston gained fame for defeating General Antonio López de Santa Anna at the battle of San Jacinto in 1836, resulting in the independence of Texas from Mexico.

Having led a most colorful life, by the age of 39 he had already been elected governor of Tennessee and United States congressman. He died on July 26, 1863.

Mature readers will enjoy *Make Way for Sam Houston* by Jean Fritz, illustrated by Elise Primavera (Putnam's, 1986), detailing his remarkable life. An excellent bibliography is appended for adult reference.

MARCH 2, 1904
Birth Date of Theodore Seuss Geisel (Dr. Seuss)

Born in Springfield, Massachusetts, Dr. Seuss's real name is Theodore Seuss Geisel. Since 1937 he has written and illustrated scores of books under two pen names, Dr. Seuss and Theo LeSieg (Geisel spelled backwards). He has introduced his readers to such wonders as sneetches, grinches, gacks, and ooblecks. His first book, *And to Think That I Saw It on Mulberry Street* (Vanguard, 1937), was rejected by 29 publishers before it was accepted. Two of his most popular titles, *Cat in the Hat* and *Cat in the Hat Comes Back* (Random House, 1957, 1958) have been read by millions of children and adults. Dr. Seuss currently lives in an observation tower in La Jolla, California.

An excellent compendium of Seussiana appears in *Dr. Seuss from Then to Now* (Random House, 1986), which is a catalogue of the retrospective exhibition organized by the San Diego Museum of Art, covering his 60-year career.

MARCH 3

Each year on this date the Festival of Dolls takes place in Japan. This special event is just for girls and lasts three days. (Boys in Japan have their day, too. *See* May 10 for the Boys' Festival.) Girls wear their finest clothes and display collections of treasured ceremonial dolls handed down from generation to generation. The dolls represent the emperor, empress, and their court figures. Five shelves are set up in the best room in the house for display. The dolls are placed on the shelves in order of importance; the emperor and empress dolls are always placed on the highest shelf. No other dolls are allowed on these shelves; only those packed away for this specific occasion are displayed. Every Japanese girl celebrates her birthday at this time, no matter when it occurs during the year. Girls look forward to entertaining visitors and enjoying these special three days.

MARCH 3, 1845

Florida became the twenty-seventh state.

Flower: Orange Blossom
Tree: Sabal Palmetto Palm
Bird: Mockingbird

MARCH 3, 1847
Birth Date of Alexander Graham Bell

Alexander Graham Bell was born in Edinburgh, Scotland. His father was a teacher of the hearing and speech impaired. Young Bell carried on his father's work in the United States. In 1875, while working with a colleague, Thomas Watson, he accidentally discovered a method of transmitting sound through vibrations. This prompted him to invent an instrument for speaking to people far away — the telephone! The telegraph, which sent signals via electrified wires, had been invented earlier, but human speech had never been carried by wire until Bell invented the telephone.

He became a United States citizen in 1882 and lived a creative life, giving services to the hearing impaired and producing other communication devices. A story about him says that he disliked the telephone because it interrupted his experiments! (See also March 7, 1876.)

MARCH 4, 1791

Vermont became the fourteenth state.

Flower: Red Clover
Tree: Sugar Maple
Bird: Hermit Thrush

MARCH 4, 1913

The United States Congress created the Department of Labor on this date to protect the welfare of United States workers. The department is responsible for enforcing laws on child labor, minimum wages, and overtime pay. It is also responsible for ensuring that businesses do not discriminate against minorities, women, and the handicapped.

MARCH 5, 1770

The Boston Massacre was a pre-American Revolution skirmish between colonial citizens and British soldiers. A crowd had gathered in front of the customs house and was throwing snowballs at the sentries. Friction between Boston's citizens and the British soldiers had been building for some time. On the night of March 5, the irritated soldiers fired on the angry mob. Five Americans were killed and six were wounded; one of the dead was Crispus Attucks, a former slave. A monument honoring the five men — the first martyrs of the struggle for American independence — now stands in Boston Commons. In the upper right-hand corner an inscription by John Adams reads, "On that night the foundation of American Independence was laid."

MARCH 6, 1475
Birth Date of Michelangelo Buonarroti

Michelangelo was one of Italy's — and the world's — greatest artists. Although mainly interested in sculpting large marble statues, he was also a painter, an architect, and a poet. At the age of 12, after a brief classical education, he became an apprentice to popular fresco painters in Florence and then studied at an art school where he attracted the attention of Lorenzo de' Medici. At age 23 he created the famous Pietà, the most important work of his youth, which now stands in St. Peter's church in Rome. His 14-foot-high sculpture, David, was carved from a single block of marble. He was commissioned to paint the ceiling of the Sistine Chapel in the Vatican and completed this magnificent work called The Creation in 1510. Twenty-five years later he painted another huge fresco on the end wall of the same chapel, The Last Judgment. He died in Rome on March 18, 1564, at the age of 90 while working on Rondanini Pietà.

Young readers get a glimpse of the man and his work in Michelangelo by Ernest Raboff (Doubleday, 1971; Harper & Row paperback), containing 14 full-color reproductions of his work, as well as black-and-white drawings.

◆

MARCH 7, 1849
Birth Date of Luther Burbank

Luther Burbank, an American horticulturist, was a noted breeder of new trees, flowers, fruits, vegetables, grains, and grasses. Among the plants he developed are the Shasta daisy, the spineless cactus, and the white blackberry. He also improved many varieties of plants.

Burbank became a gardener to support his widowed mother. His curiosity led him to experiment with plants by crossing (uniting two plants to produce a third) and selecting (choosing the best plants and rejecting inferior ones). He lived in Santa Rosa, California, where he operated a successful nursery until his death in 1926. Parts of Burbank's original acreage in and near Santa Rosa can still be visited by the public.

Planting seeds is a good way to celebrate Burbank's birthday. You will need small plastic pots, some vermiculite, and the following surefire growers: radish, sunflower, and lima bean seeds, which normally germinate rapidly. (To speed up the process, soak the seeds for one hour before planting time.) The necessary materials are inexpensive, and children become excited when sprouts and buds begin to appear, signaling the success of their indoor gardening. Follow-up activities can include graphing growth, keeping records of observed changes, and finding out what various parts of a plant do to ensure vigorous growth.

MARCH 7, 1876

Alexander Graham Bell patented the telephone. He sent his first telephone message three days later. "Come here, Watson; I want you," he said to his assistant. Since then the telephone has become a common household item. (*See also* March 3, 1847.)

MARCH 9, 1454
Birth Date of Amerigo Vespucci

Imagine our country being called the United States of Columbia, the United States of Hudsonia, or having an early explorer's name attached to our national title. Surprisingly enough, that is what happened when a sixteenth-century German mapmaker gave Amerigo Vespucci credit for discovering the New World; in reality, he had sailed west seeking the Indies and discovered Central and South America!

MARCH 9, 1822

The first patent for artificial teeth was granted. It is doubtful that any of your students wear false teeth, but teeth are interesting to study. Start a discussion about teeth and have children research false teeth — how they are made, worn, and cared for. The discussion might encourage nonbrushers or nonflossers to take care of their teeth more regularly.

Information about teeth can be found in "Tooth Tales," Chapter Two in *The Story of Your Mouth* by Dr. Alvin Silverstein and Virginia B. Silverstein, illustrated by Greg Wenzel (Coward, 1984).

MARCH 10, 1913
Death of Harriet Tubman

Harriet Tubman was born into slavery in Dorchester County, Maryland. The tablet placed near her home in Auburn, New York, a year after her death beautifully and simply tells the story of her life:

In memory of Harriet Tubman
Born a slave in Maryland about 1821.

Died in Auburn, New York, March 10th, 1913.
Called the Moses of her people
During the Civil War. With rare
Courage she led over three hundred
Negroes up from slavery to freedom,
And rendered invaluable service
As nurse and spy.
With implicit trust in God
She braved every danger and
Overcame every obstacle. Withal
She possessed extraordinary
Foresight and judgment so that
She truthfully said
"On my Underground Railroad
I nebber run my train off de track
An' I nebber los' a passenger."
This tablet is erected
By citizens of Auburn.

Tubman lived to be over 90 years old, witnessing the passing of slavery and the beginning of hope for her people.

Middle-grade readers will enjoy the biography, *Freedom Train: The Story of Harriet Tubman* by Dorothy Sterling (Scholastic paperback, 1987).

MARCH 13, 1773

If you wear earmuffs this winter you can thank Chester Greenwood who patented "ear mufflers" on this date.

MARCH 13, 1884

Standard Time was established in the United States on this date. What is the meaning of *standard time?* Have students study the country's time zones. If it is one o'clock in your zone, what time is it east or west of you? What is meant by Daylight Saving Time?

MARCH 14, 1794

Eli Whitney patented the cotton gin on this date. As a young law student Whitney spent some time on a southern plantation where he overheard a conversation among planters about the terrible problems of cleaning cotton. Concerned, he proceeded to invent and patent a cotton gin, which could clean cotton as fast as 25 workers! Later, this machine helped make the United States the world leader in cotton production.

Students might research and report on plants, noting the many ways we use them — for clothing, food, and medicine. (*See also* December 8, 1765.)

MARCH 14, 1879
Birth Date of Albert Einstein

Albert Einstein was the physicist who formulated the theory of relativity that broadened understanding of space, time, and motion. He formulated his relativity theory in 1905 when he was 26 years old, and in 1921 he won the Nobel Prize for Physics. Born in Ulm, Germany, Einstein was forced to leave his homeland in 1933 when his German citizenship was taken away by the Nazis because he was Jewish.

He was the scientist who delved into theoretical physics; using a pencil, paper, and mathematical logic, he expanded our knowledge of matter, energy, heat, light, and atomic structure. His findings contributed to the development of such complex devices as the electric eye, sound movies, and television.

He also developed an idea that provided the basic principles for making an atomic bomb and other nuclear devices. Einstein's work on the conversion of matter into energy helped bring the world into the atomic age.

MARCH 15, 1767
Birth Date of Andrew Jackson, Seventh President

Born in:	Waxhaw, South Carolina
Occupation:	Lawyer, soldier, planter
President:	1829–1837, Democrat
Died:	June 8, 1845
	The Hermitage, near Nashville, Tennessee

About Jackson
★ Self-educated on the frontier; nicknamed "Old Hickory."
★ Commanded American forces in victory over English at New Orleans in War of 1812.
★ Received most popular votes in 1824 presidential election, but John Quincy Adams became president when election was decided by House of Representatives.

During His Terms
★ President's Mansion renamed White House.
★ Westward expansion and focus; Arkansas and Michigan became states.
★ Stopped first serious secession move by a state — South Carolina.
★ Firm believer in democracy and the rights of the farmer, artisan, and frontiersman.

MARCH 15, 1820

Maine became the twenty-third state.

◆

Flower: White Pine Cone and Tassel
Tree: Eastern White Pine
Bird: Chickadee

MARCH 16, 1751
Birth Date of James Madison, Fourth President

Born in:	Port Conway, Virginia
Occupation:	Planter, statesman, lawyer
President:	1809–1817, Democratic-Republican
Died:	June 28, 1836
	Montpelier, Virginia

About Madison
★ Frail as a youngster.
★ Graduate of Princeton University.
★ Member of the Continental Congress and Constitutional Convention.
★ Proposed nine of the ten Bill of Rights amendments.
★ Served as Jefferson's Secretary of State.

During His Terms
★ War of 1812 with England; the British burned President's Mansion in Washington, D.C.
★ First protective tariff adopted.
★ His wife, Dolley, introduced ice cream as a dessert.

MARCH 16, 1926

On this date Dr. Robert H. Goddard launched the first liquid-propellant rocket outside Auburn, Massachusetts. The designer-physicist's machine only traveled 184 feet in its 2.5-second flight, but many of today's aerospace scientists recognize it as equivalent to the Wright Brothers' achievement in the history of flight. Both feats were harbingers of today's massive flying machines and space rockets.

The launching site on his Aunt Effie Ward's farm on Paka-choag Hill is marked by a granite monument erected in 1960 by the American Rocket Society.

MARCH 17
Saint Patrick's Day

According to legend, Saint Patrick was born in the early fourth century A.D. in western England, but no one knows exactly when or where. At age 16, he was captured by Irish raiders who carried him to slavery in Ireland. Patrick escaped after six years and entered an English monastery where eventually he became a bishop. He returned to Ireland as a missionary and dedicated himself to converting the Irish to Christianity. Today celebrations and parades mark the anniversary of his death in 492. It is a national holiday in Ireland and has been celebrated in America since 1737, when a group of Irish Prot-estants met in Boston to honor Saint Patrick and founded a group called the Charitable Irish Society.

More information on the holiday appears in *Shamrocks, Harps, and Shellelaghs: The Story of Saint Patrick's Day Symbols* by Edna Barth, illustrated by Ursula Arndt (Clarion, 1977; also in paperback).

MARCH 18, 1806
Birth Date of Norbert Rillieux

Norbert Rillieux, a black scientist, invented a method of re-fining sugar in 1846 that revolutionized the sugar industry. His techniques were used in Cuba, Mexico, and throughout Europe as well as in the United States. Rillieux was born in New Orleans; he died in Paris in 1894, where he lived a good part of his life. There is a memorial to him in the Louisiana State Museum in New Orleans.

MARCH 18, 1837
Birth Date of (Stephen) Grover Cleveland
Twenty-second and Twenty-fourth President

Born in:	Caldwell, New Jersey
Occupation:	Lawyer, public official
President:	1885–1889, 1893–1897, Democrat
Died:	June 24, 1908
	Princeton, New Jersey

About Cleveland
★ Sheriff of Erie County, mayor of Buffalo, and then governor of New York State.
★ Only president to lose a bid for reelection (1888) and run again to win (1892).

During His Terms
★ Married the youngest first lady in history, twenty-two-year-old Frances Folsom, while in the White House.
★ Supported tariff and civil service reform.
★ Encouraged homesteading by recovering misappropriated lands from the railroads.
★ During his second term, he faced labor unrest and a depression, which he alleviated by imposing the gold standard.
★ Developed cancer of the mouth and was forced to wear a handmade jaw for the remainder of his life.

MARCH 21
First Day of Spring

Because the earth is tilted on its axis as it moves around the sun, different amounts of light and heat fall on different areas of our planet during the year, causing spring, summer, autumn, and winter. The arrival of new seasons is most marked in temperate regions, where the sun rises highest in the sky during summer and lowest in winter. Scientists have set approximate dates for the arrival of each of the four seasons in the Northern Hemisphere: spring, March 21; summer, June 21; autumn, September 21; and winter, December 21. The summer and winter dates are called solstices and mark the days of longest and shortest daylight. Spring and autumn occur when the sun is directly over the equator; these times are called equinoxes because the hours of the day and night are equal.

Mark the arrival of each season by taking the class on a short neighborhood field trip. Let students look for the first signs of the season and perhaps collect some materials for a science table display. Add books about the particular season to the display. Set aside time for brainstorming in which students list words to describe the season. The words can be used in creative expression exercises.

MARCH 21

The zodiac sign, Aries the Ram, begins today and ends April 19. How many of your students were born under this sign?

MARCH 21
No Ruz, Iranian New Year

Houses are cleaned and redecorated, wheat and lentil seeds are planted indoors, small cuttings of shrubbery are set afire in yards for families to jump over, and children go door to door seeking small gifts. The vernal equinox occurs on March 21, and in Iran, spring and the New Year are ushered in together. It is a festive time that lasts for 12 days. During this period people eat special foods such as apples, vinegar, olives, fish, and sweet and sour dishes from a ritual table, the haft-sin, to ensure another year of fertility and well-being for their nation. March 21, 1990, will welcome the year 1369 to Iran.

MARCH 21, 1806
Birth Date of Benito Juárez

Considered the "George Washington of Mexico," Benito Juárez was a Zapotec born in the mountains of Oaxaca. His trials as "Father of His Country" were greater than those of his North American counterpart, for he not only had to defeat an invading foreign army but had to contend with political rivals for most of his public life. In 1826, he was elected to Mexico's Congress. One of his first acts was to introduce a bill to confiscate the estate of the country's conqueror, Hernando Cortés, with all proceeds to be given over to the state. His opposition to the dictator Antonio López de Santa Anna, conqueror of the Alamo, forced Juárez to flee to New Orleans. When Santa Anna was overthrown, Juárez returned to Mexico and declared himself president.

Juárez's refusal to pay foreign debts gave the French a pretext to invade the country, and he had to flee once again. The French plan was to subjugate the nation sufficiently to proclaim an empire. French troops roamed over northern Mexico searching out Juárez, but he managed to elude them. (He sent his family to New York City for safety.) In May 1864, the Austrian archduke Maximilian arrived with his wife Carlotta to become emperor of Mexico. In 1865, a more significant event happened. In the United States, President Andrew Johnson made a veiled threat to the French government, complaining that their forces in Mexico violated the Monroe Doctrine. When Juárez's wife visited Washington, Johnson gave her a warm reception in the White House, the first since he took office. The following year French troops evacuated Mexico City. Juárez and his supporters defeated the die-hard Maximilian at Querétaro. Juárez returned to Mexico City in triumph and served as Mexico's president for five years.

MARCH 22, 1846
Birth Date of Randolph Caldecott

Randolph Caldecott was born in Chester, England, and began drawing when he was a young boy. In 1871, several of his drawings appeared in the magazine *London Society*. The following year he settled in London to work as an artist. When Washington Irving's *Old Christmas* appeared with his illustrations in 1876, Caldecott's reputation was firmly established. Two years later he began working on nursery toy books. His most famous illustrations, however, were those for William Cowper's poem "The Diverting History of John Gilpin." In 1886, Caldecott made a trip to the United States, during which he died in Florida on February 12.

The Caldecott Medal is named for this artist. This award, begun in 1938, is given annually by the American Library Association to the artist of the most distinguished picture book for children. Recent Caldecott Award-winning volumes include:

1989 *Song and Dance Man* by Karen Ackerman, illustrated by Stephen Gammell (Alfred A. Knopf, 1988).
1988 *Owl Moon* by Jane Yolen, illustrated by John Schoenherr (G.P. Putnam's Sons, 1987).
1987 *Hey, Al* by Arthur Yorinks, illustrated by Richard Egielski (Farrar, Straus & Giroux, 1986).
1986 *Polar Express* by Chris Van Allsburg (Houghton Mifflin, 1985).
1985 *Saint George and the Dragon*, adapted by Margaret

Hodges, illustrated by Trina Schart Hyman (Little, Brown, 1984).

Encourage a group of students to seek earlier titles that have won the Caldecott Medal. They can set up a display of the books, read them, and discuss the various art forms.

MARCH 23, 1775

On this date Patrick Henry delivered his famous ". . . give me liberty or give me death!" speech at St. John's Church in Richmond, Virginia. Opposition to British rule of the American colonies was an earmark of this patriot's oratory. Many rich and powerful colonists loyal to the king decried Henry's radicalism, his fight against the Stamp Act, and his treasonous effort to arm the Virginia militia. Henry's words have thrilled generations of Americans:

> Is life so dear, or peace so sweet, as to be purchased at the price of chains and slavery? Forbid it, Almighty God! I know not what course others may take, but as for me give me liberty, or give me death!

Henry's service to the people continued after independence was won; he became one of the foremost advocates of the Bill of Rights which was amended to the Constitution.

He died on June 6, 1799. An account of his life and times can be found in *Where Was Patrick Henry on the 29th of May?* by Jean Fritz, illustrated by Margot Tomes (Coward, 1975; also in paperback).

MARCH 23, 1857

On this date Elisha Graves Otis installed the first passenger elevator in the United States equipped with an automatic safety brake. The idea for the elevator came about while Otis, a master mechanic, was employed in a New York mattress factory.

MARCH 25, 1871
Birth Date of Gutzon Borglum

Gutzon Borglum, an American sculptor, is best known for the noted Mount Rushmore Memorial in South Dakota, which features the heads of four United States presidents — George Washington, Thomas Jefferson, Abraham Lincoln, and Theodore Roosevelt. The busts are the largest in the world. Other works by Borglum include the head of Lincoln in the rotunda of the Capitol Building in Washington, D.C., and a statue of Lincoln seated on a bench, which is located in Newark, New Jersey. Borglum was born John Gutzon de la Mothe Borglum to Danish parents in Idaho. He died in 1941 before the Mount Rushmore Memorial was completed. His son, who had worked with him, completed the job.

MARCH 26, 1874
Birth Date of Robert Lee Frost

> You know, I've often said that every poem solves something for me in life. I go so far as to say that every poem is a momentary stay against the confusion of the world.
> — From *A Lover's Quarrel with the World*,
> WGBH Education Foundations and
> Henry Holt, Inc., film (Holt, 1963)

Poet Robert Lee Frost was born in San Francisco. He did not attend school until he was 12 years old and never read a book until he was 14. In the early 1890s, Frost lived in New England and worked as a farmer, an editor, and a schoolteacher. Many of his experiences during this time became material for his later poems. He won the Pulitzer Prize for Poetry in 1924, 1931, 1937, and 1943. Frost is recognized as one of the most popular American poets of his time.

His participation in the inauguration of President John F. Kennedy was a highlight in his career. On March 26, 1962, his eighty-eighth birthday, he was awarded the Congressional Medal at the White House by President Kennedy. His last book, *In the Clearing* (Henry Holt, 1962), was published that same year. He died on January 29, 1963. Share some poems by Frost with the class today in honor of the poet's birth.

His selected poems for children appear in *A Swinger of Birches: Poetry of Robert Frost for Young Readers*, illustrated by Peter Koeppen (Stemmer House, 1982; also in paperback). The first picture book version of his classic work, *Stopping by Woods on a Snowy Evening*, illustrated by Susan Jeffers, appeared in 1978 (E.P. Dutton); *Birches*, illustrated by Ed Young, appeared in 1988 (Henry Holt).

MARCH 26, 1930
Birth Date of Sandra Day O'Connor

In 1981, President Ronald Reagan made his first appointment to the Supreme Court. It was a historic occasion because the nominee, Sandra Day O'Connor, a former Arizona state senator and judge, was a female — the first ever to serve on the Court.

MARCH 27, 1845
Birth Date of Wilhelm C. Roentgen

In 1895, this German physicist discovered X rays — high-frequency short-wave rays produced by a stream of electrons — and was awarded the Nobel Prize in 1901. Medical science has found countless uses for Roentgen's discovery in research, diagnosis, and treatment of disease. Today X rays are measured in units called roentgens, honoring the man who discovered them.

MARCH 28, 1797

On this date the washing machine was patented by Nathaniel Briggs of New Hampshire.

MARCH 29, 1790
Birth Date of John Tyler, Tenth President

Born in:	Charles City County, Virginia
Occupation:	Lawyer
President:	1841–1845, Whig
Died:	January 18, 1862
	Richmond, Virginia

About Tyler
★ First vice president to assume full presidential powers after the death of William Henry Harrison.
★ Champion of states' rights.

During His Term
★ Whig Party tried to direct him, then expelled him when he showed independence.
★ Weather Bureau started.
★ Feuded with Congress.
★ Annexed Texas.
★ First president to marry while in office; he had been a widower.

MARCH 30, 1820
Birth Date of Anna Sewell

Anna Sewell, author of only one book, *Black Beauty*, was born at Great Yarmouth, Norfolk, England, the daughter of Quaker parents. At an early age she sprained an ankle, which left her partially lame. By her mid-thirties she was severely lame and could only get around via a pony cart.

In 1871, she was told she had only 18 months to live. It was during the latter part of this year that she started writing *Black Beauty*. Five years later she was still alive and at work on the novel. She lived to see the book published (1877), but died several months later, never knowing the success it would become thoughout the world.

Today is a good time to share part of *Black Beauty* with the class. There are countless editions. A recent one for younger readers is *Black Beauty* adapted by Newbery Award-winner Robin McKinley, with full-color pictures by Susan Jeffers (Random House, 1987). An audiocassette is also available, narrated by Ben Kingsley (Random House, 1986).

MARCH 30, 1853
Birth Date of Vincent van Gogh

> There is nothing in the world as interesting as people . . . one can never study them enough.
> — Vincent van Gogh

Born in Groot-Zundert, Holland, Vincent van Gogh produced over 800 paintings as well as hundreds of drawings, only one of which he sold. Ironically, on November 11, 1987, his painting *Irises* was sold for $53.9 million by Sotheby's in New York City.

He led a solitary life at Arles in the south of France, suffering bouts of depression and despair, finally committing suicide by shooting himself on July 29, 1890, at the age of 37.

Steer young readers toward *Van Gogh: Art for Children* by Ernest Raboff (Harper & Row paperback, 1988), which contains a brief biography of the artist and 15 color reproductions of his work.

MARCH 30, 1858

The first pencil with an attached eraser was patented in Philadelphia, Pennsylvania, by Hyman L. Lipman. The pencil had a groove into which was secured "a piece of prepared rubber glued at one end." How did this invention change our lives?

MARCH 30, 1870

The Fifteenth Amendment became part of the United States Constitution. It forbids any state to deny citizens the right to vote because of "race, color, or previous condition of servitude."

MARCH 31, 1777

On this date Abigail Adams wrote to her husband, John, who was attending the second Continental Congress in Philadelphia,

> ... I long to hear that you have declared an independency and by the way, in the new code of laws which I suppose it will be necessary for you to make, I desire you would remember the ladies and be more generous and favorable to them than were your ancestors. Do not put such unlimited power into the hands of husbands. Remember, all men would be tyrants if they could.

John Adams responded to his wife's urging for the right of women to vote: "I can't but laugh . . ."

Discuss the evolution of women's rights in the United States since the 1770s.

MARCH 31, 1889

The Eiffel Tower built by Alexandre Gustave Eiffel was completed on this date. Eiffel built the tower for the World's Fair in Paris. At that time it was the tallest building in the world — 985 feet high. Today the tower still attracts thousands of visitors and is one of the most famous architectural structures in the world.

MARCH 31, 1927
Birth Date of César Estrada Chávez

César Estrada Chávez was born in Yuma, Arizona, the son of migrant workers. As a child he attended more than 30 elementary schools because his parents traveled around, looking for work.

In 1962, he organized farm workers into the United Farm Workers (UFW), an affiliate of the AFL-CIO. He organized boycotts of grapes, wine, and lettuce to pressure California growers to sign contracts with the UFW. Within 10 years, the UFW had over 60,000 members! Today there are over 100,000 members.

A biography of Chávez for better readers is *César Chávez* by Ruth Franchere, illustrated by Earl Thollander (T.Y. Crowell, 1970; Harper & Row Trophy paperback).

MARCH/APRIL
Easter Sunday

For Christians the world over Easter Sunday is the holiest religious holiday of the year. It celebrates the resurrection of Jesus Christ who rose from the dead to new life. Easter Sunday comes on the first Sunday after the first full moon in spring.

He Is Risen: The Easter Story, adapted from the New Testament by Elizabeth Winthrop, is beautifully illustrated by Charles Mikolaycak (Holiday House, 1985). Also look for Easter by Jon Pieńkowski (Alfred A. Knopf, 1988) and Easter by Gail Gibbons (Holiday House, 1989).

MARCH/APRIL
Passover

Pesach, the festival of Passover, is an important event in the cultural life of Jews and is the best known of the Jewish holidays. It commemorates two events of ancient and historic importance: (1) shepherds of old marked the arrival of spring by sacrificing a lamb to ensure their flocks' multiplication and (2) the Hebrews escaped from slavery in Egypt. Jews commemorate these events by holding a family gathering — the Seder — at which the flight of their ancestors is recounted. Special foods are an integral part of the Passover ritual: Matzoh or unleavened bread, roasted egg, parsley, maror (bitter herbs), choroses (nuts and apples), and wine. Their significance is explained by reading from the Haggadah, a religious account of the Hebrews' Egyptian slave experience in which God forced the Pharaoh to release the enslaved Hebrews. This story is recounted in the Book of Exodus in the Bible.

Middle-graders will find out more about the holiday in Ask Another Question: The Story and Meaning of Passover by Miriam Chaikin, illustrated by Marvin Friedman (Clarion Books, 1985).

APRIL

FLOWER   ◆   BIRTHSTONE
Sweet Pea   Diamond

Until 45 B.C., April was the second month of the Roman calendar. The meaning and origin of the word *April* is the subject of considerable debate. One authority, Jakob Grimm, stated that it may have originated from the name of a hypothetical god or hero named Aper of Aprus. Others say the name is derived from the verb *apeire* meaning "to open," referring to the opening of leaves and buds at this time of year.

APRIL POEM OF THE MONTH

from
THE MERRY WIVES OF WINDSOR

He capers,
he dances,
he has eyes of youth,
he writes verses,
he smells April and May.

    — William Shakespeare

APRIL 1
April Fool's Day

"Look! There's a lizard crawling on your slice of pizza!"
  Not really, but such exclamations are something you may have to put up with today. April Fool's Day originated in France. Prior to the adoption of the Gregorian Calendar in the late sixteenth century, the vernal equinox and the New Year occurred concurrently around April 1. This was a time of festivity and gift exchanging. After the adoption of the new calendar, people far removed from the centers of civilization continued the old practice of celebrating and gift giving. Because of their error, they were ridiculed. In time this changed to April Fool practical joking.

APRIL 1, 1578
Birth Date of William Harvey

William Harvey, an English physician, was the first to discover the function of the heart in the circulation of blood through the body. His book, *An Anatomical Treatise on the Motion of the*

Heart and Blood in Animals, first published almost four hundred years ago, is considered the most important single volume in the history of physiology. (*See also* June 3, 1904.)

Invite a nurse into the classroom to aid in the study of the heart, our largest and most important muscle. Show students models or pictures of it, explaining where it is located and how it works. Students can also listen to each other's heart and take one another's pulse.

A reference book for children is *Heartbeats: Your Body, Your Heart* by Dr. Alvin Silverstein and Virginia B. Silverstein, illustrated by Stella Ormai (Lippincott, 1983). Also, *The Magic School-bus Inside the Human Body* by Joanna Cole, illustrated by Bruce Degen (Scholastic, 1989) gives readers a unique glimpse of how a heart (and other parts of the body) work.

APRIL 1, 1990
Census Day

The U.S. Census Bureau uses this date to find out how many people live in the 3.5 million square miles of the United States.

It is a task required by our Constitution and takes place every 10 years. The official count is used to analyze the population as to age, education, housing, jobs, income, and family status. Some interesting facts the census tells us are how many babies are born and how many deaths occur every minute, how many immigrants arrive in the United States every hour, and how many people leave the country to take up residence in a foreign land every hour.

The census originated in ancient Babylonia. Our first census was made in 1790 — when 16 marshals and 200 assistants counted a population of little more than four million people. The census ensures the fair distribution of congressional representatives and today is used to reapportion the seats among the 50 states.

In 1990, 300,000 specifically hired and trained enumerators and a permanent staff of almost 9,000 will try to count every one of the projected 250-million-plus persons living in the United States.

Share with students the informative volume *Counting America: The Story of the United States Census* by Melissa Ashabranner and Brent Ashabranner (Putnam's, 1989).

APRIL 2, 1805
Birth Date of Hans Christian Andersen

Hans Christian Andersen was a poet, novelist, and playwright, but he is best known throughout the world for his many delightful fairy tales such as "The Ugly Duckling," "The Emperor's New Clothes," "The Princess and the Pea," and "The Snow Queen," most of which contain a moral. Andersen was the son of a poor Danish shoemaker. At age 11, after his father died, he stopped going to school and spent most of his time making toys and puppets. At 14, he journeyed to Copenhagen to become an opera singer. Unsuccessful at this and several other ventures, he turned to writing. His first book, *The Ghost at Palnatoke's Grave*, was published when he was 17. Andersen's first real success came in 1835 with his novel, *The Improvisatore*. That same year he also published a first installment of his *Fairy Tales*. More tales appeared the following years, and by 1845 he had written three books of fairy tales, which brought him fame throughout Europe. Although he continued writing novels and plays, they were not as popular as his fairy tales, which are known and translated all over the world.

In 1872, Andersen had a strange accident. He fell out of bed and injured himself so badly that he never fully recovered. He died three years later on August 4, 1875.

You will find many single and collected volumes of Andersen's *Fairy Tales* in your school or public library. Recent editions include the picture book *It's Perfectly True*, adapted and illustrated by Janet Stevens (Holiday House, 1988), and *The Ugly Duckling*, illustrated by Daniel Sans Souci (Scholastic, 1987). For older readers, there's *The Snow Queen*, translated by Eva Le Gallienne, illustrated by Arieh Zeldich (Harper & Row, 1985). The poignant biography of the man is told in *The Fairy Tale Life of Hans Christian Andersen* by Eva Moore (Scholastic, 1969).

Read to the class one of Andersen's tales. The moral can serve as a good discussion starter.

APRIL 3, 1783
Birth Date of Washington Irving

Washington Irving is considered to be the first successful professional American man of letters. His tales, "Rip Van Winkle" and "The Legend of Sleepy Hollow," are staples in American literature and made him famous abroad as well as in the United States.

In 1945, Irving's home, Sunnyside, a small estate on the Hudson River, was bought and restored by John D. Rockefeller, Jr. Located in North Tarrytown, New York, the house is open to visitors. Irving died on November 28, 1859.

APRIL 5, 1827
Birth Date of Joseph Lister

Joseph Lister, an English surgeon, was responsible for a surgical revolution. After studying Pasteur's theories on germs and their role in spreading disease, he realized that millions of germs were spread in surgical operations by doctors' instruments and their hands. As a result, Lister introduced the concept of sterilization with antiseptics. Before their use, the fatality rate for all surgery was about fifty percent. After his introduction of antiseptics the death rate dropped to about two or three percent. He died on February 10, 1912.

Germs Make Me Sick by Melvin Berger, illustrated in full-color by Marylin Haffner (T.Y. Crowell, 1985; also in paperback), provides young readers with a look at how bacteria and viruses affect our bodies and how the body fights back.

APRIL 5, 1839
Birth Date of Robert Smalls

Robert Smalls was born a slave in Beaufort, South Carolina, a town near the sea. When the Civil War broke out, Smalls was 23 years old. His master allowed him to work as a stevedore on the Confederate naval ship The Planter, one of the fastest and most valuable ships in the navy. Smalls devised a daring plan that he shared with the crew. One May day when the crew was alone on the ship, Smalls smuggled his family aboard, lifted anchor, sailed for Charleston Harbor, and turned the vessel over to the Union Navy. Smalls received great praise and a large reward for his heroic deed; the following year he was made captain of the ship.

After the war he served in the South Carolina legislature and became a major general in the state militia. From 1875 to 1886 he served three terms in the U.S. House of Representatives. Southern racists managed to have him jailed for "corruption," but his supporters reelected him to the House. Smalls helped to create the marine base at Parris Island, the training grounds for thousands of Americans who served in the U.S. Marine Corps. He remained active in politics until his death in 1915.

APRIL 5, 1856
Birth Date of Booker Taliaferro Washington

Educator and statesman, Booker T. Washington was Frederick Douglass's successor as the foremost black American leader of his day. Washington was born a slave in Hale's Ford, Virginia. After completing his studies at Wayland Seminary in Washington, D.C., he founded the Tuskegee Institute in 1881 and became its first president. He believed that the road to equality was through education. Tuskegee is now famous throughout the world for agricultural research.

Washington was an advisor to three presidents, was awarded an honorary doctorate from Harvard University, and shortly after his death became the first black American to be elected to the New York University Hall of Fame for Great Americans in New York City. On the base of his bust there are the following lines from one of his speeches:

> The highest test of the civilization of a race is its willingness to extend a helping hand to the less fortunate.

On April 7, 1940, the Booker T. Washington ten-cent stamp, the first of its kind honoring a black American, went on sale at Tuskegee. In May 1946, the first coin honoring a black American was issued — a 50-cent piece bearing a bust relief of Washington. Do any of your students collect stamps or coins? Is this stamp or coin in anyone's collection?

APRIL 6, 1896

The first modern Olympic Games were held in Athens, Greece. Thirteen countries were represented. Many of the sports represented had been carried on from the ancient Olympic Games, dating back to 776 B.C., including foot races, discus and javelin throwing, jumping, and wrestling. The Summer Olympics are held in a different country every four years. The last games were played in Seoul, South Korea, in 1988.

APRIL 6, 1909
Discovery of the North Pole

Robert E. Peary's expedition reached the North Pole on this date. Persistence carried this naval officer toward his goal despite several previous failures. Peary's curiosity about the far north was whetted by his 1886 discovery that Greenland was an island. He organized two expeditions to search for the North Pole in 1897 and 1905; both failed! In 1908, his third party, composed of four Eskimos and a black American, finally succeeded in reaching the North Pole.

APRIL 9, 1833

The first free public library in the United States was established on this date. Subscription or society libraries that allowed people to borrow books for a fee already existed in 1833. However, the nation's first free public library was established when citizens of Peterborough, New Hampshire, voted to use a portion of the town's tax revenue for that purpose. Today taxes remain the main source of funding for public libraries, though some philanthropists have made major contributions. Near the turn of the century, Andrew Carnegie donated nearly 50 million dollars to build libraries throughout the country.

Where are the libraries located in your community? Invite a librarian into the classroom to talk about the libraries' various programs. Find out if all the students in your class have library cards. If anyone does not, today is a good time to get one.

APRIL 10, 1790

The U.S. patent system was established on this date. Discuss the meaning of the term "patent." What things warrant being patented? Students might research such patented items as the toothpick, the safety pin, the zipper, or the eraser-tipped pencil. Findings, including the inventor's name and date of invention, could be recorded on a chart with the real items taped or glued on. This date will also tie-in with the next entry. (*See also* July 31, 1790.)

APRIL 10, 1849

Walter Hunt patented the safety pin. It took him only three hours to develop the idea and to construct a working model for this device that is used for so many different things today. Pass out safety pins to all students and ask them to list as many uses for the pin as they can.

APRIL 12, 1877

James Tyng, a Harvard catcher, wore the first face protector in baseball. This wire mask, called a "bird cage," was designed by coach Frederick Thayer. It was patented and became a forerunner of today's catcher's mask. Have your students list other athletic protective gear and the reasons athletes wear these things.

APRIL 12, 1961

Yuri Gagarin, a Soviet cosmonaut, became the first man in space. He made one orbit of the earth aboard the spacecraft *Vostok I.*

APRIL 13, 1743
Birth Date of Thomas Jefferson, Third President

Born in: Albemarle, Virginia
Occupation: Farmer, lawyer, public official
President: 1801–1809
Died: July 4, 1826
            Monticello, Virginia

About Jefferson
★ Spoke Latin, Greek, Italian, French, and Spanish.
★ One of the authors of the Declaration of Independence.
★ Founded Democratic-Republican Party.
★ Amateur scientist, architect, inventor, and book collector.

During His Terms
★ Ended much of the pomp and circumstance surrounding the presidency, including national celebration of presidents' birthdays.
★ Authorized the Louisiana Purchase and the Lewis and Clark expedition.
★ Helped plan Washington, D.C., building styles.
★ Tripolitan War against pirates in the Mediterranean concluded.
★ Protested British seizures of American ships and seamen.

APRIL 13, 1796

America saw its first elephant! It came to New York City from Bengal, India. It was two years old and stood six-and-a-half feet high. You might read the class the very funny poem "Ele-telephony" by Laura E. Richards, included in *Sing a Song of Popcorn: Every Child's Book of Poems*, selected by Beatrice Schenk de Regniers, Eva Moore, Mary Michaels White, and Jan Carr (Scholastic, 1988).

APRIL 13, 1902
Birth Date of Marguerite Henry

Marguerite Henry's many children's books, the most famous of which are about horses, have won both awards and admirers for decades. They include the 1949 Newbery Award winner, *King of the Wind*, and *Misty of Chincoteague* (1947), both illustrated by Wesley Dennis; and *Mustang, Wild Spirit of the West*, illustrated by Robert Lougheed (1971; all Rand McNally; also in paperback). How many students in your class have heard or read a story by this popular author? Today is a good day to begin to read aloud from one of the titles listed above.

APRIL 14, 1828

On this date Noah Webster completed the *American Dictionary of the English Language* after more than 20 years of work. The original dictionary contained nearly 70,000 entries, including 12,000 words that had never appeared in a dictionary before. Middle-grade readers can learn more about the man in *What Do You Mean? A Story about Noah Webster* by Jeri Ferris (Carolrhoda, 1988). How have dictionaries changed over the years? Have students think of new entries that were not part of the language at the time Webster compiled his book. Reinforce dictionary skills today! (*See* October 16, 1758.)

APRIL 14, 1865

John Wilkes Booth shot President Abraham Lincoln on this date. With older students you might discuss violence against political figures. What do the students think motivates the assassins? President John F. Kennedy, Senator Robert Kennedy, Martin Luther King, Jr., Governor George Wallace, and President Ronald Reagan were all victims of assassins or would-be assassins in recent history. Why do your students think such violence was directed at these men?

APRIL 14, 1890
Pan American Day

On this date, all the independent countries of the Western Hemisphere resolved to form an organization dedicated to peace and cooperation. Known as the Organization of American States, it is today the oldest international organization in the world. Pan American Day, first observed in 1931, provides students with the opportunity to learn about other countries in the hemisphere. Encourage them to make a flag display.

APRIL 15, 1452
Birth Date of Leonardo da Vinci

When the name Leonardo da Vinci comes to mind, one immediately thinks of his great achievements as a painter and sculptor. These include the portrait of *Mona Lisa*, which hangs in the Louvre Museum in Paris, France, and *The Last Supper*, a fresco, in Santa Maria delle Grazie in Milan, Italy. But da Vinci's interests ranged widely. As a scientist he is famous for anticipating important discoveries about blood circulation, the special functions of the brain, and several modern inventions such as the airplane, tank, submarine, and cannon.

He was born in the mountain village of Vinci, near Florence. He died on May 2, 1519.

Steer readers toward *Leonardo da Vinci: Art for Children* by

Ernest Raboff, which discusses his life and contains 15 full-color reproductions of his work (Harper & Row paperback, 1988).

APRIL 15, 1912

The Titanic, a large, lavish, "unsinkable" boat, sank after hitting an iceberg in the North Atlantic, killing 1,517 passengers because the ship had not carried enough lifeboats.

On September 1, 1985, the Titanic appeared again in the headlines, when a French-American expedition led by Dr. Robert Ballard discovered the legendary lost ship sitting proudly upright on the ocean bottom, 2.5 miles below the surface.

Dr. Ballard's riveting account of the history of the ship and the rediscovery is documented in Exploring the Titanic (Scholastic, 1988; also in paperback). The volume includes full-color illustrations and photographs. (See also September 1, 1985.)

APRIL 18, 1775

Paul Revere began his famous ride to warn the American colonists that "the British are coming." Revere left Boston at about 10:00 P.M. and arrived in Lexington at midnight, riding a borrowed horse, to warn Samuel Adams and John Hancock of the imminent danger. The event inspired Henry Wadsworth Longfellow to write one of his most famous poems, a moving ballad that became one of the best-known poems in American literature, "Paul Revere's Ride." (See February 27, 1807.)

From 1776 to 1779 Revere served as a Revolutionary soldier. He was also a craftsman of note and was the first American to discover the process of rolling sheet copper. He built the first copper rolling mill in the United States. Until that time all sheet copper had been imported. Revere was born in Boston on January 1, 1735, and died there on May 10, 1818. (*See* January 1, 1735, and April 19, 1775.)

APRIL 18, 1934

The first store equipped with public washing machines in which people could do their laundry opened in Fort Worth, Texas.

APRIL 19, 1775

On this date the Battle of Lexington and Concord took place. On a large outline map, locate these two places. Students might research the route Paul Revere took to Lexington and show it by drawing arrows on the map. They can make oaktag or construction-paper models of Redcoats and Minutemen and use these on the map to reenact the Battle of Lexington and Concord.

APRIL 20

The zodiac sign, Taurus the Bull, begins today and ends May 20. How many students were born under this sign?

APRIL 20, 1898

Pierre Curie (1859–1906) and his wife Marie (1867–1934) uncovered the elements radium and polonium. This team discovered these elements in pitchblende ore and was awarded the Nobel Prize in Physics in 1903 for its findings. After the death of her husband, Marie Curie took over his professorship at the Sorbonne. Her work on isolating metallic radium won her a second Nobel Prize in 1911, making her the first person to win this award twice.

The Curies' daughter Irène (1897–1956) inherited her parents' interest in science. She, too, married a fellow scientist, Frédéric Joliot. Together they studied high-energy radiation, and in 1935 they were awarded the Nobel Prize in Chemistry for their synthesis of new radioactive elements. These studies paved the way for the development of nuclear energy.

Ironically, both Marie Curie and her daughter Irène probably died from overexposure to the radioactive substances which they pioneered, as it has been discovered that excessive exposure to radiation causes leukemia (blood cancer).

APRIL 22, 1774

A group of New Yorkers emulated their compatriots in Boston who, just four months earlier, dumped a cargo of tea into the harbor on December 16, 1773. Both groups were protesting against the arbitrary tax imposed upon tea by Britain's Parliament. The New Yorkers' act, however, took place without the colorful Indian costumes the Bostonians used to disguise their action! (See also December 16, 1773.)

APRIL 22, 1823

The first pair of roller skates were patented on this date. This marvelous device sprang from the primitive model designed by the Belgian, Joseph Merlin, in the 1760s.

Four-wheeled skates came from James Plimpton of Bedford,

Massachusetts, in 1863. How many students in your class enjoy the sport? Are they aware of the sport's immense popularity during the early twentieth century when speed skating and competitive derbys were watched by thousands of fans?

APRIL 23, 1564
Birth Date of *William Shakespeare*

William Shakespeare was probably the greatest English poet and dramatist. His works have such universality that they have been translated into more languages than any book in the world except the Bible. Although Shakespeare wrote for adult audiences, there are many segments within his great body of work that children enjoy hearing or reading.

Even people who have never read Shakespeare are familiar with the famous line "To be, or not to be," but most people are not aware that he originated such common expressions as "catch cold," "a foregone conclusion," and "fair play."

Perhaps the following well-known lines from Shakespeare's plays will provoke a fresh discussion:

All the world's a stage,
And all the men and women merely players.
They have their exits and entrances;
And one man in his time plays many parts.
— *As You Like It*, Act II

Praising what is lost
Makes the remembrance dear
— *All's Well That Ends Well*, Act II

O, beware, my lord, of jealousy;
It is the green-eyed monster which doth mock
The meat it feeds on.
— *Othello*, Act III

Older students might present a reading of one of his plays. If you are looking for a more ambitious project, your class might produce a play by Shakespeare for a school assembly. And if you are extra-ambitious, you might plan an annual Shakespeare Festival.

Tales from Shakespeare by Charles and Mary Lamb, a classic text first published in 1807, is available in many editions.

APRIL 23, 1791
Birth Date of James Buchanan, Fifteenth President

Born in:	Cove Gap, Pennsylvania
Occupation:	Lawyer, public official
President:	1857–1861, Democrat
Died	June 1, 1868
	Lancaster, Pennsylvania

About Buchanan
★ Never married but adopted two of his sister's children and a daughter.
★ Unsuccessful in three previous presidential bids: 1844, 1848, 1852.

During His Term
★ John Brown's raid on Harpers Ferry in Virginia (now West Virginia), an antislavery protest.
★ Advocated buying Cuba for the United States.
★ Unable to handle the slavery problems splitting the country.
★ Seven southern states seceded and formed the Confederacy.

APRIL 24, 1704

The first American newspaper, the Boston *News-Letter*, was published by John Campbell, a postmaster. Have students find the date their local newspaper was founded. Can they get a copy of a first edition? Compare the articles, advertisements, and features. What has changed? What is still the same?

APRIL 26, 1785
Birth Date of John James Audubon

John James Audubon was born at Le Cayes, Santo Domingo (now Haiti). As a youngster, his father, a French sea captain, took him to France. After being educated there to become either a soldier or engineer, his father sent him to live in Philadelphia on his estate. Here Audubon found what he described as "a blessed spot, where hunting, fishing, and drawing occupied my every moment."

After marrying, he sold the estate and went into a series of unsuccessful business ventures. At 34, he began studying and sketching the different species of American birds. On a trip down the Mississippi River to New Orleans, Audubon drew pictures of native birds. His attempts to publish these in America failed, so he journeyed to England to seek support there. He was able to have his drawings printed in black-and-white and then painstakingly hand-colored the beautiful prints. Eventually a full-color volume, *Birds of America*, was issued. The complete edition contained 435 plates with 1,065 life-sized reproductions of American birds in their characteristic poses and habitats. The volume is acclaimed as the authoritative book on North American birds, wildlife, plants, soil, and water.

APRIL 27, 1822
Birth Date of Ulysses Simpson Grant, Eighteenth President

Born in:	Point Pleasant, Ohio
Occupation:	Soldier
President:	1869–1877, Republican
Died:	July 23, 1885
	Mount McGregor, New York
	Buried in New York, New York

About Grant
★ By the time he was 18, his name had changed three times. He was originally Hiram Ulysses Grant, which he later changed to Ulysses Hiram Grant, but ended up with Ulysses S. Grant because of an error on his West Point appointment.
★ Rose from Civil War captain to commander of the Union Army, who accepted Lee's surrender on April 3, 1865, at Appomattox Courthouse in Virginia.

During His Terms
★ Charges of mismanagement made against him because he appointed his friends to high posts; widespread corruption prevailed.
★ First transcontinental railroad completed in 1869.
★ Homestead Act permitted western lands to be settled by land-hungry pioneers.

APRIL 27, 1898
Birth Date of Ludwig Bemelmans

In an old house in Paris that was covered with vines,
Lived twelve little girls in two straight lines.

◆

Thus begins Ludwig Bemelmans's *Madeline* (1939), followed by *Madeline's Rescue*, *Madeline and the Bad Hat*, *Madeline and the Gypsies*, and *Madeline in London* (all Viking Penguin, all in paperback). To celebrate Bemelmans's birth date, read one of the above books to elementary students. Or, perhaps you could help a group of students adapt one of the tales into a play and put on a performance for the rest of the class or for other grades.

APRIL 28, 1758
Birth Date of James Monroe, Fifth President

Born in:	Westmoreland County, Virginia
Occupation:	Lawyer
President:	1817–1825, Democratic-Republican
Died:	July 4, 1831
	New York, New York
	Buried in Richmond, Virginia

About Monroe
★ While serving as Washington's minister to France, he freed Thomas Paine from prison there.
★ Only president other than Washington to run unopposed.

During His Terms
★ Flag of the United States was adopted.
★ Spain sold Florida to the United States in 1819.
★ Monroe Doctrine promulgated, to keep Europeans out of the Western Hemisphere.

APRIL 28, 1788
Maryland became the seventh state to ratify the Constitution.

Flower: Black-Eyed Susan
Tree: White Oak
Bird: Baltimore Oriole

APRIL 30, 1803

Napoleon, the ruler of France, concluded the largest real estate transaction in world history — sale of the Louisiana Purchase. Facing the threat of imminent war with Great Britain, Napoleon sold the French territory of Louisiana to agents of President Thomas Jefferson for about four cents an acre, a total of fifteen million dollars. The vast area, 827,987 square miles, stretched from the Gulf of Mexico to Canada, and from the Mississippi River to the Rocky Mountains. Jefferson, who had only intended to purchase the key port city of New Orleans, engaged two army officers to conduct the first exploration of the American Northwest. These two men, Captain Meriwether Lewis and Lieutenant William Clark, spent the years 1804 to 1806 mapping the area. They encountered tribes of unknown Native Americans, new types of flora and fauna, and led their small expedition across an area of great natural beauty.

A group of middle-graders can present a program on Lewis and Clark's epic journey, tracing their route to the Pacific. Several students might clarify their concept of area by actually measuring a square mile area in their immediate community. Their experience will highlight the significance of Jefferson's "bargain."

APRIL 30, 1812

Louisiana became the eighteenth state.

Flower: Magnolia
Tree: Cypress
Bird: Eastern Brown Pelican

APRIL/MAY
Arbor Day

In today's ecology-conscious world Arbor Day takes on great meaning. Though there is no specific date because climates and conditions vary too greatly, it is usually celebrated in late April or early May. (In Hawaii, it is in November and in Alabama it is celebrated during the last full week of February.) To find out the date Arbor Day is celebrated in your state, have a student write to The National Arbor Day Foundation, Arbor Lodge 100, Nebraska City, NE 68410.

To add to Arbor Day festivities, contact a local greenhouse or nursery and ask it to donate a small tree — or raise money to buy one — to be planted on or near the school grounds. A tree-planting ceremony can involve all the classes in the school. Give the tree a name to honor someone special. End this ceremony with a discussion of trees — what uses they have, varieties, and so on.

Younger children will enjoy hearing or reading aloud *A Tree Is Nice* by Janice May Udry (Harper & Row, 1956; also in paperback). This book won Marc Simont the 1957 Caldecott Award. *Once There Was a Tree* by Natalia Romanova, illustrated by Gennady Spirin (Dial Books for Young Readers, 1985) relates the story of a tree stump that attracts many living creatures, even man. When it is gone, in its place a new tree attracts the same creatures. *Arbor Day* by Diane L. Burns, illustrated by Kathy Rogers (Carolrhoda, 1989) is another resource for young readers.

MAY

FLOWER   ◆   BIRTHSTONE
Lily of the Valley   Emerald

May's name and the number of days it contains
have a mixed history. The name can be traced
back to Maia, the goddess of "growth and in-
crease." Some authorities, however, maintain
that May was named to pay tribute to the Majores
or Maiores, the older branch of the Roman Senate. The number of days has varied from 22 to
30 to today's 31. Romans associated this month
with flowers, fertility, and the rich gifts of nature.

MAY POEM OF THE MONTH

LAST LAUGH

They all laughed when I told them
I wanted to be

A woman in space
Floating so free.

But they won't laugh at me
When they finally see
My feet up on Mars
And my face on TV.

— Lee Bennett Hopkins

MAY 1
May Day

May Day originated in the rites of the ancient Romans and Druids who called upon nature during this period to bring forth another life-giving spring. Trees were a central object of worship in their rituals. The English changed the custom by erecting maypoles in villages around which all danced and frolicked. They transformed the day into such a spirited festival that Puritan leaders barred the celebration in the mid-seventeenth century. Today May Day is celebrated in most areas of the world as a day to honor labor. The United States honors American workers in September. (*See* the first Monday in September.)

MAY 1, 1931

The Empire State Building was opened to the public. The skyscraper, located on Fifth Avenue in New York City, is one of the tallest buildings in the world. It has 102 stories and towers 1,250 feet high; a 222-foot television tower brings the total height to 1,472 feet — more than a quarter of a mile high. The Empire State Building was the tallest building in the world until the World Trade Center opened in New York City in 1972. These buildings are now surpassed in height by the Sears Tower in Chicago, which opened in 1974.

Children will glean interesting information about the construction of skyscrapers in *Up Goes the Skyscraper* by Gail Gibbons (Four Winds, 1986).

MAY 3, 1898
Birth Date of Golda Meir

When she was eight, Golda Meir's family emigrated from Kiev, Russia, to Milwaukee, Wisconsin. She attended the Teacher's Seminary there and later became a leader in the Milwaukee Labor Zionist party. While still young she and her husband, Morris Meyerson, emigrated to Palestine and lived on a kibbutz. She became active in politics and labor and served in many governmental capacities, including that of Israel's first ambassador to Moscow. In 1969, Meir became prime minister of Israel, a position she held until her formal resignation on June 5, 1974.

Admired throughout the world for her intelligence, leadership, and unique personality, Meir was a dominant force in the twentieth century and is a model for any era. She died on December 8, 1978, in Jerusalem.

Her autobiography, *My Life* (Dell paperback, 1976) became a nationwide bestseller. Middle-grade readers will discover more amazing facts about her in *Our Golda: The Story of Golda Meir* by David A. Adler (Viking Penguin, 1984).

MAY 4, 1626

Peter Minuit landed on Manhattan, eventually purchasing the island from the Native Americans living there for $24. He paid for it with beads and various trinkets. What a bargain!

MAY 5, 1867
Birth Date of Nellie Bly

Nellie Bly, who also used the pen name Elizabeth Cochran, was the first American woman journalist to achieve international fame. She was also a staunch crusader for women's rights and social reform.

Her best-known exploit was an attempt to travel around the world in record time, beating the time of Jules Verne's fictional character Phileas Fogg. This feat captured the country's interest and boosted her newspaper circulation at *The* (New York) *World*.

Bly started her trip on November 14, 1889, returning to New York on January 26, 1890, setting a record of 72 days, 6 hours, 11 minutes. In 1890, she wrote of her adventures in *Nellie Bly: Around the World in Seventy-two Days.* She died on January 27, 1922.

Have students discuss flight travel today. How has it changed since then? Discuss the record-setting *Concorde* and other supersonic methods of transport. (*See also* October 2, 1872.)

MAY 7, 1812
Birth Date of Robert Browning

Rats!
They fought the dogs and killed the cats,
And bit the babies in the cradles,

And ate the cheeses out of the vats,
And licked the soup from the cooks' own ladles,
Split open kegs of fish and fats,
Made nests inside men's Sunday hats,
And even spoiled the women's chats
By drowning their speaking
With shrieking and squeaking
In fifty different sharps and flats . . .

The above lines are part of the rhythmical romp, *The Pied Piper of Hamelin*, one of Robert Browning's best-known poems. In May 1842, at age 30, Browning composed the work to amuse the son of one of his friends who was confined to a sickbed.

Share some of his verse with your class. A lovely new edition of the poem has been illustrated by Terry Small in black-and-white drawings (Harcourt Brace Jovanovich, 1988). The preface traces the legend of the origin of the Pied Piper, which dates back to the 1400s.

MAY 7, 1840
Birth Date of Peter Ilich Tchaikovsky

Peter Ilich Tchaikovsky was one of Russia's first composers to gain international fame. He began composing seriously when he was 26 and produced symphonies, concertos, operas, and overtures. His ballet scores — *Swan Lake*, *Sleeping Beauty*, and *Nutcracker* — have become classics. His famous overtures include *1812* and *Romeo and Juliet*. In 1891, he visited the United States and was received with great enthusiasm. He died two years later in St. Petersburg (now Leningrad).

Celebrate Tchaikovsky's birthday with the class by listening to a selection from some of his work. (*See* December 18, 1892.)

MAY 8, 1884
Birth Date of Harry S. Truman, Thirty-third President

Born in: Lamar, Missouri
Occupation: Businessman, public official
President: 1945–1953, Democrat
Died: December 26, 1972

About Truman
★ Small-town background where he was "Mr. Average Citizen."
★ Hardships of Depression years ended his small haberdashery business leading him to politics and the Senate.
★ As vice president during Roosevelt's fourth term, he succeeded to the office upon the president's death.

During His Terms
★ Made decision to use atomic bomb on August 6, 1945, at Hiroshima and three days later at Nagasaki to end the war with Japan.
★ Inaugurated Truman Doctrine in post-World War II period against communist expansion in Europe.
★ Won reelection in 1948 against Republican Thomas E. Dewey, New York's governor, despite polls showing he would lose.

MAY 9, 1800
Birth Date of John Brown

John Brown's passionate antislavery stance was inherited from his father, Owen, an active abolitionist who sheltered runaway slaves. John Brown and his five sons moved to the Kansas Territory in 1855 and took part in the widespread fighting between pro- and antislavery forces in that area. On October 16, 1859, together with 21 other abolitionists, Brown made his most daring move — the capture of a United States government arsenal at Harpers Ferry, Virginia (now West Virginia). With the arms they seized, the band hoped to spark slave revolts all over the South. Colonel Robert E. Lee, who later served as a general for the Confederacy, led the U.S. Marines who captured Brown and his men. Brown was hanged in December, but he was considered by many to have been a martyr. Less than 18 months after his death Union soldiers marched off to fight in the Civil War singing a song praising John Brown. Sing the song "John Brown's Body" with your students:

John Brown's body lies a-moldering in the grave.
John Brown's body lies a-moldering in the grave.
John Brown's body lies a-moldering in the grave.
His soul is marching on.

Glory, glory, hallelujah!
Glory, glory, hallelujah!
Glory, glory, hallelujah!
His soul is marching on!

MAY 9, 1914
Mother's Day

Mother's Day became a public holiday. Julia Ward Howe, who wrote the words to "The Battle Hymn of the Republic" (*see* May 27, 1819), is said to have been the first to suggest a Mother's Day in the United States in 1872. The English had been honoring mothers on a day called Mothering Sunday; other countries had also been observing similar days. In 1915, President Woodrow Wilson signed a joint resolution of Congress recommending that Mother's Day be a holiday. He proclaimed it an annual observance to be held on the second Sunday in May.

Share some poems about mothers with the class. You will find 20 in *Poems for Mothers*, selected by Myra Cohn Livingston, illustrated by Deborah Kogan Ray (Holiday House, 1988). Also share with students the fact that 145 million Mother's Day cards are sent each year in the United States.

MAY 10

Boys' Festival is a holiday celebrated in Japan and Hawaii. Large carps made of paper or cloth are flown from tall poles. Families having one or more boys fly a carp for each one— the largest carp represents the oldest, the smallest carp, the youngest. The carp signifies strength and courage because the fish swims upstream and against strong currents. Boys display treasured dolls on this festival day — dolls that represent ancient warriors and heroes. Girls, too, have their day in Japan. (*See* March 3 for the Festival of Dolls.)

MAY 11, 1858

Minnesota became the thirty-second state.

Flower: Pink and White Lady's-Slipper
Tree: Red Pine
Bird: Common Loon

MAY 12, 1812
Birth Date of Edward Lear

How pleasant to know Mr. Lear!
Who has written such volumes of stuff!

Some think him ill-tempered and queer,
　But a few think him pleasant enough.

His mind is concrete and fastidious,
　His nose is remarkably big;
His visage is more or less hideous,
　His beard it resembles a wig.

He has two ears, and two eyes, and ten fingers,
　Leastways if you reckon two thumbs,
Long ago he was one of the singers,
　But now he is one of the dumbs . . .

The above stanzas are from Edward Lear's "How Pleasant To
Know Mr. Lear!," a witty ditty he wrote about himself!

Lear, the man whose name is synonymous with limericks,
was born in London, the youngest of 21 children. Early in life
he became an artist, painting birds and illustrating the works
of naturalists. At 21, he published a large collection of colored
drawings of birds. While doing similar work for the Earl of
Derby, he lived at the earl's home where he became popular
with the children of the family because of the absurd poems
and drawings he created for them. These became the nucleus
of his Book of Nonsense (1846). Later Lear moved to Italy, where
he continued to write and illustrate books, mainly about his
travels.

Children enjoy the whimsy of Lear. The youngest will love
his nonsense alphabet, which begins:

A was once an apple pie,
　　　Pidy
　　　Widy
　　　Tidy
　　　Pidy
Nice Insidy
Apple Pie!

Readers will enjoy the complete "A Was Once an Apple Pie," which can be found in *Side by Side: Poems to Read Together*, collected by Lee Bennett Hopkins, whimsically illustrated by Hilary Knight (Simon & Schuster, 1988). Also look for three sparkling editions of Lear's narrative poem, *The Owl and the Pussycat*; one is illustrated by Paul Galdone (Clarion Books, 1987), another by Lorinda Bryan Cauley (G.P. Putnam's Sons, 1986), and a pop-up version appears with illustrations by Claire Littlejohn (Harper & Row, 1987).

Older readers will enjoy *The Quangle Wangle's Hat*, illustrated by Janet Stevens (Harcourt Brace Jovanovich, 1988) and *The Scroobious Pip*, illustrated by Nancy Elkholm Burkert (Harper & Row, 1968; paperback), which is based on the handwritten manuscript of this poem discovered in a nearly finished state among Lear's papers after his death. This edition was completed by Ogden Nash.

A bountiful collection of varied works appears in *How Pleasant to Know Mr. Lear!: Edward Lear's Selected Works with an Introduction and Notes* by Myra Cohn Livingston (Holiday House, 1982).

Share some Lear limericks with the class. Here is one:

There was a Young Lady whose chin,
Resembled the point of a pin;
    So she had it made sharp,
    And purchased a harp,
And played several tunes with her chin.

Students can create limericks of their own. The form consists of five lines. Lines one, two, and five rhyme. Lines three and four may or may not rhyme.

MAY 12, 1820
Birth Date of Florence Nightingale

Florence Nightingale, the founder of modern nursing, was

named for Florence, Italy, where she was born. Nightingale was one of the greatest women of England's Victorian Age. During the Crimean War (1854), British soldiers referred to her as "The Lady with the Lamp" because of her constant devotion — night and day — to aiding the wounded. Within five months after her arrival in the Balkans, the military death rate fell from 40 percent to about 2 percent. When the war ended in 1856, she returned to England. Though quite ill, she continued to work on improving the nursing profession through writing and lecturing. Shortly before her death in 1910, King Edward VII presented her with the Order of Merit; she was the first woman to be so honored. Steer middle graders to *The Value of Compassion: The Story of Florence Nightingale* by Ann D. Johnson (Oak Tree, 1987).

MAY 14, 1686
Birth Date of Gabriel Daniel Fahrenheit

As the temperature is warming outside, it is the perfect day to teach your class about the thermometer and its use. In 1714 Fahrenheit, a German physicist, invented the type of thermometer used today.

Explain the difference between the Fahrenheit and Celsius scales. The Celsius scale is based on the metric system. (On this scale, 0° is the freezing point of water and 100° is its boiling point.) Discuss why the United States, Canada, and England use the Fahrenheit scale, while most other countries use the Celsius scale, which was invented in 1742. Older students might want to watch weather reports at home, then report their findings to the class. How often was the word *Fahrenheit* used by the weather forecaster?

MAY 14, 1908

Charles W. Furnas became the first passenger to fly in an airplane. He flew with Wilbur Wright on a flight that lasted 28.6 seconds.

MAY 14, 1948

Israel became an independent nation. On this date, it was founded as a homeland for Jews around the world who wanted a refuge from persecution. Have students locate Israel on a world map and compare its size with one of the United States. (Many children will be amazed to find out that Israel is just about the size of New Jersey.)

MAY 15, 1856
Birth Date of L. Frank Baum

L. Frank Baum had such success with his book *The Wonderful Wizard of Oz* (1900), that he followed it with 13 other books about Oz. Read portions of the book to your class. Ask students why they think it has become such a favorite story for generations of readers. How many have seen the film *The Wizard of Oz*? Compare the book and the film.

MAY 15, 1930

Ellen Church, a registered nurse, became the world's first flight attendant on a Boeing 80A trimotor flight from San Francisco to Cheyenne, Wyoming. She and seven other registered nurses were hired by United Airlines. Invite a local flight attendant to come to the class to answer children's questions about flight travel and the duties plane crews perform in the skies.

MAY 17, 1954

The landmark Supreme Court decision in the case of *Brown vs. Board of Education of Topeka, Kansas* was declared. The Supreme Court ruled that racial segregation in public schools was unconstitutional.

Through the 1930s and 1940s the National Association for the Advancement of Colored People (NAACP) fought for educational opportunities through the courts.

On this date came the decision by the Supreme Court that persons "required on the basis of race to attend separate schools were deprived of the equal protection of the laws guaranteed by the Fourteenth Amendment." Racial segregation in the public schools was outlawed. The "separate but equal" law, which the Court had upheld, was set aside.

School desegregation happened slowly. Ten years after the Court's decision only 9.2 percent of children in public schools in the southern and border states were attending desegregated classes. (*See also* July 2, 1908.)

Discuss this decision and why it was made. What changes have been made since it was declared?

MAY 19, 1925
Birth Date of Malcolm X

Malcolm X, born Malcolm Little, became famous as a leader of the black religious movement named the Nation of Islam (Black Muslims). Many Muslims took the letter X as a last name to reject the family names given by white owners to their slaves. A powerful spokesman for black nationalism, in 1964

Malcolm X formed the Organization of Afro-American Unity — a protest movement that advocated separation of the races to unify, dignify, and reshape the character of the black masses. The following year, at age 39, Malcolm X was killed while delivering a speech to his followers in New York City. His dedication to his people is admired by many Americans.

Students can read more about his life and work in the easy-to-read biography, Malcolm X, by Arnold Adoff (T.Y. Crowell, 1970; paperback).

MAY 20, 1768
Birth Date of Dolley Payne Madison

Wife of the fourth president, Dolley Payne Madison is famous for saving the portrait of George Washington when the British burned the capital in 1812 and for her gracious parties. A little-known fact about Madison is that she started the Easter custom of rolling colored eggs on the White House lawn.

MAY 20–21, 1927

Good days for flight! Charles Lindbergh made the first solo flight across the Atlantic Ocean in his plane, *The Spirit of St. Louis*. He flew from Roosevelt Field on Long Island, New York, to Le Bourget Field near Paris. The flight of about 3,610 miles was made in 33.5 hours. His definitive account of the flight, *The Spirit of St. Louis* (Scribner, 1954), won the 1954 Pulitzer Prize in American biography. Middle-graders will enjoy *The Wright Brothers at Kitty Hawk* by Donald J. Sobol (Scholastic, 1961).

Born in Detroit on February 4, 1902, Charles Augustus Lindbergh had always been interested in air travel. In 1920, he entered the University of Wisconsin as a mechanical engineering student but left in 1922 to enroll in a flying school in Lincoln, Nebraska. In 1924, he entered the United States Air Service Reserve and graduated with the rank of second lieutenant the following year. In 1925, Lindbergh graduated from the Army's flight-training school at Brooks and Kelly Fields as the best pilot in his class. After completing his Army training, the Robertson Aircraft Corporation of St. Louis hired him to fly the mail between St. Louis and Chicago.

MAY 20, 1932

Amelia Earhart began the first solo flight ever by a woman. (*See* July 24, 1898.)

MAY 21

The zodiac sign, Gemini the Twins, begins today and ends June 21. How many students were born under this sign?

MAY 23, 1788

South Carolina became the eighth state to ratify the Constitution.

Flower: Carolina Jessamine
Tree: Palmetto
Bird: Carolina Wren

MAY 23, 1975

Junko Tabei, a Japanese housewife, became the first woman to reach the top of Mt. Everest, the highest mountain in the world. A member of an expedition of 15 Japanese women, she reached the summit of the 29,028-foot mountain by taking the southeast route used by Sir Edmund Hillary and Sherpa Tenzing Norgay, the first to scale Everest, in 1953.

MAY 26, 1951
Birth Date of Sally Kirsten Ride

Sally Kirsten Ride, born in Encino, California, became the first woman candidate to become an astronaut on January 16, 1978.

A graduate of Stanford University with undergraduate degrees in English and physics, and master's and doctoral degrees in physics, Ride had not considered becoming an astronaut while choosing her courses. However, when she read in the campus newspaper that NASA was accepting astronaut candidates, she applied. Although she mailed her application on a whim, she was one of the 35 applicants chosen from a field of 8,037. (See also January 16, 1978.)

In June 1983, she became the first woman in space when she traveled on the space shuttle *Challenger* with four other astronauts. Her second flight was October 5–13, 1984.

After serving several years on NASA commissions, she left in 1987 to join the Stanford University Center for International Security and Arms Control.

Now that men, women, and animals have served on space flights, ask students if they think it might be possible for a child to accomplish this feat? Read to them the May Poem of the Month, "Last Laugh," to evoke further feelings.

MAY 27, 1819
Birth Date of Julia Ward Howe

Born in New York City, Julia Ward Howe was a writer, lecturer, and social reformer. Moved by the plight of the Civil War widows, she worked for women's rights in the professions and business. She wrote varied books of drama, verse, biography, and travel. Howe introduced the idea of Mother's Day in America (*see* May 9, 1914) and wrote the words to "The Battle Hymn of the Republic" to the tune of "John Brown's Body" in 1861. It was published in the *Atlantic Monthly* and soon became the war song of the Union forces. She married Dr. Samuel Gridley Howe, another American social reformer.

MAY 28, 1886
Birth Date of Jim Thorpe

Jim Thorpe was one of the greatest all-around athletes in history. Born near Prague, Oklahoma, Thorpe began his athletic career at the Carlisle (Pa.) Indian Industrial School. There he led the small school to national fame in football. Among his many athletic accomplishments, Thorpe played major-league baseball, professional football, and excelled at track and field events.

MAY 29, 1790

Rhode Island became the thirteenth state to ratify the Constitution.

Flower: Violet
Tree: Red Maple
Bird: Rhode Island Red

MAY 29, 1848

Wisconsin became the thirtieth state.

◆

Flower: Wood Violet
Tree: Sugar Maple
Bird: Robin

MAY 29, 1917
Birth Date of John Fitzgerald Kennedy, Thirty-fifth President

Born in:	Brookline, Massachusetts
Occupation:	Congressman, senator
President:	1961–1963, Democrat
Died:	November 22, 1963
	Dallas, Texas
	Buried in Arlington, Virginia

About Kennedy
★ Son of wealthy, politically involved parents.
★ PT boat commander in World War II.
★ Won 1957 Pulitzer Prize for *Profiles in Courage*.
★ First Roman Catholic president. Won election by narrow margin of 118,550 votes.

During His Term
★ Started "New Frontier" program of social legislation.
★ Encouraged southern black voter registration.
★ "Bay of Pigs" invasion of Cuba and Soviet missile crisis.
★ Assassinated in Dallas on November 22, 1963.

MAY 30
Memorial Day

The day was first observed on May 30, 1868, when it was initiated to honor Civil War veterans. Memorial Day, by presidential proclamation, is now observed on the last Monday in May. Graves of American soldiers are decorated with flowers on this day.

MAY 30, 1922

The Lincoln Memorial in Washington, D.C., was dedicated on this date.

MAY 30, 1903
Birth Date of Countee Cullen

The poet Countee Cullen was born Countee Porter in Baltimore, Maryland. Orphaned at an early age, he was adopted by Reverend Frederick Cullen in New York City. After attending public school, Cullen went on to New York University and then to Harvard University, where he received a Master of Arts degree. *Color*, his first volume of poetry, was published in 1925 while he was still a student. His *The Lost Zoo* (Harper & Row, 1940) is considered a children's classic. Look for a copy in your local library. At the time of his death in January 1946, Cullen was a teacher of French at a public high school in Harlem. Five years later the 136th Street Branch of the New York Public Library was renamed for him.

MAY 31, 1819
Birth Date of Walt Whitman

> The United States themselves are essentially the greatest poems.
>
> — Walt Whitman

Walt Whitman, an American poet, wrote *Leaves of Grass*, a collection considered one of the world's major literary works. It sings the praises of the United States and of democracy. Whitman began working on *Leaves of Grass* in 1848. Since no publisher would issue it, he brought out his own edition containing only 12 poems in 1855. Between this time and his death on March 26, 1892, he published several revised editions.

On May 7, 1984, he became one of the first writers to be admitted to the American Poets Corner, which is housed in the Cathedral of St. John the Divine in New York City.

Voyages: Poems by Walt Whitman includes 53 selections for better readers, selected by Lee Bennett Hopkins, illustrated in black-and-white engravings by Charles Mikolaycak (Harcourt Brace Jovanovich, 1988).

JUNE

FLOWER   ◆   BIRTHSTONE
Rose   Pearl

Like April, June's name is a matter of some debate. Some authorities believe the name honors Juniores, the lower branch of the Roman Senate; others claim it is connected with the Consulate of Junius Brutus or with Juno, wife of Jupiter, king of the gods. Originally June had 26 days. Rome's first king, Romulus, added four more to it; Numa Pompilius took one from it; Julius Caesar restored the total to 30 days.

JUNE POEM OF THE MONTH

from
STAY, JUNE, STAY!

    Stay, June, stay! —
If only we could stop the moon
And June!

                  — Christina G. Rossetti

JUNE 1, 1070

It is recorded that on this date cheese makers in southern France learned to make what is now known as Roquefort cheese. Nearly all cheeses, except cheddar, cottage, and cream cheese, are referred to as foreign-type cheeses in the United States because their production methods originated in other countries. Roquefort is one of them, of course; it is called blue cheese when made in America. Today millions of pounds of foreign-type cheese is made in the United States; approximately one hundred million pounds are imported.

This might be a good day for a cheese-and-cracker snack in the classroom!

JUNE 1, 1792

Kentucky became the fifteenth state.

Flower: Goldenrod
Tree: Kentucky Coffee Tree
Bird: Cardinal

JUNE 1, 1796

Tennessee became the sixteenth state.

Flower: Iris
Tree: Tulip Poplar
Bird: Mockingbird

JUNE 3, 1851

The New York Knickerbockers, a baseball team, introduced the first baseball uniforms. They wore straw hats, white shirts, and blue trousers. Compare these uniforms with the ones worn today.

JUNE 3, 1904
Birth Date of Charles Richard Drew

Charles Richard Drew was an important black surgeon chiefly known for his research on blood preservation and for the development of blood banks. Born more than three hundred years after William Harvey (*see* April 1, 1578), Drew was a pioneer in the study of blood plasma and set up the world's first blood bank at the American Red Cross. He served as a professor and head of the Howard University surgery department and as chief surgeon at Freedman's Hospital in Washington, D.C., from 1914 until his death in 1950.

Ironically, Drew was injured in an automobile accident near Burlington, North Carolina. In dire need of a blood transfusion, he was turned away from a local hospital because he was black and died en route to an all-black hospital.

JUNE 4, 1965

Major Ed White became the first American to walk in space. His flight aboard the *Gemini 4* spacecraft was made with fellow astronaut James McDivitt.

Shortly thereafter, on January 27, 1967, White was among those tragically killed in a flash fire on the launching pad as his *Apollo* spacecraft was being fine-tuned for a future flight under his command.

JUNE 5, c. 469 B.C..
Birth Date of Socrates

Socrates was born and lived in Athens. The wisest of the Greek philosophers, he left no writings of his own. Fortunately his pupil, Plato, recorded his eloquent dialogs with intellectuals of the time. His teachings reflected his ethical views; he was devoted to seeking truth, beauty, and goodness.

In 399 B.C., he was sentenced to death by the rulers of ancient Athens for supposedly corrupting the youth of the city with his ideas. He accepted his fate and peacefully drank a cup of hemlock poison.

Several quotes from Socrates' teachings can be shared to start class discussions:

> Know thyself.
> Courage is knowing what not to fear.
> There is only one good, knowledge, and one evil,
>   ignorance.

JUNE 7, 1917
Birth Date of Gwendolyn Brooks

The poet deals in words with which everyone is familiar.

We all handle words. And I think the poet, if he wants
to speak to anyone, is constrained to do something with
those words so that they will "mean something," will *be*
something that a reader may touch.

— Gwendolyn Brooks

Gwendolyn Brooks was born in Topeka, Kansas, but at an
early age moved to Chicago. Brooks is best known for her
poetry for adults. In 1950, she became the first black to win
the Pulitzer Prize for Poetry for her book *Annie Allen* (Harper
& Row, 1949). She was named Poet Laureate of the State of
Illinois, succeeding the late Carl Sandburg.

She has only written one book of poetry for children, *Bronze-
ville Boys and Girls* (Harper & Row, 1956). Each poem in the
book expresses a poignant feeling for children living in American inner cities.

Teachers and better readers in the middle grades can read
her autobiography, *Report from Part One* (Broadside Press, 1972).
Today, she spends her time writing poetry, lecturing at col-
leges, and encouraging young poets.

JUNE 8, 1786

On this date ice cream was first advertised and sold in America.
Ice cream has been eaten since 64 A.D. when Nero Claudius
Caesar was emperor of Rome, but it wasn't until the end of
the eighteenth century that several retail establishments in
New York City began to sell it. Dolley Madison is credited
with being the first woman to serve ice cream in the White
House; it was a favorite dessert at Mount Vernon, the home
of George and Martha Washington.

In 1848, Nancy Johnson invented a freezer that changed the
future of ice cream; and in 1851, Jacob Fussell established the
first wholesale ice cream factory in the world. In Baltimore, a

plaque erected by the Maryland Historical Society reads in part: "Birthplace of the Ice Cream Industry." Share some of these other facts about ice cream with your students:

- ◆ The ice cream cone was introduced in 1904 at the World's Fair in St. Louis, Missouri.
- ◆ More than 10 percent of all milk products in the United States is used by the ice cream industry.
- ◆ The United States consumes more ice cream than any other country.

Children can read additional facts about the history of ice cream in *Ice Cream* by William Jaspherson (Macmillan, 1988). This book takes readers on a photographic journey through Ben and Jerry's ice cream plant in Waterbury, Vermont, and explains where ice cream comes from and how it is made. Another reference is *The Scoop on Ice Cream*, by Vicki Cobb, illustrated by G. Brian Karas (Little, Brown, 1985).

JUNE 8, 1869
Birth Date of Frank Lloyd Wright

Many outstanding buildings throughout the world bear the stamp of Frank Lloyd Wright, an innovator in the field of architecture. Born in a small Wisconsin town, Wright brought his love of nature to architecture. His aim was to meld a structure and its surroundings into a unified entity, and his buildings achieved this goal.

He also introduced new materials, such as precast concrete, and new concepts of space and the use of mass-produced items. His works ranged from residential homes to office buildings, from churches to factories, to an ultramodern plan for a mile-high skyscraper. Among the buildings he designed were a house jutting out over a waterfall at Bear Run, Pennsylvania; the Imperial Hotel in Tokyo, Japan; the Guggenheim Museum in New York City; and the Marin County Civic Center in California.

JUNE 11, 1880
Birth Date of Jeannette Rankin

Born and brought up on a ranch near Missoula, Montana, Jeannette Rankin was the first woman to be elected to the U.S. House of Representatives. She served two terms — 1917–1919 and 1941–1943 — as a Republican congresswoman from Montana. Active throughout her entire life in the women's suffrage and pacifist movements, she was the only member of Congress to vote against entering both World War I and World War II.

JUNE 12, 1924
Birth Date of George Herbert Walker Bush, Forty-first President

Born in:	Milton, Massachusetts
Occupation:	Businessman, oilfield owner
President:	1989– , Republican

About Bush
★ Ronald Reagan's vice president for eight years.
★ First incumbent vice president in decades to win office of president.
★ Navy's youngest officer; pilot at the age of 18.

During His Term
★ Emphasis on "duty, sacrifice, commitment, and patriotism," as cornerstones of his administration.
★ Vowed to end widespread drug abuse.

★ Continued policy of exploring improved relationships with the U.S.S.R.

JUNE 14, 1777
Flag Day

According to legend, Betsy Ross created the first United States flag when she sewed together the stars and stripes in 1776. (*See* January 1, 1752.) On June 14, 1777, her design was accepted, and a resolution was adopted by the Continental Congress ". . . that a flag of the United States be 13 stripes, alternate red and white, that the 'Union' be 13 stars, within a blue field, representing a new constellation." The resolution did not, however, specify the arrangement of the 13 stars on the blue field. After the admission of Kentucky and Vermont, another resolution was adopted in January 1794, making the flag one of 15 stars and 15 stripes.

Realizing the flag would become unwieldly with a stripe for each new state, Captain Samuel C. Reid of the U.S. Navy suggested to Congress that the number of stripes remain the same (13) to represent the original colonies and that a star be added to the blue field for each new state joining the Union. A law to this effect was passed on April 4, 1818. The flag of the United States has changed many times since this date. The last change was made on July 4, 1960, when the fiftieth star, representing Hawaii, was added.

JUNE 15, 1215

On this date the Magna Carta was written. The Magna Carta or Great Charter is a document that marked a decisive step in the development of constitutional government in England. In it King John of England was compelled to grant many rights to the English aristocracy. The Magna Carta confirmed feudal traditions and defined the limits of an English king's powers, thus preventing the development of absolute monarchy in England.

Four original copies of the charter are still in existence; two are in the British Museum in London.

JUNE 15, 1752

On this date Benjamin Franklin reached out into the heavens to prove that lightning was a form of electricity. Scientists of Franklin's time called the electrical discharges that pass from one storm cloud to another, or between a cloud and the earth, "electrical fire." People believed these fiery flashes had magical qualities. Franklin and his son, William, thought the discharges were a form of natural electricity. They built a special, silk handkerchief kite with which they proved their point at considerable risk. The kite had a piece of wire attached to its tip, which served as a lightning rod that conducted the storm's electrical energy down the string to a key attached several feet above the holder's hand. Standing in an open field, the two guided the kite into a dark storm cloud above. As the storm's intensity developed, the elder Franklin rapped the key with his knuckles. Suddenly sparks leapt from the key. Electrical energy had been drawn from the sky above! (*See also* January 17, 1706.)

JUNE 15, 1836

Arkansas became the twenty-fifth state.

Flower: Apple Blossom
Tree: Pine
Bird: Mockingbird

JUNE 16, 1963

"It is I, Sea Gull . . ." These historic words electrified the world on this date for they were spoken by Valentina Tereshkova, the first woman in space. Tereshkova began her three-day, forty-eight-orbit flight in *Vostok* 6. The twenty-six-year-old Soviet cosmonaut had been a textile worker whose hobby was parachuting. She wrote to the directors of the Soviet space program volunteering to train for space flight, and they accepted!

JUNE 17, 1673

Explorers Father Jacques Marquette and Louis Joliet discovered the Mississippi River. Their work was the basis for French claims to the Louisiana Territory.

JUNE 17, 1775

The Battle of Bunker Hill began. After the first shots of the War for Independence were fired at Lexington and Concord, Continental troops laid seige to Boston. When British reinforcements arrived, American troops stationed themselves upon Breed's Hill overlooking Boston. Although outnumbered, they withstood two assaults by General Howe's men on their outpost. Then their ammunition gave out, and they were forced to retreat when the British seized the hill in their third attack. This conflict became known at the Battle of Bunker Hill. In 1825, a monument was dedicated at the site in the presence of the Marquis de Lafayette who was visiting the United States, a nation he helped create. (*See* September 9, 1757.)

JUNE 17, 1972

The arrest of five burglars in the offices of the Democratic National Committee in the Watergate building in Washington, D.C., just five months prior to the presidential election, began a scandal that rocked the American political structure and led to President Richard M. Nixon's resignation in August 1974. Nixon's landslide victory over Senator George McGovern in the 1972 election failed to prevent the facts from emerging. The president's closest advisors had organized a group called "the plumbers" who regularly indulged in wiretapping and other illegal acts. Officials of the Nixon administration and the president himself attempted to deny these activities. It took over two years of Senate hearings, several special prosecutors, grand jury trials, impeachment proceedings, the revelation of White House tape recordings, and a ruling by the Supreme Court that the tapes must be surrendered to reveal the truth that brought about the downfall of the Nixon presidency. Many leading Nixon associates were sentenced to jail terms for their roles in what were called "the White House horrors" and subsequent attempts to cover them up.

JUNE 19, 1846

"One — two — three strikes you're out!" These words might have been yelled at the first recorded baseball game played on the Elysian Fields in Hoboken, New Jersey. This date is considered the beginning of organized baseball in the United States. Two amateur teams met and played under rules established by Alexander J. Cartwright, a surveyor and amateur athlete who umpired the game. The Knickerbockers were beaten by the New York Nine with a score of 23 to 1. The game ended in the fourth inning as 21 runs constituted a game according to the rules then current.

◆

JUNE 19, 1910

Father's Day was first celebrated in Spokane, Washington. In 1924, President Calvin Coolidge recommended that the day be observed as a holiday in all states. Traditionally Father's Day is held on the third Sunday in June, and it is a day for all to acknowledge how special fathers are.

JUNE 20, 1863

West Virginia became the thirty-fifth state.

Flower: Big Rhododendron
Tree: Sugar Maple
Bird: Cardinal

JUNE 21
First Day of Summer

For some suggestions on welcoming the season in, see the entry for March 21.

JUNE 21, 1788

New Hampshire was the ninth state to ratify the Constitution.

Flower: Purple Lilac
Tree: White Birch
Bird: Purple Finch

◆

JUNE 22

The zodiac sign, Cancer the Crab, begins today and ends July 22. How many students were born under this sign?

JUNE 24, 1916
Birth Date of John Ciardi

Born in Boston, Massachusetts, John Ciardi was one of America's foremost contemporary poets. His translation of Dante's *Divine Comedy* brought him international recognition. In 1982, he was the sixth recipient of the National Council of Teachers of English Award for Excellence in Poetry.

Ciardi's poetry appeals to children as well as adults. Young children will enjoy *I Met a Man* (Houghton Mifflin, 1961), a volume that remained among his personal favorites, which was written on a first-grade vocabulary level for his daughter, Myra. Other titles by the poet include *You Read to Me, I'll Read to You*, illustrated by Edward Gorey (J.B. Lippincott, 1962; paperback), and *Doodle Soup*, illustrated by Merle Nacht (Houghton Mifflin, 1985). He can be heard on two recordings available from Spoken Arts, *You Read to Me, I'll Read to You* and *You Know Who, John J. Plenty and Fiddler Dan and Other Poems.*

He died on March 30, 1986. The posthumously published *The Hopeful Trout and Other Limericks*, illustrated by Susan Meddaugh (Houghton Mifflin, 1989), is a book of 41 limericks for all ages.

JUNE 25, 1788

Virginia was the tenth state to ratify the Constitution.

Flower: Dogwood
Tree: Dogwood
Bird: Cardinal

◆

JUNE 27, 1872
Birth Date of Paul Laurence Dunbar

Paul Laurence Dunbar was an American novelist and poet who was born in Dayton, Ohio. He was one of the first writers to portray black life with realism. All of his poetry is contained in *The Complete Poems of Paul Laurence Dunbar* (Dodd, Mead, 1965). This edition also includes the famous William Dean Howells' preface on Dunbar, which did so much to bring him to the attention of readers everywhere. In 1975, a United States commemorative stamp was issued honoring this famous black American writer, who died at the early age of 32.

In 1988, a biography for better readers, *Paul Laurence Dunbar* by Tony Gentry, appeared (Chelsea House).

JUNE 27, 1880
Birth Date of Helen Keller

Despite several handicaps, Helen Keller became an author, lecturer, and educator. She suffered a severe illness before she was two years old that left her visually and hearing impaired. When she was seven, she was placed in the care of Annie Sullivan of the Perkins Institute for the Blind, and by the time she was 10, she had learned to speak. Ten years later, with Sullivan, she attended Radcliffe College where she graduated with honors. After Sullivan's death in 1936, Keller's new companion was Polly Thomson; she had become her secretary in 1914. Keller authored many books, bringing her message of courage and hope to the handicapped everywhere. In 1962, MGM released *The Miracle Worker*, a film depicting Annie Sullivan's struggle to teach the young Helen Keller to speak. Keller died in Westport, Connecticut, at the age of 88.

Younger readers will enjoy *Helen Keller* by Margaret Davidson (Scholastic, 1973), and middle-grade readers might like

Helen Keller's Teacher by the same author (Scholastic, 1972) or Keller's own account, *The Story of My Life*, written in 1903 (New American Library paperback).

JUNE 29, 1577
Birth Date of Peter Paul Rubens

Born in Seigen, Germany, Peter Paul Rubens became one of the greatest Flemish painters of the 1600s. Besides creating paintings, tapestries, occasional illustrations for books, architecture, and sculpture, he was also a noted scholar and respected diplomat. The ancient Roman sculpture he studied in Italy in 1600 as well as the works of the Renaissance artists Michelangelo and Raphael influenced his style. His paintings are known for their monumental scale, brilliant colors, and feeling of movement and vitality. During his lifetime he completed an enormous amount of work dealing with a variety of subjects such as hunting scenes, landscapes, biblical and mythical episodes, and portraits.

Rubens greatly influenced contemporary tastes, and although his hands were crippled with arthritis and gout, he still worked diligently until his death in 1640 — a time when all of Europe mourned his passing.

JUNE 30, 1859

Imagine walking across Niagara Falls — that roaring chasm between New York State and Canada. People have! They have sailed over the falls — which drop 500,000 tons of water a minute — in flimsy barrels, in rafts, and in barges. However, a French tightrope walker, Blondin, is remembered as the greatest daredevil of all. On this date, he made his first crossing on a rope 1,100 feet long. In July, he repeated the amazing feat several times adding new obstacles — Blondin carried a man on his back, he pushed a wheelbarrow, and for a finale he sat down in the middle of his rope and cooked an omelette. The great high rope-walker started performing on ropes at six years old and continued until he was 72.

July

FLOWER	◆	BIRTHSTONE
Larkspur		Ruby

Originally the seventh month was the fifth on the Roman calendar. It was called *Quintilis* meaning "fifth" and had 36 days. Romulus reduced the number to 31, Numa Pompilius cut it back to 30, and later Julius Caesar restored one day, giving it 31. Marc Anthony complimented Julius Caesar by naming the month July after him as Caesar's birthday fell on the fourteenth. The month officially became July in 44 B.C., the year Caesar was stabbed and killed by Brutus.

JULY POEM OF THE MONTH

TO JULY

Here's to July,
Here's to July,
For the bird,
And the bee,
And the butterfly;
For the flowers
That blossom
For feasting the eye;
For skates, balls,
And jump ropes,
For swings that go high;
For rocketry
Fireworks that
Blaze in the sky,
Oh, here's to July.

— Anonymous

JULY 1, 1863

The Battle of Gettysburg began. General Robert E. Lee was ready to make his second attempt to invade the North, and he marched with his troops to the town of Gettysburg, Pennsylvania. When a group of soldiers rode ahead of him in search of supplies, they ran into the Union cavalry. The battle that started by chance lasted for three days. It was one of the bloodiest of the entire Civil War, but it was the turning point that eventually led to victory for the Union Army. (*See* November 19, 1863, for Lincoln's Gettysburg Address.)

JULY 2, 1908
Birth Date of Thurgood Marshall

Thurgood Marshall studied dentistry at Lincoln University, but then changed his mind and entered Howard University Law School where he graduated at the top of his class in 1933. Beginning in 1938, he spent 23 years as special counsel at NAACP. He argued 32 cases for the association before the U.S. Supreme Court and won 29 of them! His most famous victory was *Brown vs. Board of Education of Topeka*, the school desegregation case that defeated the "separate but equal" doctrine that had been in effect for 60 years. (*See also* May 17, 1954.) On October 2, 1967, Marshall became the first black member of the U.S. Supreme Court, on which he still serves.

JULY 3, 1890

Idaho became the forty-third state.

Flower: Syringa
Tree: White Pine
Bird: Mountain Bluebird

JULY 4, 1776
Independence Day

The United States celebrates its birthday on this day, which commemorates the signing of the Declaration of Independence by members of the Second Continental Congress meeting in Philadelphia, Pennsylvania. The American Fourth of July is one of the oldest independence days in the world. The Declaration of Independence, written by Thomas Jefferson, was eventually signed by 55 other men in defiance of Britain's

King George III, who threatened them with death for their action.

Two of the best-known early American leaders, John Adams and Thomas Jefferson, who were both past presidents, died on July 4, 1826, the fiftieth anniversary of the nation they helped to conceive.

Many special events have taken place in the United States on this date:

1817 Ground was broken for the Erie Canal.
1828 The Baltimore and Ohio Railroad began operating.
1832 "America" was sung for the first time.
1848 The cornerstone of the Washington Monument in Washington, D.C., was laid.
      The first Women's Rights Convention met at Seneca Falls, New York.
1858 The first baseball series began.
1861 The Battle of Bull Run was fought.
1863 Vicksburg surrendered.
      Battle of Gettysburg was fought.
1884 The United States received an important birthday gift — the Statue of Liberty.
1976 The United States celebrated the two hundredth anniversary of the adoption of the Declaration of Independence.

Several references for students about the country's birthday include *The Fourth of July Story* by Alice Dalgliesh, illustrated by Marie Nonnast (Aladdin paperback, 1987); *America's Birthday: The Fourth of July* by Tom Shactman, illustrated with full-color photographs by Chuck Saaf (Macmillan, 1986); and *Fireworks, Picnics, and Flags: The Story of the Fourth of July Symbols* by James Cross Giblin, illustrated by Ursula Arndt (Clarion Books, paperback, 1983).

JULY 4, 1872
Birth Date of (John) Calvin Coolidge, Thirtieth President

Born in: Plymouth, Vermont
Occupation: Farmer, lawyer
President: 1923–1929, Republican
Died: January 5, 1933
                     Northampton, Massachusetts
                     Buried in Plymouth, Vermont

About Coolidge
★ Became president upon Harding's death in office. Father, a notary public, administered oath of office in a Vermont farmhouse.

During His Terms
★ Called "Silent Cal" because of his conservative, retiring manner.
★ Encouraged business expansion and government's non-interference in stock market.

JULY 7, 1881

Carlo Lorenzini, whose pen name was Collodi, published the first chapter of his classic tale *Pinocchio*, which is about a puppet who comes to life on this date. There are many versions of this story. One of the loveliest editions is the large-sized *The Adventures of Pinocchio* (Macmillan, 1969). It is illustrated by Attillio Mussino, whose artwork has been hailed as the perfect interpretation of the story and earned him a gold medal at the International Exposition at Turin, Italy, in 1908. (*See also* November 24, 1826.)

JULY 8, 1835

The Liberty Bell cracked while tolling the death of Chief Justice John Marshall. The Liberty Bell has become a symbol of the American fight for independence because it was rung on July 8, 1776, to announce independence. The large metal bell, which weighs 2,080 pounds, was brought to Philadelphia, Pennsylvania, in 1752 from England. It bears the inscription from the Bible's book of Leviticus: "Proclaim Liberty throughout all the land unto all Inhabitants Thereof."

During the British occupation of the city (1777–1778), the bell was moved to Allentown, Pennsylvania, and hidden under the floor of a church for safety. After its return to Philadelphia, it was rung on Independence Day and on other special occasions — until it cracked! On D day, June 6, 1944, during World War II, the bell was tapped by the mayor, and the tone was broadcast by radio throughout the nation.

JULY 10, 1875
Birth Date of Mary McLeod Bethune

Mary McLeod Bethune, a black educator, founded the Bethune-Cookman College in Daytona, Florida, a school that grew into one of the largest institutions for training black teachers in the southeastern United States. During the Depression of the 1930s, Bethune worked with President Franklin D. Roosevelt to help minority groups. She served as director of the Negro Affairs Division of the National Youth Administration, an organization that helped more than half a million black students stay in school during these difficult years. Bethune died on May 18, 1955. Part of her last will and testament reads:

I leave you love; I leave you hope; I leave you the challenge of developing confidence in one another; I leave you a thirst for education; I leave you a respect for the use of power; I leave you faith; I leave you racial dignity; I leave you a desire to live harmoniously with your fellow men; I leave you a responsibility to our young people.

JULY 10, 1890

Wyoming became the forty-fourth state.

Flower: Indian Paintbrush
Tree: Cottonwood
Bird: Meadowlark

JULY 11, 1767
Birth Date of John Quincy Adams, Sixth President

Born in:	Braintree, Massachusetts
Occupation:	Lawyer, statesman
President:	1825–1829, Democratic-Republican
Died:	February 23, 1848
	Washington, D.C.
	Buried in Braintree, Massachusetts

About Adams
★ Foreign service as United States minister to the Netherlands, Sweden, Britain, Germany, Portugal, and Russia.
★ Elected president by the House of Representatives — of four candidates running in 1824, none won a majority of the Electoral College vote.
★ Leading antislavery advocate.
★ After his presidential term, he served as a congressman for 17 years in the House of Representatives.

During His Term
★ Great rivalry with Andrew Jackson, who received the largest popular vote in the presidential election.
★ Was the only president in history who did not have the congressional support of a political party while in office, so accomplished very little.

JULY 11, 1899
Birth Date of Elwyn Brooks White

Elwyn Brooks White, best known as E.B. White, was born in Mount Vernon, New York, the sixth and last child of Samuel Tilly and Jessica Hart White.

In 1921, after graduating from Cornell University, he moved to New York City for a year before traveling around the country. After several years of trying many jobs, he joined the staff of The New Yorker magazine. He wrote continually for the magazine and was still on the staff writing from his home in North Brooklin, Maine, shortly before his death on October 1, 1985.

Although a prolific writer of adult works, he is best known for his three children's classics: Stuart Little (1945), Charlotte's Web (1952), and The Trumpet of the Swan (1970; all Harper & Row, paperbacks).

In 1963, President John F. Kennedy named him one of 31 Americans to receive the Presidential Medal of Freedom — the highest honor a civilian can receive from the government in time of peace. In 1970, he was given the Laura Ingalls Wilder Award, an award presented to "an author or illustrator whose books, published in the United States, have over a period of years made a substantial and lasting contribution to literature for children." In 1978, he received a special Pulitzer Prize for his body of work.

Adult readers will enjoy Letters of E.B. White, edited by Dorothy Guth (1976), and Poems and Sketches of E.B. White by White

(1981; both Harper & Row). The *Elements of Style*, which White co-authored with William Strunck (3rd ed. 1979, Macmillan) is considered by many to be one of the best books on English writing and composition ever written.

JULY 14, 1789
Bastille Day

Today is Bastille Day in France. On this date, citizens of Paris stormed the royal prison, the Bastille, where political enemies of the king were imprisoned. The prison had become the hated symbol of the king's absolute power. The French were emulating the struggle of American colonists who had achieved independence from Britain in 1776, and the taking of the Bastille signaled the beginning of the French Revolution. Today in France, Bastille Day is celebrated with mammoth parades, the display of the tricolor flag, and the singing of "La Marseillaise," the national anthem.

JULY 14, 1913
Birth Date of Gerald Rudolph Ford, Thirty-eighth President

Born in: Omaha, Nebraska
Occupation: Lawyer
President: 1974–1977, Republican

About Ford
★ Name changed from Leslie King, Jr., to Gerald Rudolph Ford, Jr., when his mother remarried.
★ Football player; linebacker and center on the University of Michigan team; offered professional contract in 1932–1933.
★ Conservative Republican congressman.

- ★ Member of the Warren Commission that investigated assassination of President Kennedy.
- ★ Chosen as vice president-designate by Nixon after resignation of Agnew. First appointed vice president in history, October 1973.

During His Term
- ★ Became president when Nixon resigned on August 10, 1974, because of his Watergate involvement and certain impeachment.

JULY 15

An English saying goes:

> Saint Swithin's Day, if thou dost rain,
>   for forty-days it will remain;
>
> Saint Swithin's Day, if thou be fair,
>   for forty-days 'twill rain nae mair.

Saint Swithin was buried, so legend tells, by his own request in the churchyard of Winchester Cathedral in England. When he was made a saint, the monks decided to move his body into the cathedral. This event took place on July 15, a day when it rained heavily. The rain kept falling for the next 40 days, leading many people to believe that Saint Swithin would have preferred to be out in the open. Look out for rain today!

JULY 16, 1935
Birth Date of Arnold Adoff

In November 1988, Arnold Adoff received the eighth National Council of Teachers of English Award for Excellence in Poetry for Children. A former high school teacher in New York City, he began his writing career as an anthologist, collecting mainly poetry of black experiences. Among his diverse works are *Eats: Poems*, illustrated by Susan Russo (1979); *All the Colors of the Race*, illustrated by John Steptoe (1982); *Sports Pages*, illustrated by Steve Kuzma (1986; all J.B. Lippincott); and *Chocolate Dreams*, illustrated by Turi MacCombie (Lothrop, Lee & Shepard, 1989).

Adoff is married to Newbery Award winner Virginia Hamilton. They live in Yellow Springs, Ohio.

Celebrate the poet's birthday today by sharing some of his stylized poetry.

JULY 16, 1945

The first atom bomb exploded at Alamogordo Air Force Base in a desolate portion of New Mexico. After Germany's surrender in early May 1945, the Allies still faced a long, arduous war against Japan. To shorten the conflict they issued an ultimatum telling the Japanese "the alternative to surrender is prompt and utter destruction." When this peace initiative was rejected, President Harry S. Truman authorized the use of the new weapon. On August 6, 1945, at 8:15 A.M., an atomic bomb was dropped on Hiroshima; more than 160,000 people were killed or injured. Three days later the city of Nagasaki was similarly destroyed. The Japanese surrendered on August 14. World War II was ended by using the most devastating weapon ever developed by humankind.

Middle-graders will learn a great deal about this event and its aftermath from *Sudako and the Thousand Cranes* by Eleanor B. Coerr (G.P. Putnam's Sons, 1977; also in paperback from Dell).

JULY 18, 1976

At the age of 14, Nadia Comaneci became the first gymnast to receive a perfect score in the Olympic Games. At the Games held in Montreal, Canada, Comaneci received perfect scores of 10 on the uneven bars and balance beam. Are there any gymnasts in your class?

JULY 19, 1916
Birth Date of Eve Merriam

> When something is too beautiful or too terrible or even too funny for words, then it is time for poetry.
> — Eve Merriam

Eve Merriam always wanted to be a poet, and while in school her work was published in a variety of student publications. Her first book of adult poetry, *Family Circle* (Yale University Press, 1946), won the Yale Younger Poets Prize. Other books followed in rapid succession, including nonfiction children's books and poetry for adults and children. In 1981, she received the fifth National Council of Teachers of English Award for Excellence in Poetry for Children.

Two excellent books to share with readers are the Dell paperbacks *Jamboree: Rhymes for All Times* (1984) and *A Sky Full of Poems* (1986), both illustrated by Walter Gaffney Kessell.

Older children will enjoy reading her essay "Writing a Poem" in *A Sky Full of Poems*, which describes how she created the poem "Landscape" from start to finish.

Born in Germantown, a suburb of Philadelphia, Pennsylvania, Merriam currently lives in New York City.

JULY 19, 1932
Birth Date of Karla Kuskin

Karla Kuskin, a native New Yorker, is a writer of prose and poetry. A treasury of her work for children appears in *Dogs & Dragons, Trees & Dreams* (Harper & Row, 1980).

Kuskin is the recipient of the third National Council of Teachers of English Award for Excellence in Poetry for Children. She lives in Brooklyn, New York. Look for other titles by Kuskin in the library.

JULY 20, 1969

A man monitoring a receiver in Houston, Texas, heard one of humankind's most historic messages: "Tranquility Base here. The Eagle has landed." *Apollo II*'s lunar module, *Eagle*, had set down upon the moon's Sea of Tranquility. Six hours later the first human set foot upon the lunar crust and declared, "That's one small step for a man, one giant leap for mankind." Neil A. Armstrong relayed these words to Earth shortly before he was joined by his copilot, Colonel Edwin E. Aldrin, Jr., of the Air Force. Together Armstrong and Aldrin explored a small area around the module. A worldwide audience witnessed these first steps across the powdery surface as the spacemen planted an American flag and gathered rock samples. A dream was attained — space exploration became a reality.

JULY 22, 1849
Birth Date of Emma Lazarus

> Give me your tired, your poor,
> Your huddled masses yearning to breathe free,

The wretched refuse of your teeming shore,
Send these, the homeless, tempest-tost to me,
I lift my lamp beside the golden door!

These words are part of Emma Lazarus's most famous poem, "The New Colossus," which appears on a plaque on the Statue of Liberty pedestal on Liberty Island (formerly Bedloes Island) in New York City.

Born in New York City to a wealthy family, Lazarus was a precocious child. She wrote her first collection of poetry between the ages of 14 and 16. Her poems captured the attention of Ralph Waldo Emerson, and the two became lifelong friends.

The persecution of Russian Jews during 1879–83 turned her interest to the plight of Jewish refugees. The words to "The New Colossus" reflect her belief that the U.S. is the home for the world's oppressed. She died in New York City on November 19, 1887.

A biography for middle-grade readers is *I Lift My Lamp: Emma Lazarus and the Statue of Liberty* by Nancy Smiler Levinson (Lodestar, 1986).

JULY 23

The zodiac sign, Leo the Lion, begins today and ends August 22. How many students were born under this sign?

JULY 24, 1898
Birth Date of Amelia Earhart

Amelia Earhart, a famous American aviator, was the first woman to cross the Atlantic in an airplane (1928), to fly over the Atlantic alone (1932), to make a nonstop flight across the United States (1932), to fly from Hawaii to California (1935), and to receive the Distinguished Flying Cross. During her lifetime she also established both altitude and transcontinental speed records. On July 1, 1937, she set out from Miami for a flight around the world. On July 3, her airplane disappeared in the South Pacific Ocean. No positive trace has ever been found of her or her plane. Earhart was declared dead in 1939.

A biography for middle-graders is *Lost Star: The Story of Amelia Earhart* by Patricia Lauber (Scholastic, 1988).

JULY 25, 1952

Puerto Rico became a commonwealth. Puerto Rico's history and culture are a synthesis of the varied peoples and events that have affected this island in the West Indies. Arawak Indians, Spaniards, and Americans have all ruled it. Until the 1950s self-government was withheld by the United States, which acquired the island after the Spanish-American War. Puerto Ricans then wrote their own constitution and chose to be associated with the United States as a commonwealth rather than as a state. Statehood and independence are still serious questions under discussion by Puerto Ricans.

JULY 26, 1788

New York became the eleventh state to ratify the Constitution.

Flower: Rose
Tree: Sugar Maple
Bird: Bluebird

JULY 26, 1965

Great Britain granted independence to the Maldive Islands, which lie four hundred miles southwest of Ceylon in the

Indian Ocean. Older children can locate these islands on a map. After they have found them, they might research the Maldivian word *atoll*. Atolls are coral clusters built entirely on the skeletons of sea animals; when these organisms die, their naturally cemented remains form the foundation of many coral isles.

JULY 28, 1973

Skylab 2 was launched from Cape Kennedy (now called Cape Canaveral), Florida. Its crew spent a record-breaking 59 days in space. Navy Captain Alan L. Bean shared the adventure with two others, Major Jack R. Lousma of the Marines and a civilian scientist, Dr. Owen K. Garriott. Their flight covered twenty-four million miles and surpassed *Skylab I*'s 28-day journey around the earth. On September 25, 1973, the spaceship splashed down.

Steer elementary readers to the delightful picture book *I Want to Be an Astronaut* by Byron Barton (T.Y. Crowell, 1988). Middle-grade readers will enjoy *My Life as an Astronaut* by Alan L. Bean (Pocket Books, 1988), the fourth person to walk on the moon.

JULY 31, 1790

The first federal patent issued by the United States was granted to Samuel Hopkins of Vermont for a soapmaking process using potash and pearl ash. Today more than 100,000 inventors contact the U.S. Patent Office each year. To obtain a patent, inventions must be both new and useful. Approximately 70,000 patents ranging from the ridiculous to the sublime are issued annually, for inventions such as a self-cleaning chalkboard, a pair of shoes with sundial tops by which the wearer can tell the time of day, and a hula hoop with an orbiting satellite.

A 1980 Supreme Court decision ruled that genetic engineering of organisms could be patented when they upheld the creation of an oil-eating bacterium to assist in cleaning up oil spills.

Students might look toward the future and "invent" their own products. They might provide a written description of their idea and accompany it with a diagram or drawing showing how it works. Anyone for a talking cereal bowl that says "Good morning"? (See April 10, 1790.)

Young inventors can send their ideas to the U.S. Patent Office at this address: Patent and Trademark Office, Commerce Department, 2021 Jefferson Davis Highway, Washington, DC 20231.

AUGUST

FLOWER   ◆   BIRTHSTONE
Poppy   Sardonyx

Julius Caesar's adopted nephew and heir, Gaius Julius Caesar Octavianus, was the first Roman emperor to receive the title *Augustus*, meaning "reverend," from the Senate. The senators changed the name of the sixth month of their calendar, Sextilis, to August to honor their leader. Augustus took a day from February to give his month 31 days so that it would be as long as July, which honored Julius Caesar.

AUGUST POEM OF THE MONTH

NO MATTER

No matter
how hot-burning
it is
outside

when

you peel a
long, fat cucumber

or

cut deep into
a fresh, ripe watermelon

you can
feel
coolness
come into your hands.

— Lee Bennett Hopkins

AUGUST 1, 1876

Colorado became the thirty-eighth state.

Flower: Rocky Mountain Columbine
Tree: Colorado Blue Spruce
Bird: Lark Bunting

AUGUST 2, 1873

The inventor Andrew Hallidie piloted San Francisco's first cable car down Nob Hill at 5:00 A.M. He chose this early morning hour for good reason — there would be fewer people around if anything went wrong. Fortunately nothing did! Has anyone in your class visited San Francisco? Have them share their experiences about the city and its cable cars.

AUGUST 6, 1945

The atomic bomb was dropped on Hiroshima, Japan. (*See* July 16, 1945.)

AUGUST 7, 1904
Birth Date of Ralph Johnson Bunche

Ralph Johnson Bunche, an internationally famous diplomat and United Nations mediator, was born in Detroit, Michigan, the grandson of a slave. In 1950, he became the first black American to receive the Nobel Peace Prize for his years of working for peace throughout the world and for his role in settling the Arab-Israeli dispute of 1950. From 1967, until his resignation in 1971, he was a key United Nations diplomat until shortly before his death on December 9, 1971. Young readers can learn more about his many contributions in *The Value of Responsibility: The Story of Ralph Bunche* (Oak Tree, 1978).

AUGUST 10, 1821

Missouri became the twenty-fourth state.

Flower: Hawthorn
Tree: Dogwood
Bird: Bluebird

AUGUST 10, 1874
Birth Date of Herbert Clark Hoover, Thirty-first President

Born in:	West Branch, Iowa
Occupation:	Engineer, mine owner
President:	1929–1933, Republican
Died:	October 20, 1964
	New York, New York

About Hoover
- ★ From poverty to mining engineer in Australia and China, he became a millionaire mine owner.
- ★ Humanitarian relief work during and after World War I.

During His Term
- ★ Stock market crash in October 1929 marked beginning of the Great Depression.
- ★ By 1932, twelve million Americans were unemployed. He refused to sanction relief measures and relied on individual initiatives to overcome the financial crisis.

AUGUST 17, 1786
Birth Date of David (Davy) Crockett

In 1836, when the ruins of the Alamo were searched, the diary of a legendary frontiersman, David Crockett, was found. It related how 187 Texans had fought to the death against the superior forces of Mexican dictator Antonio López de Santa Anna. Crockett — a scout, army officer, and congressman from Tennessee for three terms — died as he had lived, immersed in adventure.

After growing up in Tennessee, Crockett plunged into frontier life where he hunted bears, fought Native Americans, and cast aside the fetters of town life. Middle-graders can read about more of his adventures in *Davy Crockett: Young Rifleman* by Aileen W. Parks (Macmillan, 1986).

AUGUST 17, 1926
Birth Date of Myra Cohn Livingston

Myra Cohn Livingston was born in Omaha, Nebraska. When she was 11, her family moved to California, where she still lives in Beverly Hills with her husband. In addition to her writing life, she teaches classes in creative writing and poetry throughout the country. In 1980, Livingston became the fourth recipient of the National Council of Teachers of English Award for Excellence in Poetry for Children. For a discussion of poetry and the ways she has used it with children and educators, see her adult book, *The Child As Poet: Myth or Reality?* (Horn Book, 1985).

Livingston has written many volumes of poetry for children including *Celebrations*, illustrated by Leonard Everett Fisher (Holiday House, 1985; paperback); *Worlds I Know*, illustrated by Tim Arnold (1986); and the poignant *There Was a Place and Other Poems* (1988; both Margaret K. McElderry Books); *Sky Songs* (1984), *Sea Songs* (1986), and *Earth Songs* (1986), all illustrated by Leonard Everett Fisher (all Holiday House).

Anthologies she has compiled are *These Small Stones*, with Norma Farber (Harper & Row, 1987); *Halloween Poems*, illustrated by Stephen Gammell (Holiday House, 1989).

AUGUST 18, 1934
Birth Date of Roberto Clemente

Born in the little town of Carolina, Puerto Rico, Roberto Clemente pursued a baseball career from early childhood. He was spotted on the island in 1954 by the National League's

Brooklyn Dodgers and was assigned to their Montreal farm team. After joining the Pittsburgh Pirates, he helped that team become world champions in the 1960 World Series against the New York Yankees, and again in 1971 against the Baltimore Orioles. Clemente was a four-time batting champion of the National League and one of 11 men in baseball history to make 3,000 hits. His lifetime batting average of .317 led to his being named National League Most Valuable Player in 1966. He was also voted most valuable player in the World Series.

The star's death in a plane crash on December 3, 1972, brought grief to baseball fans. Clemente had been helping victims of the massive earthquake in Managua, Nicaragua; the plane he was on was carrying relief supplies to the stricken city. Clemente's later election in 1973 to the Baseball Hall of Fame testified to this player's greatness.

A biography of this baseball giant is *Pride of Puerto Rico: The Life of Roberto Clemente*, by Paul Robert Walker (Harcourt Brace Jovanovich, 1988).

AUGUST 19
National Aviation Day

To mark the birth date of Orville Wright, today is celebrated as National Aviation Day. When one thinks of aviation, Orville and Wilbur Wright immediately come to mind. They were bicycle manufacturers, mechanics, and pilots who pioneered in aviation. They made their first flight in a power-driven aircraft, Flyer, near Kitty Hawk, North Carolina, on December 17, 1903. The plane, driven by a small gasoline engine, had a wingspan of 40 feet, 6 inches. Orville piloted the first of four flights. He was in the air for 12 seconds and covered 120 feet. Wilbur followed with a thirteen-second flight of 195 feet. Then Orville flew more than 200 feet in 15 seconds. The fourth and final flight, with Wilbur at the controls, was the most successful — 852 feet in 59 seconds. The aircraft can be seen in the National Air and Space Museum in Washington, D.C. Here is the telegraph message Orville sent to his father:

> Success   four flights   Thursday morning   all against 21-mile wind   started from level with engine power alone   average speed through air 31 miles longest 59 seconds   inform press   home Christmas.

AUGUST 19, 1902
Birth Date of Ogden Nash

Ogden Nash, born in Rye, New York, was an inimitable writer of light verse. He also co-wrote the libretto for the 1943 Broadway musical *One Touch of Venus*.

Introduce students to his outrageous rhymes by sharing his works from *Custard & Company: Poems by Ogden Nash*, selected and illustrated by Quentin Blake (Little, Brown, 1980; paperback).

He died on May 19, 1971, in Baltimore, Maryland.

AUGUST 20, 1833
Birth Date of Benjamin Harrison, Twenty-third President

Born in:	North Bend, Ohio
Occupation:	Lawyer
President:	1889–1893, Republican
Died:	March 13, 1901
	Indianapolis, Indiana

About Harrison

★ His grandfather was William Henry Harrison, ninth president of the United States.

★ He lost the presidential election by 100,000 popular votes but won in the Electoral College against Grover Cleveland.

During His Term
★ A weak leader with no program of his own.
★ United States population expanded westward; North and South Dakota, Montana, Washington, Idaho, and Wyoming became states.
★ First Pan-American Conference.
★ White House wired for electricity.

AUGUST 21, 1959

Hawaii became the fiftieth state.

Flower: Hibiscus
Tree: Kukui, "Candlenut"
Bird: Nene, "Hawaiian Goose"

AUGUST 23

The zodiac sign, Virgo the Virgin, begins today and ends September 22. How many students were born under this sign?

AUGUST 26, 1920

The Nineteenth Amendment went into effect, giving women the right to vote.

AUGUST 27, 551 B.C.
Birth Date of Confucius

Confucius, an ancient Chinese philosopher, devoted many years to thinking about and studying humans, their place in the universe, and his relationship to them. As a young man he organized a school where others could study academic subjects as well as examine duty, love, manners, and how they relate to human life. Some of Confucius's thoughts are embodied in his oft-quoted "sayings" such as "The superior man understands what is right, the inferior man understands what is profitable." Confucius's real name was K'ung Ch'iu. Confucius is a Latin form of the title K'ung-fu-tzu, which means Great Master K'ung. Although Confucius received some minor official appointments during his lifetime, at the time of his death, he was largely unknown throughout China. His disciples spread his teachings. None of his writings were preserved, but his conversations and sayings were compiled by his followers in a book titled The Analects.

AUGUST 27, 1908
Birth Date of Lyndon Baines Johnson, Thirty-sixth President

Born in:	Stonewall, Texas
Occupation:	Congressman, senator, rancher
President:	1963–1969, Democrat
Died:	January 22, 1973
	Johnson City, Texas

About Johnson
★ Texas ranch background.
★ Elementary school teacher.
★ First congressman to enter the armed forces in World War II.
★ Senate Majority Leader.
★ Elected vice president and became president when John F. Kennedy was assassinated.

During His Terms

★ The 1964 Civil Rights Bill outlawed racial discrimination in public accommodations and employment.

★ Won the 1964 election against Senator Barry Goldwater by the largest number of popular votes ever.

★ "Great Society" program of social legislation: Job Corps, Medicare, Voting Rights Bill, aid to education.

★ Appointed first black cabinet member, Robert Weaver, Department of Housing and Urban Development, and first black Supreme Court Justice, Thurgood Marshall.

★ The Vietnam War escalated during his terms — with mounting casualties and costs.

AUGUST 28, 1963
March on Washington, D.C.

More than 200,000 Americans marched in Washington, D.C., and gathered in front of the Lincoln Memorial to tell the world that they wanted liberty, freedom, and justice for all. This date was one of the most significant in the history of the civil rights struggle in America. Among the leaders of the march were Jesse Jackson and the Reverend Dr. Martin Luther King, Jr., who addressed the crowd with the now historic speech that began with the words, "I have a dream . . ." and ended with:

> When we allow freedom to ring — when we let it ring from every village and from every hamlet, from every state and every city, we will be able to speed up that day when all of God's children, black men and white men, Jews and Gentiles, Protestants and Catholics, will be able to join hands and sing in the words of the old Negro spiritual: "Free at last, Free at last! Thank God almighty, we are free at last."

(*See also* January 15, 1929.)

SEPTEMBER

FLOWER   ◆   BIRTHSTONE
Aster   Sapphire

The name September comes from the Latin word *septem* meaning "seven." September was the seventh month in the Roman calendar until 45 B.C., when Julius Caesar revised the calendar.

SEPTEMBER POEM OF THE MONTH

NOW

Close the barbecue.
Close the sun.
Close the home-run games we won.

Close the picnic.
Close the pool.

Close the summer.

Open school.

— Prince Redcloud

THE FIRST MONDAY IN SEPTEMBER
Labor Day

This legal holiday is observed on the first Monday in September to honor American workers. In 1886, the American Federation of Labor, one of America's earliest and largest unions, proclaimed, "It shall be as uncommon for a man to work on that day as on Independence Day." The nation's first Labor Day parade was held on September 5, 1882, in New York City, although the holiday was not made a national one until 1894 when President Grover Cleveland signed a bill making it a legal holiday. The founder of Labor Day was Peter J. Maguire, a carpenter and founder of the United Brotherhood of Carpenters and Joiners. Each Labor Day, memorial services are held at Maguire's grave in Philadelphia, Pennsylvania.

SEPTEMBER 1, 1939
World War II Began

German troops crossed the Polish frontier launching the beginning of a six-year war that killed almost forty million people. Adolf Hitler, the Nazi dictator, succeeded in seizing most of Europe almost effortlessly as the forces allied against him— the British Commonwealth, France, and the U.S.S.R. — reeled under the new type of war the Germans had invented. The blitzkrieg, or lightning war, of 1940 introduced air bombings that destroyed major cities; massive tank attacks that crushed ill-equipped armies in France, Scandinavia, and the Balkans; and the ruthless suppression of civilian populations.

On December 7, 1941, the Japanese attack on Pearl Harbor brought the United States into the war on the side of Great Britain and the U.S.S.R. Opposing the Allies were the Axis Powers of Japan, Italy, and Germany. After almost six long years of widespread conflict, the Allies were victorious on all fronts in 1945.

There are scores of books for children about this period of history. Blitzcat by Robert Westall (Scholastic, 1989) is a compelling novel for young adult readers, revealing the courage and cowardice, greed and generosity of humans during wartime.

SEPTEMBER 1, 1985

The Titanic was discovered by Dr. Robert Ballard. (See April 15, 1912.)

SEPTEMBER 2, 1838
Birth Date of Queen Liliuokalani

Queen Liliuokalani, the last of the Hawaiian Islands' monarchs, refused to recognize the constitutional reforms that lessened the power of the Hawaiian monarchy. She was dethroned in 1893, a year before Hawaii became a republic. Her people, the Polynesians, are today the island's smallest group in a multiethnic population of European, Japanese, and Filipino descent.

The queen was a prolific songwriter. Her works include the popular "Aloha Oe" and "Farewell to Thee," which for many symbolize the island state.

Listen to these songs and more Hawaiian music today.

SEPTEMBER 3, 1783
The Treaty of Paris

The Treaty of Paris was signed by Great Britain on one side, and by the United States, France, Spain, and Holland on the other. The treaty ended the American Revolutionary War and acknowledged the independence of the United States.

SEPTEMBER 4, 1888

Today marks the day that George Eastman patented his Kodak camera, the forerunner of today's snapshot camera. This camera was preloaded with enough film for 100 exposures and took a round picture 2.5 inches in diameter. The camera cost $25.00 and included a memorandum book for a record of photos taken and a leather carrying case.

Celebrate today by taking pictures of your students or have them bring in photos from home. It will make a great back-to-school bulletin board display. Have someone take a picture of you, too!

SEPTEMBER 5, 1847
Birth Date of Jesse Woodson James

Jesse Woodson James, an American outlaw and legendary figure, was born at Centerville (now Kearney), Clay County, Missouri. At the outbreak of the Civil War the James family favored the South. Jesse and his brother Frank joined the guerilla band led by William Clarke Quantrill and served with it until the end of the war. In 1866, he was declared an outlaw. For the next 16 years he carried out a campaign of banditry that made him infamous. In 1873, James, along with a group of confederates, staged a new kind of highway robbery when they held up their first train. Nine years later he moved to St. Joseph, Missouri, changed his name to Tom Howard, and posed as a cattle buyer. Later that year he was shot in the head by Robert Ford, a member of the band who had turned against him.

SEPTEMBER 6, 1620

The Pilgrims sailed on the *Mayflower* from Plymouth, England, to settle in the New World. An account of what the voyage was like is given in *If You Sailed on the Mayflower* by Ann McGovern (Scholastic, 1969).

SEPTEMBER 6, 1860
Birth Date of Jane Addams

Jane Addams, one of the country's first female college graduates, was a social reformer who, in 1889, established Hull House, a settlement in a slum neighborhood of Chicago, Illinois.

Winner of many national prizes for her work, she received a Nobel Peace Prize in 1931. Her major written work, *Twenty Years at the Hull House* (1910), became a classic in social reform; its sequel, *The Second Twenty Years at Hull House,* was published in 1930. She died on May 21, 1935. Thirty years later she was elected to the Hall of Fame.

SEPTEMBER 6, 1988

Thomas Gregory, an eleven-year-old English boy, crawled ashore at Shakespeare Beach, setting a record as the youngest person to swim the English Channel. He did it in 11 hours, 45 minutes, setting out from Cape Gris-Nez, France.

SEPTEMBER 7, 1860
Birth Date of Anna Mary Robertson Moses

Anna Mary Robertson Moses, better known as Grandma Moses, began to paint in 1938 at age 78. She was one of 10 children born on a farm in Greenwich, New York. Her education was limited for, in her own words, "Little girls did not go to school much in winter owing to the cold and not enough clothing." Her feeling for art showed itself when she was quite young, but she was discouraged by her mother.

After the death of her husband in 1927, Moses began to embroider to fill empty hours. When her hands became too crippled from arthritis to hold a needle, she turned to oil painting. Her first oil was done on thresher cloth with some old paints she found in the barn on her farm. Later she ordered paint and some brushes from a mail order house and began to copy postcard scenes and Currier and Ives prints. She soon turned to painting scenes representing experiences from her own life. In 1939, her work was discovered, and when she was 80 years old her first one-woman show was held. Since then her work, described as "authentic American primitive," has become an American legend. She died on December 31, 1961, at the age of 101 in upstate New York. *Grandma Moses: Painter of Rural America* by Zibby Oneal, illustrated by Donna Ruff, with paintings by Grandma Moses (Viking, 1986) provides an engaging portrait of the artist.

◆

SEPTEMBER 8
International Literacy Day

This day is observed by the organizations of the United Nations in honor of worldwide reading.

SEPTEMBER 9, 1757
Birth Date of the Marquis de Lafayette

By the time French-born Lafayette reached the age of 30, he had made himself one of the world's foremost fighters for freedom. He served in George Washington's army as a major general, suffered the hardships of Valley Forge (1777–1778), and supported his fellow Frenchmen's desires for justice and equality after Americans won their fight for independence. (See June 17, 1775.)

SEPTEMBER 9, 1850

California became the thirty-first state.

Flower: Golden Poppy
Tree: Californian Redwood
Bird: California Valley Quail

SEPTEMBER 9, 1875
Birth Date of Edward E. Kleinschmidt

How rapidly can news be sent to all parts of the world? Edward E. Kleinschmidt's invention of the teletype printer made it possible to report events almost immediately. His printer transmitted words through telephone wires.

A prolific inventor, Kleinschmidt held 118 patents in the

field of electronics. Born in Bremen, Germany, he came to the United States at the age of eight and launched his career without a formal education. He died on August 10, 1977, at the age of 101.

SEPTEMBER 9, 1906
Birth Date of Aileen Fisher

Poet Aileen Fisher grew up around the little town of Iron River on the Upper Peninsula of Michigan, near the Wisconsin border. Currently she lives in Boulder, Colorado, where she enjoys woodworking, hiking, mountain climbing, and all forms of nature.

Since Fisher has written poetry for all age levels, why not celebrate her birthday by reading one of her poems? Two of her titles for younger readers are *Rabbits, Rabbits*, illustrated by Gail Niemann (Harper & Row, 1983), and *The House of a Mouse*, illustrated by Joan Sandin (Harper & Row, 1988).

In 1978, Fisher received the second National Council of Teachers of English Award for Excellence in Poetry for Children.

SEPTEMBER 10, 1846

Elias Howe patented the sewing machine. His apprenticeship as a machinist and cotton mill worker in Massachusetts helped him develop a machine that revolutionized the sewing industry. His invention took five years to perfect. He sold his patent for $1,250 in England because little interest was shown in it in the United States. Later, American manufacturers tried using his invention free; he sued for royalties and won the case.

SEPTEMBER 12, 1913
Birth Date of Jesse Owens

Born in Danville in Morgan County, Alabama, Jesse Owens became a world track record holder in sprinting, hurdling, and jumping. In addition, he won four gold medals at the 1936 Olympic Games in Berlin. Because of his great sports accomplishments he became a symbol for black American athletes, and America became known to the rest of the athletic world as a place where blacks were given the opportunity to compete on equal terms.

SEPTEMBER 13, 1895

The first professional game of football was played at Latrobe, Pennsylvania, between the local YMCA team and the Jeannette (Pennsylvania) Athletic Club. Each player received $10. The game, played by two teams of 11 players each on a rectangular field, apparently began in ancient Greece and Rome. It was brought to America as early as the seventeenth century.

Today the professional game is a complex, highly profitable operation. Interested students might research the history of football from ancient times to the present and prepare a time line of "Great Events and Great Players in Football."

SEPTEMBER 13, 1948

Margaret Chase Smith became the first woman elected to the U.S. Senate without having served a prior appointed term. Before her election to the Senate, Smith, a Maine Republican, served as a U.S. representative. In 1971, a Harris poll named her one of the three most respected women in the world.

Have students find out about some of the women officeholders in your city or state. This information can be obtained by calling the local League of Women Voters or the Chamber of Commerce. (*See also* December 14, 1897.)

SEPTEMBER 14, 1814

Oh, say, can you see by the dawn's early light,
What so proudly we hail'd at the twilight's last
  gleaming?

Francis Scott Key, a Baltimore attorney, wrote the words to "The Star-Spangled Banner" in a Baltimore, Maryland, hotel room after witnessing the British bombardment of Fort McHenry from a ship in Chesapeake Bay. Key gave the manuscript to his brother-in-law, J.H. Nicholson, the next day. The manuscript remained in the Nicholson family for almost one hundred years. In 1953, the Maryland Historical Society bought it for $26,400. Key made three additional copies of the poem; one is owned by the Pennsylvania Historical Society, another by the Library of Congress, and the third disappeared. The words were sung to the tune of an old English tavern refrain, "To Anacreon in Heaven." It was sung for the first time in Baltimore.

On March 3, 1931, President Herbert Hoover signed a bill making "The Star-Spangled Banner" the national anthem. Today the flag that inspired the song is displayed in the Museum of History and Technology in Washington, D.C.

The Star-Spangled Banner (Doubleday, 1973; paperback) is gloriously illustrated by Peter Spier. Music is provided at the back of the book and includes guitar chords. The volume also contains a historical note about the song and a reproduction of Key's original manuscript. Endpapers depict full-color reproductions of "A Collection of Flags of the American Revolution and Those of the United States of America, Its Government, and Armed Forces."

174

◆

SEPTEMBER 14, 1988

Hurricane Gilbert roared into the Gulf of Mexico. The storm's wind of more than two hundred miles an hour ranked it as a Category 5 hurricane, capable of doing catastrophic damage.

The Gulf Coast had also been the site of the worst natural disaster in United States history. On September 8, 1900, a storm killed 6,000 people in the Galveston, Texas, area.

Only two other Category 5 hurricanes have hit the United States since meteorological records have been kept. The first occurred in Florida in 1935; the second, on the Mississippi coast in 1969.

Hurricane Watch by Franklyn M. Branley, illustrated by Giulio Maestro (T.Y. Crowell, 1985; paperback), simply describes the origin and nature of hurricanes and ways of staying safe when threatened by one of these dangerous storms.

MID-SEPTEMBER
National Hispanic Heritage Week

This week provides opportunities for students to study some of the Hispanic cultures in the United States. A display of pictures and crafts, or sharing of dishes such as tortillas, corn, and other national specialties can spark interest in studying the immigrant contributions and how it affects our national texture.

Many ideas regarding some of the traditions, customs, and rich heritage of Hispanics can be gleaned from *Arroz con Leche: Popular Songs and Rhymes from Latin America*, selected by Lulu Delacre (Scholastic, 1989). This attractive feast of Latin-American folk culture captures the spirit of 12 ear-catching songs and rhymes, printed in Spanish and English. The English lyrics are by Elena Paz; musical arrangements by Ana-María Rosado. You will find songs and rhymes from Puerto Rico, Mexico, and Argentina in this attractive book with full-color illustrations.

SEPTEMBER 15, 1857
Birth Date of William Howard Taft, Twenty-seventh President

Born in:	Cincinnati, Ohio
Occupation:	Lawyer, professor, judge
President:	1909–1913, Republican
Died:	March 8, 1930
	Washington, D.C.
	Buried in Arlington, Virginia

About Taft
★ Only president to serve as chief justice of the Supreme Court after his term of office.
★ First governor general of the Philippines.

During His Term
★ Continued Theodore Roosevelt's antitrust and conservation policies.
★ Started custom of president throwing out the first ball to start the new baseball season.

SEPTEMBER 16, 1810
Mexico's Independence Day

In 1519, Hernando Cortés led a small army of conquistadores, or conquerors, from the east coast of Mexico to its capital in the interior. They soon crushed the Aztec Empire and its legendary leader, Montezuma. This set the stage for 300 years of autocratic rule over Mexico by Spain. The first serious challenge to Spanish domination was made on this date by Miguel

Hidalgo, a village priest of Indian background. He issued his *Grito de Dolores* ("Call of Dolores"), calling upon all Mexicans to revolt against the Spaniards who had oppressed them for so long. Although Hidalgo's crusade attracted thousands of armed supporters and liberated many major towns and cities, the revolution failed. Hidalgo was executed in 1811, and Mexico endured 10 more years of Spanish rule.

Annually, Mexico's president reenacts Hidalgo's heroic act, the *Grito* is read, and the Independence Day bell originally rung by the priest is rung again. Mexicans thus honor the call for freedom issued by the simple priest from the Parish of Dolores.

SEPTEMBER 17–23
Constitution Week

This week celebrates the anniversary of the signing of the Constitution of the United States on September 17, 1787. This document was drawn up by members of the Constitutional Convention who met in Philadelphia, Pennsylvania. The Constitution went into effect nine months later, June 21, 1788, when it was ratified by nine states and replaced the Articles of Confederation. The Constitution spells out the responsibilities of the three branches of the federal government — the executive, legislative, and judicial — and how they check and balance each other. It also defines the relations of the states to the federal government and sets forth the amendment process by which the Constitution can be changed, added to, and brought up to date. Twenty-six such changes have been made since the Constitution was adopted. Because it can be altered, people feel the Constitution will never become old-fashioned or rigid. What do your students think about this?

Students might prepare a time line showing when the 50 states entered the Union. (All information is given within this book.) Traced outlines of the individual states can be transferred to colored construction paper, cut out, and placed in chronological order to depict the growth of the United States.

SEPTEMBER 20, 1519

Ferdinand Magellan, a Portuguese nobleman, set forth on his epic three-year voyage around the world. Dissatisfied with his treatment by the Portuguese king, Magellan had sought support from neighboring Spain. Flying the Spanish flag, his five ships and 270 seamen sailed west to reach the Eastern Spice Islands. In the process they dramatically demonstrated that the earth is round! The voyage entailed finding a passage around the tip of South America (today's Strait of Magellan), entering a new ocean (which he named the Pacific), and exploring new lands, among them the Philippines, where Magellan was murdered. Only one of his ships completed the voyage; it returned to Spain in September 1522. (*See also* September 25, 1513.)

SEPTEMBER 21
Beginning of Autumn

For some suggestions on welcoming the season in, see the entry for March 21.

SEPTEMBER 21, 1988

On this date, the U.S. Senate unanimously confirmed the nomination of the first person of Hispanic descent to serve as a cabinet member.

Dr. Lauro F. Cavazos, a former college president and native

Texan, became Secretary of Education. His brother was the first Hispanic to become a four-star general in the U.S. Army.

SEPTEMBER 23

The zodiac sign, Libra the Scales, begins today and ends October 23. How many students were born under this sign?

SEPTEMBER 23, 480 B.C.
Birth Date of Euripides

Euripides was the last of the three most famous Greek dramatists of the ancient world. The first was Aeschylus, the second Sophocles. It is said that Euripides was born on this day — the day the Greeks defeated the Persians in the great sea battle of Salamis. The plays of Euripides are still widely read and performed throughout the world.

SEPTEMBER 23, 1838
Birth Date of Victoria Claflin Woodhull

Did a woman ever run for president of the United States? Yes, indeed! Victoria Claflin Woodhull attempted this on May 10, 1872. She was an unconventional reformer who fought for women's rights. In later years she became an early patron of aviation and offered a prize of $5,000 in 1914 for the first transatlantic flight.

Open discussion by asking students which women they might like to see nominated for president — either from the past or the present.

SEPTEMBER 23, 1846

The planet Neptune was accidentally discovered because of its neighbor Uranus's strange behavior — Uranus failed to reappear where mathematicians and astronomers calculated its orbit would take it. Scientists were very puzzled and remained so for 20 years. This mystery was solved with the discovery of Neptune by two German astronomers. Neptune's strong gravitational pull accounted for Uranus's erratic orbit. Neptune, a greenish mass, is the eighth most distant planet from the sun, has two satellites (Triton and Nereid) and takes about 165 years to revolve around the sun. Suggest *A Book about Planets and Stars* by Betty Polisar Reigot (Scholastic, 1988) to younger students who want more information.

SEPTEMBER 24, 1898
Birth Date of Harry Behn

It wasn't until Harry Behn was 50 years old that he began writing poetry for children. At that time he moved to Connecticut to devote his life to writing and traveling. Celebrate his birthday by sharing one of his poems from *Crickets and Bullfrogs and Whispers of Thunder: Poems and Pictures* by Harry Behn, selected by Lee Bennett Hopkins (Harcourt Brace Jovanovich, 1984).

SEPTEMBER 25, 1513

Vasco Nuñez de Balboa, a Spanish conqueror and explorer, became the first European to see the eastern shore of the Pacific Ocean. Four days later he waded into the ocean and claimed it and all its shores for Spain. His discovery paved the way for the Spanish exploration and conquest of the western coast of South America. The Spanish called the ocean the South Sea because it lay south of the Isthmus of Panama, a strip of land connecting North and South America. Later in 1520, Ferdinand Magellan sailed across the ocean and found its waters quiet and calm. He renamed it the Pacific, meaning "peaceful."

SEPTEMBER 26, 1774
Birth Date of John Chapman

John Chapman, better known as Johnny Appleseed, was an American frontier nurseryman who became a major folk hero because of his interest in growing apple trees. He is considered the first planter of orchards across America. He died in March 1845, near Fort Wayne, Indiana, where a city park and other monuments honor his unmarked grave.

Younger readers will delight in *Johnny Appleseed: A Tale Retold*, illustrated by Steven Kellogg (Morrow, 1988) or *Johnny Appleseed* by Eva Moore (Scholastic, 1964). Share the tale with the class — while all munch on apples, of course!

SEPTEMBER 26, 1888
Birth Date of Thomas Stearns Eliot

Thomas Stearns Eliot, best known as T.S. Eliot, was born in St. Louis, Missouri. By the time he was 34, he had set the course for modern poetry with the publication of *The Waste Land* (Harcourt, 1922), a 433-line work that remains a landmark in literature.

Adult readers will glean much about his life and work from *The Letters of T.S. Eliot: Volume I*, edited by his widow, Valerie Eliot (Harcourt Brace Jovanovich, 1988).

Introduce students to the poet's work via the classic *Old*

Possum's Book of Practical Cats, illustrated by Edward Gorey (Harcourt, 1982, new edition; paperback), or listen to the recording produced by Caedmon with readings by Sir John Gielgud and Irene Worth. Some of your students may have seen the hit musical, *Cats*, which is based on the book. Parts of the recording of the show can be played.

Another volume to share with readers is *Growltigers Last Stand, with the Pekes and the Pollicles, and the Song of the Jellicles*, illustrated by Errol Le Cain (Harcourt Brace Jovanovich, 1987).

SEPTEMBER 27, 1822
Birth Date of Hiram Rhodes Revels

Hiram Rhodes Revels was born free in Fayetteville, North Carolina. On February 25, 1870, he took office as a United States senator, the first black to achieve this position. Until March 3, 1871, he represented Mississippi, the state he adopted after the Civil War. A great deal of his life was devoted to church work. He was an ordained minister in the African Methodist Church and organized many black churches.

END OF SEPTEMBER
Native American Day

Native American Day, formerly American Indian Day, usually celebrated the last Friday in September, honors Native Americans. It is not a universal holiday in the United States — the states that note the holiday are those with large Native American populations, such as Arizona, California, and Connecticut. It is not a religious or ceremonial day, but rather a day to awaken interest in and knowledge of Native Americans. This is an excellent time to discuss the history of Native Americans, past and present.

For better readers, suggest *In the Trail of the Wind: American Indian Poems and Ritual Orations* by John Bierhorst (Farrar Straus & Giroux, 1971) and *Indian Chiefs* by Russell Freedman (Holiday House, 1987), which features six biographies of Western Indian chiefs who led their people in a historic moment of crisis, when a decision had to be made about fighting or cooperating with the white pioneers encroaching on their hunting grounds. The volume is elegantly and lavishly illustrated with black-and-white photographs and drawings. Students will enjoy *Dancing Teepees: Poems of American Youth*, selected by Virginia Driving Hawk Sneve, with art by Caldecott-Award-winning artist Stephen Gammell (Holiday House, 1989).

SEPTEMBER/OCTOBER
Jewish Holidays

Two important Jewish holidays, Rosh Hashanah and Yom Kippur, fall during the month of September or October. They have been celebrated for more than five thousand years. (Check your calendar to find the exact dates for this year.)

The blowing of the *shofar*, a trumpet made from a ram's horn, calls Jews to gather in their synagogues to mark Rosh Hashanah, the beginning of a new year. This holiday commences with the start of the seventh Hebrew month, Tishri — September or October of today's calendar. Traditionally God was asked to provide rainfall for crops, spare those who committed minor sins, and grant a new year of happiness. Believers have 10 days, until Yom Kippur, to seek forgiveness. God opens the "Book of Life" on this holiday, reads all deeds and thoughts of his followers, and determines their fate for the coming year.

Annually ancient Hebrews selected a goat to send into the wilderness; this specially selected creature was thought to carry the sins of the community away with it. Today Yom Kippur celebrates this ritual of ancient times. It is the Day of Atonement for all Jews — a 24-hour period of fasting and asking God to forgive personal and general sins. Translated, Yom means "day," and Kippur, "cleansing from sin." Jews gather in synagogues to commit themselves to living according to the rules of the *Torah* (Bible).

A good resource for older readers is *Sound the Shofar: The Story and Meaning of Rosh Hashanah and Yom Kippur* by Miriam Chaikin, illustrated by Erika Weihs (Clarion Books, 1986).

OCTOBER

FLOWER   ◆   **BIRTHSTONE**
Marigold   Opal

October comes from the Latin word *octo* meaning "eighth." October was the eighth month in the Roman calendar.

OCTOBER POEM OF THE MONTH

THREE GHOSTESSES

Three little ghostesses,
Sitting on postesses,
Eating buttered toastesses,
Greasing their fistesses,
Up to their wristesses,
Oh, what beastesses
To make such feastesses!

— Anonymous

OCTOBER
Fire Prevention Week

Usually during the early part of October, one week is designated Fire Prevention Week. Statistics show that awareness of fire prevention techniques is important. There are approximately 550,000 residential fires a year in the United States that cause billions of dollars worth of damage and loss of life. Forest fires are another area of great concern.

Discuss the positive and negative uses of fire with the class. Discuss ways people can help prevent fires. Walk around the school and community to look at fire hydrants, extinguishers, alarm boxes, fire exits, and the location of the nearest firehouse. Younger children learn a great deal from a visit to the local fire station; for middle-graders, invite a fire fighter to speak to the class on fire prevention practices and the duties fire fighters perform. All children can create fire prevention posters to display around the classroom, school, or community. For a detailed look into the life and work of a fire fighter, younger readers will enjoy *Fire Fighters*, written and photographed by Robert Maass (Scholastic, 1989).

OCTOBER 1, 1908

Henry Ford introduced his Model T automobile. By developing an assembly line that mass-produced inexpensive automobiles, Ford paved the way to the mobile world of today. Discuss with students how their lives would be different if there were no motor vehicles. How would people get from one place to another? How might our lives be better without automobiles?

Help students prepare a bulletin board display on the many types of vehicles we use today.

OCTOBER 1, 1924
Birth Date of Jimmy (James Earl) Carter, Jr., Thirty-ninth President

Born in:	Plains, Georgia
Occupation:	Farmer, engineer, businessman, naval officer, state senator, governor
President:	1977–1981, Democrat

About Carter
★ Relatively unknown outside of the South. He promised to remove the taint left on the high office by the Nixon years.
★ The first southerner to win the presidency in this century.

During His Term
★ Helped bring peace to the conflict between Israel and Egypt through face-to-face meetings of their leaders.
★ Attempted to negotiate release of 52 Americans held hostage by Iran. They were finally freed on President Reagan's Inaugural Day in 1981.
★ Human rights became a central issue during his term of office.

OCTOBER 2, 1800
Birth Date of Nat Turner

One of the major slave revolts of nineteenth-century America was led by Nat Turner, a slave-preacher in Virginia. He declared God had told him to lead his people out of bondage. On Sunday, August 21, 1831, Turner, four disciples, and two other slaves attacked and killed Turner's master and his entire family. The group then attracted more slaves. All that night and the following day they went from plantation to plantation, freeing slaves and slaying whites in an abortive attempt to lead a liberation movement of southern slaves. When the rebellion was suppressed, Turner went into hiding for two months. He was finally captured and hanged in Jerusalem, Virginia, along with other participants in this uprising. Nat Turner's revolt is early evidence of black people's determination to win freedom at any cost.

OCTOBER 2, 1869
Birth Date of Mohandas Karamehand Gandhi

Gandhi, an intensely religious man, opposed any form of violence. The Indian people looked upon him as a saint and called him *mahatma*, meaning "great soul." Gandhi was instrumental in gaining India's independence from the British. He urged his followers to boycott anything English. His tactics of nonviolent resistance served as models for nonviolent social change in many parts of the world, and his philosophy inspired the late Dr. Martin Luther King, Jr.

Gandhi was the son of an Indian merchant. He studied law in England and in 1893 went to South Africa where he first encountered racial discrimination. In 1915, he returned to India's Congress Party, a political organization working for independence. After one of his campaigns against British rule, he was jailed. In fact, he spent many years of his life in prison for his beliefs.

In 1934, Gandhi resigned from the Congress. He did so partly to devote full time to encouraging village industries, hoping this would make India economically independent of the British. Britain finally granted independence to India in 1947. The following year Gandhi was assassinated by a fanatical Hindu youth.

OCTOBER 2, 1872

On this date, Jules Verne's fictional character Phileas Fogg stated: "I will bet twenty thousand pounds against anyone who wishes, that I will make the tour of the world in eighty days or less," beginning one of the greatest travel adventures of all time. Fogg started out from a local club in London, England, and returned on December 21, 1872 — 79 days, 23 hours, 59 minutes, and 59 seconds later!

Children will be fascinated by this story. Better readers can read one of many versions of Verne's *Around the World in Eighty Days*. (*See also* May 5, 1867.)

OCTOBER 3, 1950

Happy Birthday Charlie Brown!

On this date the first "Peanuts" comic strip created by Charles M. Schulz was published. Share *Happy Birthday, Charlie Brown* by Lee Mendelson in association with Charles M. Schulz (Random House, 1979) with students of all ages. In addition to lavish full-color illustrations, all the great moments in "Peanuts" history are included: the origins of Snoopy, Lucy, Charlie Brown, Linus, and the rest; the gang's first television debut in

A Charlie Brown Christmas, Snoopy's flight on *Apollo* 10 — and more!

Does "Peanuts" appear in your local newspaper? If so, clip out several cartoon strips to make a "Happy Birthday, Charlie Brown" bulletin board display.

OCTOBER 4, 1181 or 1182
Birth Date of Saint Francis of Assisi

Each year the feast of Saint Francis is celebrated in memory of Saint Francis of Assisi. The son of a wealthy merchant, he was 20 when he fought for his native Assisi in a battle with the neighboring city of Perugia. Assisi lost, and Francis was captured and imprisoned for a year. When he returned home, he became gravely ill and decided to dedicate his life to prayer and service to the poor. He and his many followers formed the Franciscan Order of monks, which is devoted to poverty and prayer. The hilltop town of Assisi in central Italy where Saint Francis was born and died is visited by travelers from throughout the world each year. Today the Franciscan Order and the separate order for women, the Poor Clares, are still widely known for their charity, education, and missionary work.

OCTOBER 4, 1822
Birth date of Rutherford Birchard Hayes, Nineteenth President

Born in:	Delaware, Ohio
Occupation:	Lawyer, general, governor
President:	1877–1881, Republican

Died: January 17, 1893
               Fremont, Ohio

About Hayes
★ Unpaid defense attorney for fugitive slaves.
★ Civil War general.
★ Governor of Ohio for three terms.
★ Became president in disputed election against Samuel J. Tilden. Neither received an electoral majority until three days before Inauguration Day when an electoral commission finished their investigation of the voting returns in three southern states.

During His Term
★ Ended Reconstruction period by taking troops out of the South.
★ The first telephone was installed in the White House. Alexander Graham Bell gave the president a personal demonstration.

OCTOBER 4, 1957

A device the size of a basketball was rocketed into orbit around the earth by the Soviet Union. *Sputnik 1*, meaning "fellow-traveler," was the first man-made satellite. Its 184 pounds completed a trip around the earth every 96 minutes at 18,000 miles per hour. It fell to earth on January 4, 1958, setting the stage for later manned flights by Russian and American astronauts.

OCTOBER 4, 1987

A larger-than-lifesize bronze sculpture of Mrs. Mallard and her eight ducklings, characters from Robert McCloskey's 1942

Caldecott-Award-winning book *Make Way for Ducklings* (Viking Penguin, 1941; paperback) was dedicated at the Boston Public Garden in Boston, Massachusetts. The installment coincided with the park's 150th anniversary.

A plaque at the sculpture site carries the dedication: "This sculpture has been placed here as a tribute to Robert Mc-Closkey whose story *Make Way for Ducklings* has made the Boston Public Garden familiar to children throughout the world."

Born on September 14, 1914, in Hamilton, Ohio, McCloskey illustrated the well-known picture books *Blueberries for Sal* (Viking Penguin, 1948; paperback) and *One Morning in Maine* (Viking Penguin, 1952; paperback). Have your students look for them in your school or public library.

OCTOBER 5, 1830
Birth Date of Chester Alan Arthur, Twenty-first President

Born in:	Fairfield, Vermont
Occupation:	Lawyer
President:	1881–1885, Republican
Died:	November 18, 1886
	New York, New York

About Arthur
★ Elected vice president and became president when James A. Garfield died, seven months after being shot by an assassin.

During His Term
★ Fought for establishment of the Civil Service Commission to end an era of widespread corruption and patronage in federal jobs.

* ★ Most elegantly dressed president since Washington.
* ★ Refurnished the White House in Victorian splendor.

OCTOBER 6, 1914
Birth Date of Thor Heyerdahl

Thor Heyerdahl, a Norwegian explorer-ethnologist, risked his life several times to test his theory that Polynesia might have been settled by Peruvians in the distant past.

He used the *Kon-Tiki*, an exact duplication of an ancient sailing vessel, to make this voyage of 4,300 miles successful! Other dangerous voyages included trips in a reed boat from Morocco to Barbados, and from Egypt to South America.

OCTOBER 8, 1941
Birth Date of Jesse L. Jackson

In 1984, Jesse L. Jackson, an ordained Baptist minister, sought the Democratic Party's nomination for the presidency of the United States. He followed the same path in 1988, but this time his "Rainbow Coalition" attracted many more votes, giving him victory in some state primaries.

Jackson participated in Dr. Martin Luther King, Jr.'s Southern Christian Leadership Conference where his charismatic manner enhanced the struggle for civil rights. His more recent efforts to achieve economic power for masses of blacks led him to organize People United to Save Humanity (PUSH), which seeks economic parity for black citizens. An extremely helpful biography for middle-grade readers is *Jesse Jackson: A Biography* by Patricia McKissack (Scholastic, 1989).

OCTOBER 9
Leif Erikson Day

Leif Erikson Day was proclaimed in 1964. Erikson, a Norse adventurer, was nicknamed Leif the Lucky. Around the year 1000, he unintentionally discovered North America while attempting to sail to Greenland from Norway. He called his discovery Vinland, and historians think he landed at Labrador or Newfoundland. Recently he has been given credit for being one of several individuals who touched upon the North American continent before Christopher Columbus.

Have students trace Erikson's route on a world map and compare his voyage with that of Columbus. (*See* October 12, 1492.) A good discussion among middle-grade students is the subject of great things people find by accident.

OCTOBER 10, 1973

Vice President Spiro T. Agnew, serving under President Richard M. Nixon, resigned from his office due to charges of tax evasion on payments made to him by Maryland contractors when he was governor of that state. He became the second vice president in the country's history to resign. The first was John C. Calhoun, the famed southern orator who stepped down from his office on December 28, 1832, after a political feud with President Andrew Jackson over the issue of states' rights.

OCTOBER 11, 1884
Birth Date of Eleanor Roosevelt

As America's famous First Lady from 1933 to 1945, Eleanor Roosevelt, wife of President Franklin Delano Roosevelt, became a legend in her own time. She was not content to merely be the White House hostess. She spent a great deal of time being the "legs and eyes" for her husband, who was crippled with polio. She traveled extensively, investigating many types of institutions and localities during the Depression. During World War II she acted as an ambassador of goodwill to other countries and visited military camps abroad. After her husband's death, President Truman appointed her United States delegate to the United Nations. Her major accomplishments were with the Commission on Human Rights, where she worked on problems of resettling refugees of World War II. She died in 1962.

Better readers will enjoy *Eleanor Roosevelt, First Lady of the World* by Doris Faber, illustrated by Donna Ruff (Viking Kestral, 1985).

OCTOBER 12, 1492

Christopher Columbus sighted San Salvador Island in Central America as a result of his quest for a short route to the Indies in Asia. Columbus referred to the indigenous inhabitants of the region as Indians, coining the words used to refer to Native Americans for many centuries. The year 1992 marks the 500th anniversary of the explorer's feat.

Steer younger readers to *Christopher Columbus* by Ann McGovern (Scholastic, 1962), *A Book about Christopher Columbus* by Ruth Belov Gross (Scholastic, 1975), and *Christopher Columbus* by Lisl Weil (Macmillan, 1983).

Middle-grade readers will enjoy *Where Do You Think You're Going, Christopher Columbus?* by Jean Fritz, illustrated by Margot Tomes (G.P. Putnam's Sons, 1980; paperback).

OCTOBER 13, 1754
Birth Date of Mary Ludwig Hays McCauley

Mary Ludwig Hays McCauley, better known as Molly Pitcher, was a heroine of the War for American Independence. Born near Philadelphia, she met her husband John Hays near there. She then traveled with him to Valley Forge, where both endured the harsh conditions forced upon the Continental Army. On June 28, 1778, at the Battle of Monmouth, she was given the name Molly Pitcher by Washington's soldiers because of her ceaseless work providing water to the exhausted troops. In this same fight she manned her husband's cannon after he was wounded and continued firing the weapon until the battle was over.

OCTOBER 14, 1644
Birth Date of William Penn

One might wonder why the son of a famous English admiral would endure prison, ostracism, and poverty for his religious beliefs. William Penn, founder of the Pennsylvania Colony, pursued this course when he became a Quaker in his native Britain. In 1682, when Penn's father died, King Charles II gave young Penn title to an enormous area of land in the American colonies to wipe out a royal debt to the elder Penn. Penn named the area *Sylvania*, meaning "woods," because of its immense forests. Pennsylvania, as it came to be known, became a refuge for thousands of Europeans seeking religious freedom; even Native Americans were treated fairly in this Quaker-dominated state.

OCTOBER 14, 1744

The Earl of Sandwich, in England, took two slices of bread and placed meat between them, thus creating the world's first sandwich!

OCTOBER 14, 1890
Birth Date of Dwight David Eisenhower, Thirty-fourth President

Born in:	Denison, Texas
Occupation:	Soldier
President:	1953–1961, Republican
Died:	March 28, 1969
	Washington, D.C.
	Buried in Abilene, Kansas

About Eisenhower
★ Came from a poor family.
★ West Point education led to an army career.
★ Supreme Commander of Allied forces in Europe during World War II.
★ President of Columbia University.

During His Terms
★ Ended Korean War.
★ Started space program when Russians launched first Sputnik I.
★ Historic Supreme Court decision made against segregation in public schools, May 17, 1954.

OCTOBER 14, 1947

Chuck Yeager broke the sound barrier on this date. This veteran of World War II broke the "Barrier" by flying for one minute in a rocket-powered plane at 700 miles per hour. He was only 24 years old at the time.

Yeager served the U.S. Air Force first as a fighter pilot, later as a test pilot. His dangerous work cleared the way for today's supersonic aircraft, the Concorde, that flies at twice the speed first attained by the daring young airman.

Invite a pilot to visit your class to talk about air travel. Find out about the extensive and rigorous training program all pilots go through.

Students can read about the man and his exploration in *Chuck Yeager: Fighter Pilot* by Carter M. Ayres (Lerner, 1988), illustrated with black-and white photographs.

OCTOBER 16, 1758
Birth Date of Noah Webster

In 1828, Noah Webster, a farm boy who became a teacher, published his *American Dictionary of the English Language*, a job that had taken him 50 years to complete. New editions of Webster's dictionary are still issued periodically. Celebrate Webster's birthday by having each student in class look through a dictionary to find a new word she or he likes and can use.

Readers can glean more about Webster's life in *What Do You Mean: A Story About Noah Webster* by Jeri Ferris (Carolrhoda, 1988). (See April 14, 1828.)

OCTOBER 19, 1850

On this date Annie Smith Peck, a mountain climber, became the first person to conquer Peru's Mount Coropona, at 21,250 feet. She was 61 years old.

OCTOBER 19, 1987

The New York Stock Exchange "crashed" on this date sending markets all over the world into a sharp decline. The panic following the crash saw many investors lose faith in the market as a sound investment.

The Dow Jones Industrial Average plunged 508 points between the opening bell at the Stock Exchange at 9:30 A.M. and the closing at 4:00 P.M. The Dow Jones Industrial Average is the oldest index of stock market activity in United States history. The New York State Department of Labor estimated the loss of 10,800 jobs in the securities and commodities industry as a result of the crash. Certainly many more jobs were lost in related fields.

OCTOBER 20, 1891
Birth Date of Sir James Chadwick

Sir James Chadwick spent much of his life doing research on radioactivity. In 1932, he discovered an unknown part of the atomic building block of all matter — the neutron. He later demonstrated that neutrons carry no electrical charge. He received the Nobel Prize in Physics for that discovery in 1935 and later applied his findings to develop the atomic bomb. As head of the British team that worked in the United States on atomic weapon research — the Manhattan Project, as it was called — he always hoped that these efforts would be unsuccessful. Many scientists shared his feelings and envisioned atomic power being used for peaceful purposes only.

Students can research ways atomic energy is used to benefit humankind today or can brainstorm possible applications for the future. Better readers will glean much information from *Understanding Radioactivity* by Lorus J. and Margery Milne, illustrated by Bruce Hiscock (Atheneum, 1989).

OCTOBER 21, 1833
Birth Date of Alfred Nobel

This Swedish inventor's will has provided funds since 1901 for annual Nobel prizes in the field of physics, chemistry, physiology, medicine, literature, peace, and economics. The man who developed and manufactured explosives thus hoped to encourage the peaceful use of science and technology.

Middle-graders can do research on the following people who have won Nobel prizes and report their findings to the class:

Physics: Wilhelm Roentgen for discovering X rays (Germany, 1901); Albert Einstein for work in mathematical physics (Switzerland, 1921).

Chemistry: Frédéric and Irène Joliot-Curie for work on radioactive elements (France, 1935).

Literature: Rudyard Kipling (Great Britain, 1907); Sir Winston Churchill (Great Britain, 1953); Isaac Bashevis Singer (United States, 1978).

Peace: Theodore Roosevelt for helping end the Russo-Japanese War (United States, 1906); Woodrow Wilson for helping found the League of Nations (United States, 1919); Ralph J. Bunche for mediating in Palestine in 1948–1949 (United States, 1950); Albert Schweitzer for his humanitarian work in Africa (France, 1952); Martin Luther King, Jr., for his work to gain black civil rights by nonviolent direct action (United States, 1964); Mother Teresa for years of service to children, refugees, and the poor (United States, 1979).

OCTOBER 22, 1811
Birth Date of Franz Liszt

Franz Liszt, a nineteenth-century Hungarian, was a composer and pianist who gave his first piano concert at the age of nine. Acclaimed as the greatest pianist of his day, his works greatly influenced many of the twentieth century's greats. His "Hungarian Rhapsodies" are familiar to many. He died on July 31, 1886.

In 1989, over 100 years after Liszt's death, Jay Rosenblatt, a doctoral candidate at the University of Chicago, discovered a new Liszt concerto, tentatively dated 1839. The work was given its world premiere in 1989.

OCTOBER 24

The zodiac sign, Scorpio the Scorpion, begins today and ends November 21. How many students were born under this sign?

OCTOBER 24, 1788
Birth Date of Sara Josepha Hale

Sara Josepha Hale was born in the small town of Newport, New Hampshire. In addition to her strong nineteenth-century battle to make Thanksgiving a national holiday, she was also the creator of countless articles, books, poems, and songs, including the popular song "Mary's Lamb," which was written in 1830, and more familiarly known as "Mary Had a Little Lamb." Hale was the editor of a popular women's magazine, *Godey's Lady's Book*, the country's first magazine for women, which within a few years had a circulation of 150,000. She held the position of editor until her retirement at the age of 90. Hale died in 1879. (*See also* November/Thanksgiving Day.)

OCTOBER 24, 1945
United Nations Day

By presidential proclamation, this date honors the United Nations, which was conceived as an organization to prevent the bloodshed and chaos of another world war. In an attempt to avoid future conflicts, 50 nations drew up the organization's charter in San Francisco, California, on this date. The first formal meeting was held in London in 1946. Now based in New York City, the United Nations continues its attempt to keep world peace, promote human rights, and serve as the forum where words can take the place of military action.

The United Nations has six main divisions to carry out its programs: the General Assembly, the Security Council, the Trusteeship Council, the International Court of Justice, the Economic and Social Council, and the Secretariat. Have students research the powers allocated to these divisions and present information about some of the United Nations' successes and shortcomings.

The United Nations also has many agencies. One of the best known is UNICEF, the United Nations International Children's Emergency Fund. Financed by governments and individuals, UNICEF provides food, medical treatment, raw materials, emergency aid, and funds for education of the world's needy children.

Many books for children have been written about the United Nations. Since the United Nations is an ever-changing organization, direct students to look carefully at the latest ones for the most accurate information. (For additional information on the United Nations, see December 10, Human Rights Day.)

OCTOBER 25, 1881
Birth Date of Pablo Ruiz y Picasso

Pablo Ruiz y Picasso was born in Málaga, Spain, the son of the artist José Ruiz and María Picasso. Rather than using the common name, Ruiz, young Picasso took the rarer name of his mother.

A prodigy, Picasso, at the age of 14, completed the one-month qualifying examination of the Academy of Fine Arts in Barcelona in one day!

During his lifetime he adapted and created more styles than any other artist. His works are categorized as follows: the Blue Period, Rose Period, Primitivism, Cubism, Classicism, Surrealism, Sculpture — and more. In the 1960s he produced a monumental 50-foot sculpture for the Chicago Civic Center. In 1970, he donated more than eight hundred of his works to the Berenguer de Aguilar Palace Museum in Barcelona.

When he died on April 8, 1973, in Mougins, France, he was a very wealthy man.

An easy-to-read account of his life appears in *Pablo Picasso* by Ernest Raboff (J.B. Lippincott, 1987). The volume also features 15 full-color reproductions of the artist's work, and many smaller drawings and designs.

OCTOBER 25, 1888
Birth Date of Richard Evelyn Byrd

After graduating from the U.S. Naval Academy, Richard Evelyn Byrd devoted his life to aviation and polar exploration. His efforts brought him world acclaim. Below are several of his accomplishments:

1925 Commander of a flight over Greenland.
1926 Together with Floyd Bennett, he flew over the North Pole.
1927 Carried first air mail from New York to Paris. Flew over the South Pole.
1934 First man to spend a winter in Antarctica, the coldest place on earth.
1947 Led a thirteen-ship exploratory expedition to Antarctica.

Admiral Byrd died in 1957 and was buried at Arlington National Cemetery. He was a direct descendant of William Byrd (1652–1704), one of the earliest plantation owners in Virginia.

OCTOBER 26, 1911

The New York Public Library opened its doors. By 1962, it had outgrown its 88 miles of stacks. By 1990, part of its collection will be underground. Books stored in the underground stacks will be whisked to the main library on a custom-designed conveyor system. The new extension will hold 3.2 million books. Each year the library acquires 150,000 books. Younger readers can explore the subject more in I Like the Library by Anne Rockwell (E.P. Dutton, 1977).

OCTOBER 26, 1919
Birth Date of Edward W. Brooke

Edward W. Brooke returned to Washington, D.C., the city of his birth, in 1966. His election as a Republican senator from Massachusetts marked a momentous occasion — a black man sitting in the U.S. Senate for the first time in the twentieth century. Only two other blacks, Hiram Revels (see September 27, 1822) and Blanche Kelso Bruce (see March 1, 1841), had ever been elected to this important body. While attorney general of Massachusetts, Brooke proved his ability as a capable vote-getting member of his party. Brooke served until 1978, when false charges of fiscal fraud led to his defeat in his bid for reelection.

OCTOBER 26, 1927

The first sound motion picture was shown to the public at Warner's Theater in New York City. It was titled *The Jazz Singer* and starred Al Jolson in his screen debut.

OCTOBER 27, 1858
Birth Date of Theodore Roosevelt, Twenty-sixth President

Born in:	New York City
Occupation:	Public official, lawyer
President:	1901–1909, Republican
Died:	January 6, 1919
	Oyster Bay, New York

About Roosevelt
★ Sickly childhood; spent years building his health, became a great boxer, outdoorsman, and advocate of exercise.
★ Cattle rancher in the Dakota Territory after his first wife's death.
★ New York City police commissioner.
★ Led Rough Riders, a volunteer fighting group, in the Spanish-American War.
★ Became nation's youngest president on September 14, 1901, after assassination of William McKinley.

During His Terms
★ Acted against trusts — monopolies that dominated business, industry, and politics.
★ Great conservationist — acquired western lands for public use as national parks.
★ Initiated construction of the Panama Canal.
★ Won Nobel Peace Prize in 1906 for his efforts to end Russo-Japanese War.

OCTOBER 28, 1914
Birth Date of Jonas Salk

In 1952, 58,000 American children contracted the crippling disease of poliomyelitis (polio). Thirteen years later only 121 cases were reported. The miracle of the polio vaccine invented by Dr. Jonas Salk was responsible for this dramatic decrease. Dr. Salk dedicated a major portion of his adult life to research viruses — tiny organisms one millionth of an inch in size. He was on a research team that pioneered the development of a flu vaccine made of weakened disease germs that cause the body to build up natural immunity, and he envisioned doing the same with the polio virus. After Dr. John Enders of Boston grew polio viruses in a test tube — a feat that won him a Nobel Prize — Salk's team developed a three-step procedure for polio prevention: They grew a virus in a test tube, they killed the virus with disinfectant to create a vaccine, and they injected this substance into people to form antibodies. In 1952, Salk and his family injected themselves with the vaccine to test its effectiveness. Two years later the vaccine was approved for mass use with over a million people. Polio is now a conquered disease.

OCTOBER 29, 1656
Birth Date of Edmund Halley

This contemporary of Sir Isaac Newton has a comet named after him. Comets are small, celestial bodies that travel around the sun in a regular orbit. The ancients viewed them as harbingers of great events to come.

In 1705, Halley predicted that a long-period comet, a comet that appears perhaps only once in a lifetime, would return in 1758 and every 76 years after, calculating that it was the same object that had been seen in 1682, 1607, and 1531. At that time most people thought that a comet was only visible once and never returned. Halley's theory, however, was proved correct. His findings are corroborated with each regular "visit" by Halley's comet.

OCTOBER 29, 1929

The New York Stock Market collapsed, signaling the beginning of the Great Depression of the 1930s and early 1940s.

OCTOBER 30, 1735
Birth Date of John Adams, Second President

Born in:	Braintree, Massachusetts
Occupation:	Farmer, teacher, lawyer
President:	1797–1801, Federalist
Died:	July 4, 1826
	Quincy, Massachusetts

About Adams
★ Successfully defended perpetrators of Boston Massacre.
★ One of five authors of the Declaration of Independence.
★ Lived to 90 years of age, making him the longest-surviving president.
★ His son, John Quincy Adams, became sixth president.

During His Term
★ First to live in the White House in Washington, D.C.
★ First U.S. Navy ship launched, *The United States.*
★ U.S. Marine Corps was established.
★ Library of Congress started.

OCTOBER 31
Halloween

Be on the lookout for goblins and ghosts, pioneers and princesses, witches and wizards, and for tricks and treats tonight! This is the evening before the feast of All Saints Day, initiated by the Roman Catholic Church in the 700s. Tales and customs concerning Halloween are derived from a wide variety of sources. Younger readers will enjoy *Halloween* by Gail Gibbons (Holiday House, 1984), which presents many traditions associated with the holiday. Middle-grade readers are presented with the history and origins of Halloween symbols in *Witches, Pumpkins and Grinning Ghosts: The Story of Halloween Symbols* by Edna Barth (Clarion Books, 1981; paperback).

Children will enjoy creating jack-o'-lanterns. Help children carve the face. Scoop out the pumpkin seeds and save them for roasting and eating, or planting. Place a candle inside the finished pumpkin. Before the school day ends, turn out the classroom lights, light the jack-o'-lantern, and read the class a spooky story.

OCTOBER 31
National Magic Day

Today marks the death of the great magician Harry Houdini (1926). Houdini, an American escape artist and one of the greatest showmen of all time, was named Erich Weiss and claimed to be born in Appleton, Wisconsin. Some researchers, however, believe he was born in Budapest, Hungary. Even his birth date in April 1874 has been debated. He died from advanced appendicitis caused by a seemingly minor injury.

Harry Houdini: Master of Magic by Robert Kraske (Scholastic, 1989) recounts the life of this great magician from his boyhood through his years as an escape artist. It is a fascinating biography for middle-grade readers.

OCTOBER 31, 1864

Nevada became the thirty-sixth state.

Flower: Sagebrush
Tree: Single-Leaf Piñon
Bird: Mountain Bluebird

NOVEMBER

FLOWER   ◆   BIRTHSTONE
Chrysanthemum   Topaz

November derives its name from the Latin word
novum meaning "nine." November was the ninth
month in the Roman calendar.

NOVEMBER POEM OF THE MONTH

GOOD BOOKS, GOOD TIMES!

Good books.
Good times.
Good stories.
Good rhymes.
Good beginnings.
Good ends.
Good people.
Good friends.
Good fiction.
Good facts.
Good adventures.
Good acts.
Good stories.
Good rhymes.
Good books.
Good times.

— Lee Bennett Hopkins

NOVEMBER 1, 1800

The White House in Washington, D.C., became the official residence of the U.S. presidents. The first full-time occupants were John and Abigail Adams, who moved in on this date, even though work on the building had not been completed.

Students are fascinated to learn about the capital's other locations — New York, New York, and Philadelphia, Pennsylvania. Researching other White House facts might lead them to discover which presidents' children shared the residence.

211

◆

NOVEMBER 2, 1734
Birth Date of Daniel Boone

Daniel Boone was an explorer and frontiersman, one of the daring people who constantly wondered what was behind the next mountain. In 1769, he journeyed west from North Carolina. His "highway" through the Cumberland Mountains was an Indian trail, the Warrior's Path. His curiosity and bravery opened up an unsettled area of Kentucky for thousands of pioneers who followed in his footsteps to settle there. Boone died in Missouri at age 86. He was elected to the Hall of Fame in 1915.

Younger children might enjoy mapping an area of their immediate environment to show streets and familiar landmarks. Older students can discuss frontier areas that remain today. A recent biography for middle-grade readers is *Daniel Boone* by Laurie Lawlor (Whitman, 1989). One for younger readers is *Daniel Boone: Young Hunter and Tracker* by Augusta Stevenson (Macmillan, 1986).

NOVEMBER 2, 1795
Birth Date of James Knox Polk, Eleventh President

Born in:	Mecklenburg County, North Carolina
Occupation:	Lawyer, congessman
President:	1845–1849, Democrat
Died:	June 15, 1849
	Nashville, Tennessee

About Polk
★ Deeply religious.
★ Always in poor health.

212
◆

★ First "dark horse" candidate, the result of a Democratic Party stalemate.

During His Term
★ War with Mexico.
★ Added most territory to the United States after Thomas Jefferson — California, Utah, New Mexico, Nevada, and parts of other Rocky Mountain states.
★ U.S. Naval Academy at Annapolis opened.

NOVEMBER 2, 1865
Birth Date of Warren Gamaliel Harding, Twenty-ninth President

Born in:	Corsica, Ohio
Occupation:	Editor, publisher, teacher
President:	1921–1923, Republican
Died:	August 2, 1923
	San Francisco, California
	Buried in Marion, Ohio

About Harding
★ Fun loving, a golfer, and an avid poker player.

During His Term
★ For the first time, women voted for president.
★ Widespread corruption — Teapot Dome oil scandal.
★ First woman senator, Rebecca L. Fulton of Georgia, appointed in 1922.
★ First woman member of Congress, Ella Mae Nola of California, took office in 1923.
★ Died in office.

◆

NOVEMBER 2, 1889

Two states entered the Union on this date — North Dakota became the thirty-ninth state and South Dakota became the fortieth.

North Dakota:

South Dakota:

Flower: Wild Prairie Rose
Tree: American Elm
Bird: Western Meadowlark

Flower: Pasqueflower
Tree: Black Hills Spruce
Bird: Ring-Necked Pheasant

NOVEMBER 3, 1900

The first automobile show opened in New York City at Madison Square Garden. Five years earlier J. Frank Duryea, one of America's leading automobile manufacturing pioneers, won the first United States automobile race held in Chicago, Illinois. He drove his car at an average speed of 7.5 miles per hour!

NOVEMBER 4, 1825

I've got a mule, her name is Sal
Fifteen miles on the Erie Canal.
She's a good ol' worker an' a good ol' pal
Fifteen miles on the Erie Canal.

The refrain of this old folk song was sung by canal-boat mule drivers as they traveled along the Erie Canal, which opened on this date. The Erie Canal is a waterway stretching across northern New York State; it was the first major waterway to be constructed in the United States. It linked the Hudson River with Lake Erie to provide a transportation route between the Eastern Seaboard and the Great Lakes.

NOVEMBER 5, 1639

The first colonial post office was established in Boston, Massachusetts, on this date. Invite someone from a local post office to talk with children about the many services the post office provides. Young readers will enjoy *The Post Office Book: Mail and How It Moves* by Gail Gibbons (Harper & Row, 1982; paperback).

NOVEMBER 5, 1958

Shirley Chisholm became the first black woman to be elected to the U.S. House of Representatives.

NOVEMBER 6, 1854
Birth Date of John Philip Sousa

John Philip Sousa, born in Washington, D.C., showed an early aptitude for music. After studying the violin and trombone, he played for five years with the U.S. Marine Band. He devoted the rest of his life to musical composition, including his famed marches that earned him the title "The March King."

In 1897, he wrote "The Stars and Stripes Forever," one of his most famous marches. He died on March 6, 1932, in Reading, Pennsylvania.

NOVEMBER 8, 1889

Montana became the forty-first state.

Flower: Bitterroot
Tree: Ponderosa Pine
Bird: Western Meadowlark

NOVEMBER 9, 1906

President Theodore Roosevelt sailed on a United States battleship for the Panama Canal Zone, becoming the first United States president to leave the country while serving in office. Times have certainly changed! Today it is common for the president to make trips abroad. Encourage children to look for articles that describe presidential journeys and/or discuss the purposes of foreign travel for a nation's leader.

NOVEMBER 9, 1938

The Holocaust began. *Kristallnacht*, a term coined by the perpetrators of this outrage, means "night of shattered glass." On this date, Nazi storm troopers systematically burned synagogues, smashed the windows of Jewish shops, and opened an era of persecution for all Jews.

Remembrance and mourning for the six million Jewish victims of the Holocaust was marked 50 years later on November 9, 1988, by people everywhere. Church bells rang and candles were lit as people of all faiths pledged that never again would this be permitted to happen.

Students can develop an awareness of the events surrounding these actions in books. *The Upstairs Room* by Johanna Reiss (Viking, 1972; paperback) is a haunting novel written by a survivor; *The Diary of a Young Girl* by Anne Frank (Doubleday, 1967; paperback) contains the actual words that thirteen-year-old Frank, a Jewish girl, wrote during the two years she and her family were hiding in an old Amsterdam warehouse; *Smoke and Ashes: The Story of the Holocaust* by Barbara Rogasky (Holiday House, 1988), whose 80 photographs, many taken by Nazis at the scene, form a stark background to this chilling, objective account.

◆

NOVEMBER 10, 1903

Patent No. 743,801 was issued to Mary Anderson of Massachusetts for the windshield wiper. If it is raining today, a lot of drivers will want to thank Anderson for this wondrous invention.

NOVEMBER 11
Original Veterans Day

On November 11, 1918, an armistice was signed. World War I was over. It wasn't until November 1921, however, that Armistice Day was declared a national legal holiday by Congress to honor those who gave their lives in World War I. It was at this time that an unknown soldier was buried in a tomb in Arlington National Cemetery in Arlington, Virginia, across the Potomac River from Washington, D.C. In June 1954, President Dwight D. Eisenhower signed a bill designating the day as Veterans Day to honor also the dead of World War II and the Korean War. Today Veterans Day is celebrated on different dates. Check your calendar to see when it comes this year.

NOVEMBER 11, 1889

Washington became the forty-second state.

Flower: Western Rhododendron
Tree: Western Hemlock
Bird: Willow Goldfinch

NOVEMBER 12, 1815
Birth Date of Elizabeth Cady Stanton

American women were angered when the Fifteenth Amendment to the U.S. Constitution was passed because it granted former slaves the right to vote but continued to limit the vote to males only. The National Woman's Suffrage Association was formed in 1869 to secure that right. Elizabeth Cady Stanton was elected president of the organization, which became one of the foremost forces to educate and agitate for female voting rights. Stanton worked closely with Lucretia Mott and Susan B. Anthony (*see* February 15, 1820).

Finally on August 26, 1920, with the ratification of the Nineteenth Amendment, American women won the right to vote and have since played a vital part in the political life of the nation.

NOVEMBER 12, 1840
Birth Date of Auguste Rodin

Auguste Rodin's early sculptures were rejected by French authorities, who called them "vulgar realism." His revolutionary style, portraying people with accurate anatomical details, grew out of his youth.

His persistence led to commissions on public monuments as well as portrait sculptures of Victor Hugo, George Bernard Shaw, and Pope Benedict XV.

Paris-born, he stated: "Nothing is ugly that has life. Whatever suggests human emotions, whether of grief, or pain, goodness or anger, hate or love, has its individual seal of beauty." This statement expresses this great sculptor's belief in the humanistic nature of art. He started his career as a stonemason, progressed as a sculptor, creating realistic, free-standing figures. Among his many great works are *The Thinker*, *Bronze Age*, and *The Burghers of Calais*. His works are displayed in museums throughout the world. There is a Rodin Museum in Philadelphia, Pennsylvania, and another in Paris, France.

NOVEMBER
Election Day

Ancient Greeks voted with colored stones — black signified no, white yes. Using this device, a select portion of the male population was permitted to express preferences in civic affairs. Many colonial Americans voted similarly, using different colored corn kernels to express their wishes. The term *ballot* originated in the republics of Venice and Florence, Italy, where colored balls, *ballotta*, were used for voting.

In 1888 the Australian ballot, a paper ballot listing candidates' names, was first used in the United States. It ensured greater secrecy for voters. Today Americans over 18 years of age have the right to vote when most national, state, and local elections take place on the first Tuesday after the first Monday in November. Young readers can learn more about the event in *Voting and Elections* by Dennis B. Fradin (Children's, 1985).

NOVEMBER
Children's Book Week

Since Children's Book Week began in 1919, parents, teachers, librarians, booksellers, publishers, editors, authors, illustrators, and book reviewers have joined in to stimulate children to read. The Children's Book Council (67 Irving Place, New York, NY 10003) formulates the plans for observing Book Week. They print more than 50,000 posters to promote the celebration. Authors and illustrators make appearances, autograph parties are held, television and radio programs air, and story hours abound during this special week. Observances have greatly contributed to the improvement of books for children.

A list of the council's publications and current order forms may be obtained by sending a self-addressed, stamped envelope to the address above.

Children's Book Week is a good time to visit or revisit the school and/or public library. Plan ahead to have the librarian talk to the children about books and other items available in the library. Your students might enjoy engaging in a class activity to help celebrate this week. This is a good time to share the November Poem of the Month, "Good Books, Good Times!" by Lee Bennett Hopkins.

NOVEMBER 13, 1850
Birth Date of Robert Louis Balfour Stevenson

Born in Edinburgh, Scotland, the only son of an engineer, Robert Louis Balfour Stevenson was afflicted with a lung disease as a child and was often confined to bed. Throughout his childhood he required the care of a nursemaid. She was Alice Cunningham to whom Stevenson dedicated *A Child's Garden of Verses* (1885). Besides poetry, he wrote several classic novels: *Treasure Island* (1883), *Kidnapped* (1886), and *The Strange Case of Dr. Jekyll and Mr. Hyde* (1886). In 1880, Stevenson and his family settled in Samoa, an island in the Pacific Ocean, where he lived until his death on December 3, 1895.

There are many editions of *A Child's Garden of Verses*. A recent volume illustrated by Michael Hague is *The Land of Nod and Other Poems for Children* by Robert Louis Stevenson (Henry Holt, 1988). The single poem *Block City* is finely illustrated by Ashley Wolff (E.P. Dutton, 1988).

NOVEMBER 14, 1765
Birth Date of Robert Fulton

Born in Lancaster County, Pennsylvania, Robert Fulton first intended to become a painter, but at age 29 he became in-

220
◆

terested in canal engineering. Three years later he proposed the idea of a submarine, which he built in 1800. The next year he met Robert R. Livingston, a man who for two decades held a monopoly on steamboat navigation in the state of New York. Together they planned the construction of a steamboat, which became a reality in 1807.

NOVEMBER 15, 1897
Birth Date of David McCord

Poet David McCord was born in New York City. He grew up in New York, New Jersey, and Oregon; he was an only child. At a very young age he was stricken with malaria, having recurring bouts of fever that kept him out of school a great deal. This, however, did not stop him from graduating with high honors from Lincoln High School in Portland, Oregon, and from Harvard College in 1921. Harvard, thereafter, became an integral part of his life. Prior to his retirement in 1963, McCord spent well over 40 years at the university serving in many capacities. In 1956, Harvard conferred upon him the first honorary degree of Doctor of Humane Letters it ever granted.

Currently, he lives at the Harvard Club in Boston, Massachusetts, where he writes and conducts workshops on poetry with children.

In 1977, McCord received the first National Council of Teachers of English Award for Excellence in Poetry for Children.

Share some of his verses with your students from his delightful One at a Time: His Collected Poems for the Young, illustrated by Henry B. Kane (Little, Brown, 1977).

NOVEMBER 16, 1907

Oklahoma became the forty-sixth state.

Flower: Mistletoe
Tree: Redbud
Bird: Scissor-Tailed Flycatcher

NOVEMBER 17, 1805
Lewis and Clark Reach the Pacific Ocean

In 1803, President Thomas Jefferson proposed that Lewis and Clark explore a vast, uncharted Louisiana territory recently purchased from France. The expedition of some 40 men utilized the services of Sacagawea, a Shoshone who proved to be a valuable asset in their passage across the vast country, meetings with Native Americans, and attaining passage to the Pacific Ocean.

Scott O'Dell, the noted writer of historical fiction, recounts the expedition in his fascinating novel *Streams to the River, River to the Sea* (Houghton Mifflin, 1986), which middle-grade students will enjoy.

NOVEMBER 18, 1789
Birth Date of Louis Jacques Mandé Daguerre

In 1836, Louis Jacques Mandé Daguerre, a French painter and physicist, announced the invention of the daguerreotype, the first practical method of photography. His discovery has been acclaimed as one of the world's greatest inventions. This might be a good day to take photographs of the class!

NOVEMBER 18, 1929
Birth Date of Mickey Mouse

Mickey Mouse's road to fame started at the Colony Theatre

in New York City with the debut of the black-and-white animated cartoon *Steamboat Willie*.

The mouse, a Depression-era product, provided the foundation for Walt Disney, its creator, to begin an organization that blossomed into a multimillion dollar operation.

Disney got the idea for the cartoon character from two real mice that used to scamper about his drawing board. He made friends with them and imagined all kinds of adventures for them.

For over 60 years, Mickey Mouse has captivated children and adults everywhere. Have any of your students visited one of the Disney theme parks? Ask them to discuss their experiences.

NOVEMBER 19, 1831
Birth Date of James Abram Garfield, Twentieth President

Born in:	Orange, Ohio
Occupation:	Lawyer, congressman
President:	1881, Republican
Died:	September 19, 1881
	Elberon, New Jersey
	Buried in Cleveland, Ohio

About Garfield
★ Worked as a canal boatman, janitor, teacher of ancient languages, college president, preacher, and Union Army general, besides practicing law.

During His Term
★ Opposed the spoils system of granting federal jobs to political friends.
★ Shot by a disappointed job seeker in Washington railroad station; he lingered for 79 days before dying.

NOVEMBER 19, 1863

Abraham Lincoln delivered the Gettysburg Address at the dedication of a national cemetery on the battlefield where so many soldiers had died the summer before during the three-day battle of Gettysburg. (*See* July 1, 1863.) Lincoln's speech began with the historic words:

> Fourscore and seven years ago, our fathers brought forth on this continent a new nation, conceived in Liberty, and dedicated to the proposition that all men are created equal. . . .

The entire speech consisted of only 300 words, but it has come down through history as one of the most noble expressions of what democracy means. The complete text of the speech can be found in most encyclopedias.

NOVEMBER 20, 1925
Birth Date of Robert Francis Kennedy

> If we cannot open to youth a sense of possibility, we will have only ourselves to blame for their disillusionment; and with their disillusionment lies the danger — for we rely on our youth for all our hopes for a better future — and thus in a real and direct sense, for the very meaning of our own lives.
>
> — Senator Robert F. Kennedy

Robert Francis Kennedy shared the vision of a New Frontier held by his brother, John Fitzgerald Kennedy, the thirty-fifth president of the United States. (*See* May 29, 1917.) Bobby, as he was popularly known, served in his brother's administration as attorney general, helping to shape a new approach to poverty, civil rights, and foreign affairs. After John Kennedy's death, Robert continued to serve the nation; he was elected senator from New York State in 1964; in 1968, he entered the Democratic Party's presidential primary. While campaigning in Los Angeles, California, where he scored a victory, he was assassinated. The death of the two Kennedys has had a profound effect upon the nation's political affairs.

NOVEMBER 21, 1789

North Carolina was the twelfth state to ratify the Constitution.

Flower: Dogwood
Tree: Pine
Bird: Cardinal

NOVEMBER 22

The zodiac sign, Sagittarius the Archer, begins today and ends December 21. How many students were born under this sign?

NOVEMBER 22, 1643
Birth Date of Sieur de La Salle

Hearing tales of a "great river to the southwest," French explorer Sieur de La Salle became determined to explore it. In 1666, he sailed to Canada where he traded with the Native Americans. Years later, in 1682, he traveled down the Mississippi River to its mouth and claimed the entire valley for France, naming it Louisiana in honor of King Louis XIV. His mission was to colonize the Mississippi Valley, but he was killed on an expedition and never saw his dream become a reality.

NOVEMBER 22, 1906

SOS was adopted as the international distress signal on this date. The letters represented by the radiotelegraphic signal ...--... are used by ships and aircraft.

NOVEMBER 23, 1804
Birth Date of Franklin Pierce, Fourteenth President

Born in:	Hillsboro, New Hampshire
Occupation:	Lawyer
President:	1853–1857, Democrat
Died:	October 8, 1869
	Concord, New Hampshire

About Pierce
★ Childhood of wealth, good education, and politically prominent family.
★ Served in the Mexican War.
★ Won Democratic nomination on forty-ninth ballot as a compromise "dark horse."

During His Term
★ His failure to solve slavery issue led to the formation of a new Republican Party by its opponents.
★ Opened first World's Fair in the United States — the Crystal Palace Exposition in New York City, July 1853.

NOVEMBER 24, 1716

America saw its first lion on this date in an exhibition in Boston, Massachusetts. Roar-rrrr!

NOVEMBER 24, 1784
Birth Date of Zachary Taylor, Twelfth President

Born in: Orange County, Virginia
Occupation: Soldier
President: 1849–1850, Whig
Died: Washington, D.C.
              July 9, 1850
              Buried in Springfield, Kentucky

About Taylor
★ Frontier background.
★ Little formal education.
★ General in war against Mexico.
★ Nicknamed "Old Rough and Ready."

During His Term
★ Firmly against spread of slavery; hated politics and appeasement of South.
★ Pastured his horse, Whitney, on White House lawn.
★ Died 16 months after taking office.

NOVEMBER 24, 1826
Birth Date of Carlo Lorenzini

Carlo Lorenzini is the pseudonym of Carlo Collodi, author of *Pinocchio*. Born in Florence, Italy, Collodi became a journalist, taking the name of his mother's home town.

After a great deal of writing, *Pinocchio* began as a serial, the first chapter appearing in a July 7, 1881, issue of a weekly paper for children. The tale eventually appeared in book form in 1883. His publisher is said to have made a fortune from the volume, but Collodi died in 1890, too early to witness its international success. (*See also* July 7, 1881.)

NOVEMBER 24, 1868
Birth Date of Scott Joplin

Born in Texarkana, Texas, Scott Joplin became a pianist and composer. In 1899, John Stark, a music publisher, published Joplin's "Original Rag," the first ragtime piece to appear in sheet music form, and "Maple Leaf," one of the most famous of all American jazz compositions.

He died on April 11, 1917, in New York City. Although he left a rich musical legacy to the world, he never lived to hear any of his works recorded.

Play some ragtime today so the students can get a taste of this unusual musical form.

NOVEMBER 29, 1832
Birth Date of Louisa May Alcott

Born in Germantown, Pennsylvania, Louisa May Alcott lived most of her life in New England. Ralph Waldo Emerson and Henry David Thoreau were among her friends, and Nathaniel Hawthorne was a neighbor. Because her father, a philosopher, was a poor provider, Alcott began early in life to provide for her family. As a child she earned money by making dolls' clothes. Later she taught school and eventually she turned to writing. Her first published book, Flower Fables, appeared in 1854; this was a collection of fairy stories originally told to Emerson's daughter. Hospital Sketches (1863), her first major book, was written after voluntarily serving as a nurse in the Civil War and contracting typhoid. Later several of her stories were published in Atlantic Monthly. Because of these she was asked to write a book "for girls." At first she refused the offer but because she needed money, she wrote the novel, Little Women, which is semi-autobiographical. After she handed in the manuscript, her publisher thought it unacceptable. Fortunately he allowed the children in his family to read it and they loved it! Little Women was published (1868–1869), and a classic was born. This was the first great novel for children dealing with family life.

Other books based on Alcott's early life experiences followed such as Little Men (1871) and Jo's Boys (1886), but none were as popular as Little Women. There are many editions of the volume. If you have middle-grade students who have not tasted the joys of this novel, steer them to it. They will also enjoy reading the biography of the author, Invincible Louisa by Cornelia Meigs (Little, Brown, 1933; paperback). This book won the 1934 Newbery Medal and is still popular with better readers.

NOVEMBER 30, 1835
Birth Date of Samuel Langhorne Clemens

Samuel Langhorne Clemens, also known as Mark Twain, was born in Florence, Missouri, spending most of his youth in Hannibal, on the Mississippi. His father died when he was just 12 years old causing him to leave school in order to earn money. He became a printer and worked his way to New York and Pennsylvania, writing newspaper articles.

In 1857, he apprenticed himself to a Mississippi river pilot where he spent the next four years. After the start of the Civil War, he became a reporter using the pseudonym Mark Twain, supposedly a river navigation term for "two fathoms deep."

After becoming a successful journalist and traveling around the Mediterranean and through the Holy Land, he began writing books. His first, The Innocents Abroad, comically recounting his journey, appeared in 1869. But it was The Adventures of Tom Sawyer, published seven years later in 1876 that brought him widespread public praise. The Adventures of Huckleberry Finn, the sequel, appeared in 1884. Later books include A Connecticut

Yankee in King Arthur's Court (1889) and *The Prince and the Pauper* (1882).

Share Twain's work with your middle-grade students.

NOVEMBER 30, 1874
Birth Date of Winston Churchill

Reporter, army officer, prime minister, world statesman, and architect of the policy of resistance to communist expansion (Cold War) were some of the roles Winston Churchill, this English political leader, filled during his active life.

Born in a palace because his father was a duke, he was the product of a British-American union; his mother was an American, Jennie Jerome.

Churchill's cigar-smoking countenance, his *V* for victory hand signal, and his bulldog appearance were known throughout the Western world when he served as England's prime minister during the years when Great Britain and the United States were allies during the dark days of World War II. As a young man he had joined the army because his parents thought him a poor student; he was a reporter during the Boer War in Africa and was a prolific writer and amateur painter.

NOVEMBER
Thanksgiving Day

The Pilgrims landed in the New World on December 21, 1620, after an arduous voyage from England. Governor William Bradford of the Plymouth Colony proclaimed a day of thanksgiving a year later, a day that was shared with the Native Americans. Thanksgiving Day has been celebrated on different dates in various states and was mainly a New England holiday. Sara Josepha Hale was the first to suggest that Thanksgiving be a national patriotic holiday. For almost 20 years she campaigned through editorials and letters to the president and state governors. She finally won the support of President Abraham Lincoln, who in 1864 issued a proclamation making the last Thursday in November Thanksgiving Day. (*See also* October 24, 1788.)

Each year, during the last two weeks in November, there is a daily re-creation of the Pilgrims' original thanksgiving feast at the Plimoth Plantation in Plymouth, Massachusetts. Visitors can see people engaged in everyday tasks of a seventeenth-century farming community. A full-scale reproduction of the *Mayflower* is berthed nearby and open to the public.

Today is a good time for young readers to read *Sarah Morton's Day: A Day in the Life of a Pilgrim Girl* by Kate Waters (Scholastic, 1989). It is a charming portrayal of life in the seventeenth century, photographed at Plimoth Plantation in Plymouth, Massachusetts.

Ideas for activities to celebrate Thanksgiving can be gleaned from more books. For younger readers suggest *The Thanksgiving Story* by Alice Dalgliesh, illustrated in full color by Helen Sewell (Scribners, 1945; paperback). Two other approaches to the holiday are featured in *Thanksgiving Day* by Gail Gibbons (Holiday House, 1983) and *How Many Days to America? A Thanksgiving Story* by Eve Bunting, illustrated in full color by Beth Peck (Clarion Books, 1988).

NOVEMBER/DECEMBER
Hanukkah

Hanukkah, or the "Festival of Lights," lasts eight days. It begins on the twenty-fifth day of the Hebrew month *Kislev*. On the Roman calendar, this falls at the end of November or some time during the month of December. The holiday is a joyous occasion commemorating the Hebrew victory over Syria's oppressive King Antiochus, in which the Maccabees recaptured the temple of Jerusalem.

The *menorah*, a candlestick with nine cups for candles, is an important symbol of the event. Eight candles represent the eight days the oil burned during the first *Hanukkah*. The ninth cup holds the *shamos* candle. *Shamos* means "servant" in Hebrew. Hebrew legend states that the Maccabees were miraculously able to burn one day's oil supply for eight days once their temple was cleansed of Antiochus's pagan statues. The candlelight reminds the Jewish people of their fight to pray to their own God in their own way.

Each night of *Hanukkah* the *shamos* is lit first and then used to light the other candles. One candle is lit each night until the last night of *Hanukkah*, when all nine burn brightly. Children receive gifts on each of the eight days, sing songs, and play games.

A toplike toy, the *dreidel*, might be shown to the children. It is closely associated with the holiday, and children will be fascinated to discover its role in the *Hanukkah* ritual. On each side is one Hebrew letter: *Nun*, or *N; Gimel*, or *G; Hei*, or *H; Shin* or *Sh*. These are the first letters of the Hebrew words *Nes Godal, Hayah Sham* meaning "a great miracle happened there." Students who know how to play dreidel can demonstrate to the rest of the class. Each player has a chance to spin the *dreidel*, and how it falls determines the outcome of the game.

Light Another Candle: The Story and Meaning of Hanukkah by Miriam Chaikin, illustrated by Demi (Clarion Books, 1981), and *The Hanukkah Book* by Marilyn Burns, illustrated by Martha Weston (Four Winds, 1981), are excellent resources to share with young readers.

DECEMBER

FLOWER   ◆   BIRTHSTONE
Narcissus   Turquoise

The name of the last month of the year comes from the Latin word *decem* meaning "tenth." December was the tenth month in the Roman calendar.

DECEMBER POEM OF THE MONTH

SING HEY! SING HEY!

Sing hey! Sing hey!
For Christmas Day;
Twine mistletoe and holly,
For friendship glows
In winter snows,
And so let's all be jolly!

— Anonymous

DECEMBER 3, 1818

Illinois became the twenty-first state.

Flower: Native Violet
Tree: White Oak
Bird: Cardinal

DECEMBER 5, 1782
Birth Date of Martin Van Buren, Eighth President

Born in:	Kinderhook, New York
Occupation:	Lawyer
President:	1837–1841, Democrat
Died:	July 24, 1862
	Kinderhook, New York

About Van Buren
★ Built New York political machine — a group of people working together to achieve benefits with the victory of their party's candidates.
★ Vice president during Jackson's second term.

* Helped Jackson form Democratic Party.
* Presidential candidate again in 1848 for Free Soil Party.

During His Term
* First "machine-elected" president.
* Economic depression occurred.
* Lost election of 1840 to William Henry Harrison in dirty campaign.

DECEMBER 5, 1901
Birth Date of Walter Elias Disney

Walter Elias Disney, better known as Walt Disney, was born in Chicago, Illinois. After studying art, and becoming an advertising artist, he went to Hollywood and created several cartoon characters, the first popular one being Oswald the Rabbit. He became famous in 1928 with the creation of Mickey Mouse. (*See* November 18, 1929.) A motion-picture and television producer, he was a pioneer in cartoon animation.

Disney died in Los Angeles, California, on December 15, 1966 — 10 days after his sixty-fifth birthday.

Walt Disney by Greta Walker, illustrated by Ruth Sanderson (Putnam, 1977) presents an easy-to-read biography of the man and his accomplishments.

Interested students might compare the Disney treatments of such classics as *Mary Poppins, Peter Pan, Alice in Wonderland,* or *Snow White* to the books from which they were adapted.

DECEMBER 6, 1886
Birth Date of Alfred Joyce Kilmer

Alfred Joyce Kilmer was born in New Brunswick, New Jersey. His book of poems, *Trees and Other Poems,* appeared in 1914 and it included the title poem, "Trees." This short poem became known internationally, its success due to its sentiment and simple philosophy. The music to the verse is still sung widely. Kilmer died during a battle in World War I near the village of Seringes, in France.

DECEMBER 7, 1787

Delaware was the first state to ratify the Constitution.

Flower: Peach Blossom
Tree: American Holly
Bird: Blue Hen Chicken

DECEMBER 7, 1941

Japanese bombers launched a surprise attack on Pearl Harbor, destroying the military and naval base on the island of Oahu in the Hawaiian Islands. The United States had 18 ships sunk or seriously damaged, 200 planes destroyed, and 3,700 casualties. The attack plunged the United States into World War II. President Franklin Delano Roosevelt, in a famous address, called it "a day that will live in infamy."

DECEMBER 8, 1765
Birth Date of Eli Whitney

Farmer, part-time college student, teacher, inventor, munitions maker — these all describe Eli Whitney, a pioneer in the development of modern industrial methods. Born in Westboro, Massachusetts, Whitney helped on his father's farm and in spare moments worked his way through Yale University. A lifelong fascination with mechanical things prompted him to manufacture nails. His later invention of the cotton gin, for which he is most recognized, revolutionized the cotton industry. It separated cotton fibers from seeds rapidly; previously this had been done by hand, a slow, tedious process. Whitney patented the machine on March 14, 1794, but had to sue to secure his rights. He won the case but never reaped much money from his invention. In the early 1800s, he turned to manufacturing guns for the U.S. Army and pioneered mass production of rifles with interchangeable parts. Mass production techniques are now utilized in all modern manufacturing. (*See also* March 14, 1794.)

DECEMBER 10
Human Rights Day

On December 10, 1948, the United Nations produced an international definition of the rights of humankind known as the Universal Declaration of Human Rights. Since then every December 10 has been designated Human Rights Day. The Declaration is considered one of the finest accomplishments of the United Nations. It sets forth the following human rights as goals for all governments to work toward:

◆ The right of individuals to life, liberty, and security.
◆ The right of everyone to an education and to equality before the law.
◆ The right of each person to move about freely, to worship as she or he chooses, to associate freely with other people, and to have access to information in her or his search for understanding.
◆ The right of everyone to be a citizen of a country and to work under favorable conditions with equal pay for equal work.
◆ The right to marry and raise a family.

The Declaration has influenced the shaping of the constitutions of new countries and has helped to change the practices of some countries concerned with slavery, forced labor, and women's and children's rights. (For additional information on the United Nations, *see* October 24, 1945.)

DECEMBER 10, 1817

Mississippi became the twentieth state.

Flower: Magnolia
Tree: Magnolia
Bird: Mockingbird

DECEMBER 10, 1830
Birth Date of Emily Dickinson

To live is so startling it leaves little time for anything else.
— Emily Dickinson

Though Emily Dickinson wrote more than seventeen hundred poems, only six were printed while she was alive. She preserved the others in hand-sewn leather booklets. Born in Amherst, Massachusetts, she lived there all her life and in 1860 began writing verse. Her main themes dealt with love, death, and nature. She died in 1886.

Share some of her work with your middle-graders today. You will find a good sampling in *I'm Nobody! Who Are You? Poems of Emily Dickinson for Children*, illustrated by Rex Schneider (Stemmer House, 1978; paperback).

DECEMBER 10, 1909

Red Cloud, last of the great Oglala Sioux chieftans, was buried in the Mission Cemetery on the hill above the Red Cloud Indian School in Pine Ridge, South Dakota. There is no record of his birth date. In the course of his 87 years, Red Cloud had witnessed the extermination of his people. The Sioux nation occupied the north-central portion of today's United States. They were driven to desperation by the seizures of their lands and the slaughter of their food supply, the bison. Many battles were fought as white settlers poured in the western territories after the Civil War. At the most famous, the Battle of Little Bighorn in Montana in 1876, Sitting Bull defeated General George Custer's troops. Today, there are almost one million Americans of Native American descent.

Further information about Red Cloud and five other chiefs who led their people in a historic moment of crisis — Santana of the Kiowas, Quanah Parker of the Comanches, Washakie of the Shoshonis, Joseph of the Nez Percés, and Sitting Bull of the Hunkpapa Sioux — can be found in *Indian Chiefs* by Russell Freedman (Holiday House, 1987). The volume contains many black-and-white photographs.

DECEMBER 11, 1816

Indiana became the nineteenth state.

Flower: Peony
Tree: Tulip Poplar
Bird: Cardinal

DECEMBER 12, 1787

Pennsylvania was the second state to ratify the Constitution.

Flower: Mountain Laurel
Tree: Hemlock
Bird: Ruffed Grouse

DECEMBER 12, 1901

Guglielmo Marconi sent the first radio signal across the Atlantic Ocean from Cornwall, England, to Newfoundland in North America. The work of Marconi, an Italian engineer, has saved countless lives at sea and enabled people to communicate instantly over vast distances via radio wave transmission. His company used wireless radio to bridge the English Channel and send messages from Britain to France in 1899. Because of his pioneering efforts, Marconi was awarded the Nobel Prize in Physics in 1909. Today's communications industry is possible thanks to many contributions Marconi made to media.

DECEMBER 13, 1577

Sir Francis Drake started a voyage around the world. With 160 men and five ships Drake spent the next three years sailing around South America to California, which he claimed for his country, then across the Pacific and Indian Oceans, and finally up the coast of Africa. He became the first Englishman to sail around the globe. Students can use a world map to trace Drake's route and see the enormous distances involved.

The story of Drake's adventures is told in the picture book *Sir Francis Drake His Daring Deeds* by Roy Gerrard (Farrar, Straus & Giroux, 1988).

DECEMBER 14, 1819

Alabama became the twenty-second state.

Flower: Camellia
Tree: Southern Pine
Bird: Yellowhammer

DECEMBER 14, 1919

Roald Amundsen's dog sled expedition reached the South Pole, the farthest south one can go from the equator. The Norwegian-born explorer achieved a lifelong ambition on the frozen wasteland of the Antarctic continent, a region where the earth's coldest temperature of 102° below Fahrenheit was recorded in 1957–1958. Amundsen's feat came after he had lost the race to the North Pole; an American, Robert E. Peary, reached that site in 1909. (*See* April 6, 1909.)

Children can compile a series of polar facts to share by reading about Peary, Amundsen, Robert Scott, Richard Byrd, and other polar explorers.

DECEMBER 14, 1897
Birth Date of Margaret Chase Smith

Born in Skowhegan, Maine, Margaret Chase Smith worked as a teacher and journalist prior to her political career. She was the first woman in the United States to serve in both houses: House of Representatives (1940–1949) and the Senate (1949–1973). (*See also* September 13, 1948.)

DECEMBER 16, 1770
Birth Date of Ludwig van Beethoven

Ludwig van Beethoven's early musical compositions embodied the classical style prevalent in the royal courts of Europe. Born in Bonn, Germany, the composer studied briefly with Haydn and Mozart after moving to Vienna, Austria. He composed chamber music, symphonic pieces, and piano masterpieces that expressed his feelings for humanity and foreshadowed the development of nineteenth-century ro-

mantic music. Despite the fact that Beethoven's first symptoms
of deafness had appeared before 1800 and he became totally
deaf about 1819, the great master continued to compose and
produce many works until his death in 1827.

Play a Beethoven selection for children today, such as his
famous "Moonlight Sonata." The "Ode to Joy," a Christmas
favorite, is part of his Ninth Symphony. First- through sixth-
grade students can delve into his life further with *Beethoven* by
Alan Blackwood (Franklin Watts, 1987).

DECEMBER 16, 1773

Boston's harbor became a giant teapot in an event known as
the Boston Tea Party. As a crowd of spectators watched, the
Sons of Liberty, a Patriot group disguised as Indians, boarded
a British ship and deliberately dumped 342 cases of tea into
the waters. This illegal action was a protest against a tax placed
on tea by the British Parliament. Although the tax was insig-
nificant, colonial citizens felt compelled to make a gesture of
defiance against "outside" interference in their affairs. (*See*
April 22, 1774.)

DECEMBER 18, 1787

New Jersey became the third state to ratify the Constitution.

Flower: Purple Violet
Tree: Red Ash
Bird: Eastern Goldfinch

DECEMBER 18, 1865

The Thirteenth Amendment was ratified as part of the U.S.
Constitution. Starting with the words: "Neither slavery or in-

voluntary servitude . . . ," this historic addition to the Constitution brought an end to the cruel system of forced labor that had been practiced for over two hundred years in the United States. (*See* January 1, 1863.)

DECEMBER 18, 1892

Peter Ilich Tchaikovsky's famous ballet, *The Nutcracker*, based on the story "The Nutcracker and the Mouse King" by E. T. A. Hoffman, was first performed in St. Petersburg (now Leningrad) in Russia. The holiday tale features a little girl's Christmastime dreams involving sugar plum fairies, exotic dancers, and other fantasies, as well as a dramatic battle between the nutcracker and an army of mice.

Today in cities and towns all over the United States, *The Nutcracker* has become a part of the Christmas tradition.

An excellent volume to share is *The Nutcracker: A Story and a Ballet* by Ellen Switzer (Atheneum, 1985), with dramatic black-and-white and full-color photographs featuring the heralded performance staged by the New York City Ballet, choreographed by George Balanchine. (*See also* May 7, 1840.)

DECEMBER 19, 1958

The United States satellite *Atlas* broadcast the first radio voice from space, a recorded Christmas greeting from President Dwight D. Eisenhower.

DECEMBER 21
First Day of Winter

For some suggestions on welcoming the winter season, *see* the entry for March 21.

DECEMBER 21, 1620

After a journey from England aboard the *Mayflower*, the Pilgrims landed at Plymouth Rock, in Plymouth, Massachusetts. (*See* September 6, 1620.)

DECEMBER 22

The zodiac sign, Capricorn the Goat, begins today and ends January 19. How many students were born under this sign?

DECEMBER 22, 1932

The doors were opened to the great theater, Radio City Music Hall located in New York City's Rockefeller Center. The first production launched in the Music Hall was a vaudeville show consisting of 19 separate acts. Among the features were appearances by Ray Bolger, The Flying Wallendas, and dancers, The Roxyettes. All 6,200 seats were filled as the premiere began 45 minutes late. The show, however, went on and on and on — until two-thirty the next morning. By this time half of the audience had left.

For over 50 years the Music Hall has been producing spectacular shows seen by people from all over the world. Have any of your students been to the Music Hall? Have them tell about their experiences.

DECEMBER 25
Christmas Day

Christmas Day celebrates the birthday of Jesus Christ, born nearly 2,000 years ago in Bethlehem. The Christmas holiday is celebrated in many parts of the world. In some countries Christmas greetings are said in this way:

		Pronunciation
Danish:	Glaedelig Jul	GLA-da-lig U-el
Finnish:	Hauskaa Joulua	HAUS-ka U-loo-a
French:	Joyeux Nöel	jo-YEUH no-EL
German:	Fröhliche Weinachten	FRO-leek-eh VY-nak-tehn
Greek:	Kala Christougenna	ka-LA chris-TOU-yeh-na
Italian:	Buon Natale	boo-ON na-TA-leh
Norwegian/ Swedish:	God Jul	gud U-el
Portuguese:	Feliz Natal	feh-LEES na-TAL
Russian:	S Rozhdyestvom Khristovym	S Ro-zhdye-STVOM krist-TOYM
Spanish:	Feliz Navidad	feh-LEES na-vi-DOD

There are many books to share about this joyous holiday. Encourage students to do research on how the holiday is celebrated throughout various parts of the world. A good place for younger readers to start is in *Christmas around the World* by Emily Kelley (Carolrhoda, 1986). *Christmas* by Barbara Cooney (Harper & Row, 1967; also in paperback) and *Christmas Time* by Gail Gibbons (Holiday House, 1982) are nice classroom read alongs. For middle-grade readers, *Holly, Reindeer, and Colored Lights: The Story of the Christmas Symbols* by Edna Barth (Clarion Books, 1981; paperback) is a fascinating look at many of the holiday symbols.

DECEMBER 25, 1642
Birth Date of Sir Isaac Newton

English-born Sir Isaac Newton is often remembered with the true anecdote about his discovery of gravity while sitting under an apple tree. The apple's fall initiated his monumental investigation of gravity — the mysterious force that holds the universe together. While attending Cambridge University, where he was a mediocre student, often spending hours under apple trees, Newton made three of his most important contributions to science: the invention of calculus, his theory of gravitation, and the discovery of the spectrum — a pioneering effort in a new field. Newton's accomplishments won him a professorship at Cambridge as well as world fame. He died on March 20, 1727, in Kensington, England.

DECEMBER 25, 1821
Birth Date of Clara Barton

Clara Barton's lifelong interest in the nursing profession made her internationally famous as the founder and leading spirit of the American Red Cross. This organization was founded on May 21, 1881.

Barton did not become a nurse until she was almost 40 years old. During the Civil War, she became a heroine as she cared for the sick and wounded. The soldiers called her the Angel of the Battlefield. Barton lived to be 91 years old. She died on April 12, 1912.

DECEMBER 27, 1822
Birth Date of Louis Pasteur

The most numerous living things are bacteria, of course. They are one-celled organisms that are both harmful and helpful to humans.

Louis Pasteur, the French chemist, pioneered the discovery and control of these microscopic life forms. His studies of fermentation in wine led him to conclude that the process was caused by airborne bacteria. Pasteur's name is closely associated with immunization or vaccination — producing resistance to disease by injecting weakened germ cultures. Pasteurization — the killing of harmful germs by heating — and the development of a cure for rabies are also credited to the scientist.

Encourage children to look for the word *pasteurized* on milk containers and other dairy products. Another topic for investigation is how bacteria helps human beings.

DECEMBER 28, 1846

Iowa became the twenty-ninth state.

Flower: Wild Rose
Tree: Oak
Bird: Eastern Goldfinch

DECEMBER 28, 1856
Birth Date of (Thomas) Woodrow Wilson, Twenty-eighth President

Born in:	Staunton, Virginia
Occupation:	Educator, lawyer
President:	1913–1921, Democrat
Died:	February 3, 1924
	Washington, D.C.

About Wilson
★ Only president with a PhD degree.
★ President of Princeton University, Princeton, New Jersey.
★ Writer of political science texts.

During His Terms
★ Started press conferences.
★ Women obtained the right to vote.
★ United States entered World War I.
★ Pioneered for peace and for the creation of the League of Nations.
★ Suffered crippling stroke during the middle of his second term, leaving the nation with a disabled president.

DECEMBER 29, 1808
Birth Date of Andrew Johnson, Seventeenth President

Born in:	Raleigh, North Carolina
Occupation:	Tailor, public official
President:	1865–1869, Democrat
Died:	July 31, 1875
	Carter Station, Tennessee

About Johnson
★ Because of his bleak poverty, he was called "a working man's champion."
★ The only southern senator to stick with the Union; 21 others left.
★ Became Lincoln's vice president on March 4, 1865, one month before the president was assassinated.

During His Term
★ Conflict with radical Republicans over the treatment of the defeated Confederate states and alleged misuse of presidential power led to an impeachment trial in which the Senate vote on removing him failed by one vote.
★ Alaska purchased from Russia in 1867; the cold area was called "Johnson's polar bear garden," reflecting its lack of appeal.

DECEMBER 29, 1845

Texas became the twenty-eighth state.

Flower: Bluebonnet
Tree: Pecan
Bird: Mockingbird

DECEMBER 29, 1876
Birth Date of Pablo Casals

Pablo Casals's name is synonymous with the cello, an instrument this musician mastered early in life. Born in a Catalan town in Spain, forty miles from Barcelona, Casals was introduced to the flute, piano, violin, and cello by his father, who was a choirmaster. The young Casals could sing in tune before he could talk clearly; at age five he was a soprano in a church choir. In the 1930s he chose self-exile from his native Spain rather than accept Franco's totalitarian regime. His cello performances, particularly Bach solos, won him world acclaim. In 1956, he adopted Puerto Rico as his home and organized an annual music festival on the island. He died there in 1973 at the age of 97.

An excellent autobiography is *Joys and Sorrows by Pablo Casals: His Own Story* as told to Albert E. Kahn (Simon & Schuster, 1970; paperback).

DECEMBER 30, 1865
Birth Date of (Joseph) Rudyard Kipling

Although Rudyard Kipling wrote several successful adult novels and a large amount of poetry, it was his stories for children that earned him an international and lasting reputation. These include the popular *Jungle Books* (1894, 1895) and *Just-So Stories* (1902). Kipling's writings about nature and the habitats of animals, particularly his tales in the *Jungle Books*, are very accurate. He was born in India where his father was a British official. When he was six he was brought to England for his education. School life was an unhappy experience, and he drew upon it later in several books including *Stalky and Company* (1899). In 1882, he returned to India as a journalist. Along with the pressures of work, he began to write poems and short stories. Then in 1892 he moved to the United States. He married an American woman and lived in Vermont for four years. In later life he became a champion of the British Empire. Kipling was England's first winner of the Nobel Prize for Literature in 1907.

Children still enjoy Kipling's stories. The *Jungle Books* contain the classic tales of Mowgli, a boy adopted by a wolf pack and taught the way of the jungle, and "Rikki-Tikki-Tavi," a tale about a mongoose. Younger girls and boys will delight in hearing *Just-So Stories*, which include "The Elephant's Child," "How the Camel Got His Hump," and "How the Leopard Got His Spots." With older children these tales might spark creative writing; have them make up their own "how-the's "!

An easy-to-read account of his life appears in *Kipling: Storyteller of East and West* by Gloria Kamen (Atheneum, 1985).

DECEMBER 31

> Ring out the old, ring in the new,
>   Ring, happy bells across the snow:
> The year is going, let him go;
>   Ring out the false, ring in the true.
> > — Alfred, Lord Tennyson
> > In Memorium *CVI*

Tonight is the night when Western peoples celebrate the coming of the New Year. It is usually marked by parties, jolly celebrations, and New Year's resolutions.

Happy, happy New Year!

INDEX

Abolitionists. *See* Brown, John; slavery; Tubman, Harriet.

Adams, Abigail, March 31, 1777; November 1, 1800

Adams, John, March 5, 1770; March 31, 1777; October 30, 1735

Adams, John Quincy, March 15, 1767; July 11, 1767; October 30, 1735

Addams, Jane, September 6, 1860

Adoff, Arnold, July 16, 1935

Agnew, Spiro T., January 9, 1913; July 14, 1913; October 10, 1973

airplanes. *See* Wright, Orville; Wright, Wilbur.

Alabama, December 14, 1819

Alaska, January 3, 1959; December 29, 1808

Alcott, Louisa May, November 29, 1832

Aldrin, Edwin E., Jr., July 20, 1969

Ali, Muhammad, January 17, 1942

amendments, Constitutional. *See* United States — Constitution.

American Magazine, The, February 13, 1741

American Revolution, January 1, 1735; March 5, 1770; March 23, 1775; April 18, 1775; April 19, 1775; April 22, 1774; June 17, 1775; September 3, 1783; September 9, 1757; December 16, 1773. *See also* Declaration of Independence.

Amundsen, Roald, December 14, 1819

Andersen, Hans Christian, April 2, 1805

Anderson, Marian, February 17, 1902

Anderson, Mary, November 10, 1903

Antarctica, October 25, 1988

Anthony, Susan B., February 15, 1820; November 12, 1815

Apollo II, July 20, 1969

April Fool's Day, April 1

Appleseed, Johnny. *See* Johnny Appleseed.

Aquarius, January 20

Arbor Day, April/May

Aries, March 21

Arizona, February 14, 1912

Arkansas, June 15, 1836

Armstrong, Neil, July 20, 1969

Arthur, Chester A., October 5, 1830

Atlas (communications satellite), December 19, 1958

atomic bomb, May 8, 1884; July 16, 1945; August 6, 1945; October 20, 1891

Attucks, Crispus, March 5, 1770

Audubon, John James, April 26, 1785

Australia, January 26, 1788

Automobile Show, November 3, 1900

automobiles, October 1, 1908; November 3, 1900

autumn, September 21

aviation. *See* National Aviation Day; Wright, Orville; Wright, Wilbur.

Balboa, Vasco Nunez de, September 25, 1513

Ballard, Robert, September 1, 1863

Barton, Clara, December 25, 1821

baseball, June 19, 1846; August 18, 1934
baseball uniforms, June 3, 1851
Bastille Day, July 14, 1789
"Battle Hymn of the Republic, The"
  May 9, 1914; May 27, 1819
Baum, L. Frank, May 15, 1856
Beethoven, Ludwig von, December 16,
  1770
Behn, Harry, September 24, 1898
Bell, Alexander Graham, March 3, 1847;
  March 7, 1876
Bemelmans, Ludwig, April 27, 1898
Bethune, Mary McLeod, July 10, 1875
Bill of Rights, March 16, 1751
Black History Month, February
Blackwell, Elizabeth, January 23, 1849;
  February 3, 1821
Blondin, June 30, 1859
blood banks, June 3, 1904
Bly, Nellie, May 5, 1867; October 2, 1872
Boone, Daniel, November 2, 1734
Booth, John Wilkes, April 14, 1865
Borglum, Gutzon, March 25, 1871
Boston Massacre, March 5, 1770
Boston News-Letter, April 24, 1704
Boston Public Garden, October 4, 1987
Boston Tea Party, January 1, 1735; De-
  cember 16, 1773. See also New York-
  ers' Act.
Boys Festival, March 3; May 10
Braille, Louis, January 4, 1809
Brooke, Edward W., October 26, 1919
Brooks, Gwendolyn, June 7, 1917
Brown, John, January 19, 1807; April 23,
  1791; May 9, 1800
Brown vs. the Board of Education of Topeka,
  Kansas, May 17, 1954; July 2, 1908
Browning, Robert, May 7, 1812
Bruce, Blanche Kelso, March 1, 1841;
  October 26, 1919
Buchanan, James, April 23, 1791
Buffalo Bill. See Cody, William F.
Bunche, Ralph, August 7, 1904
Bunker Hill, Battle of, June 17, 1775
Buonarroti, Michelangelo. See Michelan-
  gelo Buonarroti.
Burbank, Luther, March 7, 1849
Bush, George H., June 12, 1924

Byrd, Richard E., October 25, 1888

cable cars, August 2, 1873
Caesar, Gaius Julius, February 29
Caldecott, Randolph, March 22, 1846
calendars, February 29
Calhoun, John C., October 10, 1973
California, September 9, 1850. See also
  Gold Rush, California.
cameras. See Kodak cameras.
Campbell, John, April 24, 1704
Cancer, June 22
Capricorn, December 22
Caraway, Hattie, January 12, 1933
Carnegie, Andrew, April 9, 1833
Carroll, Lewis. See Dodgson, Charles
  Lutwidge.
Carter, Jimmy, February 17, 1902;
  October 1, 1924
Carver, George Washington, January 5,
  1864
Casals, Pablo, December 29, 1876
catcher's mask, April 12, 1877
Cavazos, Lauro F., September 21, 1988
Census Day, April 1, 1990
Chadwick, James, October 20, 1891
Challenger space shuttle, January 16, 1978;
  January 28, 1986; May 26, 1951
Chapman, John. See Johnny Appleseed.
Chávez, César, March 31, 1927
cheese, June 1, 1070
Children's Book Week, November
Chinese New Year, January/February
Chisholm, Shirley, November 5, 1958
Christmas Day, December 25
Church, Ellen, May 15, 1930
Churchill, Winston, November 30, 1874
civil rights. See Black History Month;
  Brown vs. the Board of Education of To-
  peka, Kansas; King, Martin Luther, Jr.;
  March on Washington, D.C.
Civil War, U.S., January 19, 1807; Febru-
  ary 12, 1809; February 20, 1895;
  March 23, 1791; April 27, 1822; May
  30; July 1, 1863; November 19, 1863
Clay, Henry, January 7, 1800
Clemens, Samuel Langhorne (Mark
  Twain), November 30, 1835

Clemente, Roberto, August 18, 1934
Cleveland, Grover, March 18, 1837; First Monday in September
Cody, William F. (Buffalo Bill), February 26, 1846
Collodi, Carlo, July 7, 1881; November 24, 1826
Colorado, August 1, 1876
Columbus, Christopher, October 9; October 12, 1492
Comaneci, Nadia, July 18, 1976
Confucius, August 27, 551 B.C.
Connecticut, January 9, 1788
Constitution, U.S. See United States — Constitution.
Constitution Week, September 17–23
Coolidge, Calvin, June 19, 1910; July 4, 1872
Copernicus, Nicolaus, February 4, 1473
Cortes, Hernando, September 16, 1810
cotton gin, March 14, 1794; December 8, 1765
Crockett, Davy, August 17, 1786
Cullen, Countee, May 30, 1903
Curie, Irene, April 20, 1898
Curie, Marie and Pierre, April 20, 1898
Custer, George, December 10, 1909

D day, July 8, 1835
da Vinci, Leonardo. See Leonardo da Vinci.
Daguerre, Louis Jacques Mandé, November 18, 1789
Darwin, Charles, February 12, 1809
Declaration of Independence, January 17, 1706; January 23, 1737; July 4, 1776
Delaware, December 7, 1787
deSoto, Hernando, January 12, 1812
Dewey, Thomas E., May 8, 1884
Dickens, Charles, February 7, 1812
Dickinson, Emily, December 10, 1830
dictionaries, April 14, 1828; October 16, 1758
Disney, Walt(er), November 18, 1929; December 5, 1901
Dodge, Mary Elizabeth Mapes, January 26, 1831

Dodgson, Charles Lutwidge (Lewis Carroll), January 27, 1832
Dolls, Festival of, March 3
Douglass, Frederick, January 1, 1863; February 20, 1895; April 5, 1856. See also Black History Month.
Drake, Francis, December 13, 1577
Drew, Charles Richard, April 1, 1578; June 3, 1904
Dunbar, Paul Laurence, June 27, 1872
Duryea, J. Frank, November 3, 1900

ear muffs, March 13, 1773
Earhart, Amelia, May 20, 1932; July 24, 1898
Easter, March/April
Easter egg roll, May 20, 1768
Eastman, George, September 4, 1888
Edison, Thomas Alva, February 11, 1847
Eiffel Tower, March 31, 1889
Einstein, Albert, March 14, 1879
Eisenhower, Dwight D., January 9, 1913; February 12, 1902; October 14, 1890; December 19, 1958
Election Day, U.S., November
electricity, June 15, 1752
elephants, April 13, 1796
elevators, March 23, 1857
Eliot, T(homas) S(tearns), September 26, 1888
Emancipation Proclamation, January 1, 1863
Empire State Building, May 1, 1931
Erikson, Leif, October 9
Erie Canal, November 4, 1825
Euripides, September 23, 480 B.C.

Fahrenheit, Gabriel Daniel, May 14, 1686
false teeth, March 9, 1822
Father's Day, June 19, 1910
Fifteenth Amendment. See United States — Constitution.
Fillmore, Millard, January 7, 1800
Fire Prevention Week, October
Fisher, Aileen, September 9, 1906
Flag Day, January 1, 1752; June 14, 1777
Flag, U.S., January 1, 1752; April 28, 1758; June 14, 1777

flight attendants, May 15, 1930
Florida, March 3, 1845
football, September 13, 1895
Ford, Gerald R., January 9, 1913; July 14, 1913
Ford, Henry, October 1, 1908
Fourteenth Amendment. *See* United States — Constitution.
Francis of Assisi (Saint), October 4, 1181 or 1182
Franklin, Benjamin, January 17, 1706; February 11, 1751; June 15, 1752
French Revolution, July 14, 1789
Frost, Robert, March 26, 1874
Fugitive Slave Act, January 7, 1800
Fulton, Robert, November 14, 1765
Furnas, Charles W., May 14, 1908

Gagarin, Yuri, April 12, 1961
Galillei, Galileo, February 15, 1564
Gandhi, Mohandas Karamchand, October 2, 1869
Garfield, James A., November 19, 1831
Geisel, Theodore Seuss (Dr. Seuss), March 2, 1904
Gemini, May 21
Georgia, January 2, 1788
Gettysburg Address, November 19, 1863
Gettysburg, Battle of, July 1, 1863
Glenn, John, February 20, 1962
Gold Rush, California, January 24, 1848
Goodard, Robert H., March 16, 1926
Grand Canyon, February 26, 1919
Grant, Ulysses S., January 19, 1807; April 27, 1822
Gregory, Thomas, September 6, 1988
Grimm, Jakob and Wilhelm, January 4, 1785
Groundhog Day, February 2

Hale, Sarah Josepha, October 24, 1788
Halley, Edmund, October 29, 1656
Hallidie, Andrew, August 2, 1873
Halloween, October 31
Hancock, John, January 23, 1737; April 18, 1775
Handel, George Frideric, February 23, 1685

Hanukkah, November/December
Harding, Warren G., July 4, 1872; November 2, 1865
Harrison, Benjamin, August 20, 1833
Harrison, William Henry, February 9, 1773; March 29, 1780; August 20, 1833
Harvey, William, April 2, 1578; June 3, 1904
Hayes, Rutherford B., October 4, 1822
Hawaii, August 21, 1959
Henry, Marguerite, April 13, 1902
Henry, Patrick, March 23, 1775
Heyerdahl, Thor, October 6, 1914
Hidalgo, Miguel, September 16, 1810
Hiroshima, July 16, 1945; August 6, 1945
Hispanics. *See* National Hispanic Heritage Week.
Hitler, Adolf, September 1, 1939
Holocaust, Jewish, November 9, 1938
Hood, Thomas, February 11, 1751
Hoover, Herbert C., August 10, 1874; September 14, 1814
Hopkins, Samuel, July 31, 1790
hospitals, February 11, 1751
Houdini, Harry, October 31
Houston, Sam, March 2, 1793
Howe, Julia Ward, May 9, 1914; May 27, 1819
Hughes, Langston, February 1, 1902. *See also* Black History Month.
Human Rights Day, December 10
Hunt, Walter, April 10, 1849
Hurricane Gilbert, September 14, 1988

ice cream, March 16, 1751; June 8, 1786
Idaho, July 3, 1890
Illinois, December 3, 1818
Inauguration Day, presidential, January 20
Independence Day, July 4, 1776; July 8, 1835
Indiana, December 11, 1816
Indians, American. *See* Native Americans.
International Literacy Day, September 8
Iowa, December 28, 1846
Iranian New Year. *See* No Ruz.
Irving, Washington, April 3, 1783
Israel, May 14, 1948

Jackson, Andrew, March 15, 1767; July 11, 1767; October 10, 1973
Jackson, Jesse, August 28, 1963; October 8, 1941
James, Jesse, September 5, 1847
Jefferson, Thomas, April 13, 1743; April 30, 1803; July 4, 1776; November 17, 1805
Jewish holidays, September/October. *See also* Hanukkah; Passover.
Johnny Appleseed, September 26, 1774
Johnson, Andrew, March 21, 1806; December 29, 1808
Johnson, Lyndon Baines, August 27, 1908
Joliet, Louis, June 17, 1673
Jolson, Al, October 26, 1927
Joplin, Scott, November 24, 1868
Juárez, Benito, March 21, 1806

Kansas, January 29, 1861
Keller, Helen, June 27, 1880
Kennedy, John Fitzgerald, March 1, 1961; March 26, 1874; May 29, 1917; November 15, 1897; November 20, 1925
Kennedy, Robert F., July 11, 1899; November 20, 1925
Kentucky, June 1, 1792
Key, Francis Scott, September 14, 1886
Kilmer, Alfred Joyce, December 6, 1886
King, Martin Luther, Jr., January 15, 1929; August 28, 1963; October 2, 1869; October 8, 1941; October 21, 1833
Kipling, Rudyard, October 21, 1863; December 30, 1865
Kleinschmidt, Edward E., September 9, 1875
Kodak cameras, September 4, 1888
Kristellnacht, November 9, 1938
Kuskin, Karla, July 19, 1932

La Salle, Robert de, January 12, 1812; November 22, 1643
Labor Day, First Monday in September. *See also* May Day.

Labor Department, U.S. *See* United States — Labor Dept.
Lafayette, Marquis de, June 17, 1775; September 9, 1757
Lazarus, Emma, July 22, 1849
Leap Year Day, February 29
Lear, Edward, May 12, 1812
Lee, Robert E., January 19, 1807; February 12, 1809; April 27, 1822; July 1, 1863
Leo, July 23
Leonardo da Vinci, April 15, 1452
Lewis and Clark, April 13, 1743; April 30, 1803; November 17, 1805
Liberty Bell, July 8, 1835
Libra, September 23
libraries, public, April 9, 1833; May 30, 1903; October 26, 1911
Liliuokalani (Queen), September 2, 1838
Lincoln, Abraham, February 12, 1809; February 20, 1895; April 14, 1865; November 19, 1863; December 29, 1908. *See also* Black History Month; Thanksgiving Day.
Lincoln Memorial, May 30, 1922
Lindbergh, Charles, February 4, 1902; May 20–21, 1927
lions, November 24, 1716
Lipman, Hyman, March 30, 1858
Lister, Joseph, April 5, 1827
Liszt, Franz, October 22, 1811
literacy. *See* International Literacy Day.
Livingston, Myra Cohn, August 17, 1926
Lofting, Hugh, January 14, 1886
Longfellow, Henry Wadsworth, February 27, 1807; April 18, 1775
Lorenzini, Carlo. *See* Collodi, Carlo.
Louisiana, April 30, 1812
Louisiana Purchase, April 13, 1743; April 30, 1803; November 17, 1805

Madison, Dolley, March 16, 1751; May 20, 1768. *See also* ice cream.
Madison, James, January 20; March 16, 1751
magazines, February 13, 1741
Magellan, Ferdinand, September 20, 1519

magic. *See* National Magic Day.
Magna Carta, June 15, 1215
Maguire, Peter J., *See* Labor Day.
Maine, March 15, 1820
Malcolm X, May 19, 1925
Maldive Islands, July 26, 1965
March on Washington, D.C., January 15, 1929; August 28, 1963
Marconi, Guglielmo, December 12, 1901
Marquette, Jacques, June 17, 1673
Marshall, John, July 8, 1835
Marshall, Thurgood, May 17, 1954; July 2, 1908; August 27, 1908
"Mary Had a Little Lamb." *See* Hale, Sara Josepha.
Maryland, April 28, 1788
Massachusetts, February 6, 1788
May Day, May 1
Mayflower, September 6, 1620; December 21, 1620
McAuliffe, Sharon Christa, January 28, 1986
McCauley, Mary Ludwig, October 13, 1754
McCloskey, Robert, October 4, 1987
McCrod, David, November 15, 1897
McKinley, William, January 29, 1843; October 27, 1927
Meir, Golda, May 3, 1898
Memorial Day, May 30
Merlin, Joseph, April 22, 1823
Merriam, Eve, July 19, 1916
Metropolitan Museum of Art (New York City), February 20, 1872
Mexican Independence Day, September 16, 1810
Michelangelo Buonarroti, March 5, 1475; June 29, 1577
Michigan, January 26, 1837
Mickey Mouse, November 18, 1929
milk bottles, January 11, 1878
Milne, A.A., January 18, 1882
Minnesota, May 11, 1858
Minuit, Peter, May 4, 1626
Mississippi, December 10, 1817
Mississippi River, January 12, 1812; June 17, 1673
Missouri, August 10, 1821

Monroe, James, January 20; February 22, 1732; April 28, 1758
Monroe Doctrine, April 28, 1758
Montana, November 8, 1889
moon landing, July 20, 1969
Moses, Anna Mary Robertson (Grandma Moses), September 7, 1860
Mother's Day, May 9, 1914; May 27, 1819
motion pictures, sound, October 26, 1927
Mott, Lucretia, November 12, 1815
Mount Coropona, October 19, 1850
Mount Everest, May 23, 1975
Mount Rushmore, March 25, 1871
Mozart, Wolfgang Amadeus, January 27, 1835

Nash, Ogden, August 19, 1902
national anthem, U.S., September 14, 1814
National Aviation Day, August 19
National Hispanic Heritage Week, Mid-September
National Magic Day, October 31
Native Americans, End of September; December 10, 1909
Nebraska, March 1, 1867
Neptune, September 23, 1846
neutrons, October 20, 1891
Nevada, October 31, 1864
New Hampshire, June 21, 1788
New Jersey, December 18, 1787
New Mexico, January 6, 1912
New Year's Day, January 1. *See also* Chinese New Year; No Ruz; Rosh Hashana.
New Year's Eve, December 31
New York, July 26, 1788
New York Public Library, May 30, 1903; October 16, 1911
New York Stock Exchange, October 19, 1987; October 29, 1929
New Yorkers' Act, April 22, 1774. *See also* Boston Tea Party.
newspaper, first American, April 24, 1704
Newton, Isaac, December 25, 1642
Niagara Falls, June 30, 1859

Nightengale, Florence, May 12, 1820
Nijinsky, Vaslov, February 28, 1890
Nineteenth Amendment. *See* United States — Constitution.
Nixon, Richard M., January 9, 1913; June 17, 1972; July 14, 1913; October 10, 1973
No Ruz, March 21
Nobel, Alfred, October 21, 1833
North Carolina, November 21, 1789
North Dakota, November 2, 1889
North Pole, April 6, 1909; October 25, 1888
Nutcracker, The, December 18, 1892

O'Connor, Sandra Day, March 26, 1930
Ohio, March 1, 1803
Oklahoma, November 16, 1907
Olympic Games, February 10, 1950; April 6, 1896; July 18, 1976; September 12, 1913
Oregon, February 14, 1859
Otis, Elisha Grave, March 23, 1857
Owens, Jesse, September 12, 1913

Paine, Thomas, April 28, 1758
Pan American Day, April 14, 1890
Passover, March/April
Pasteur, Louis, December 27, 1822; April 5, 1827
Patent Office, U.S., July 31, 1790
patents, July 31, 1790. artificial teeth, March 9, 1822. catcher's mask, April 12, 1877. cotton gin, March 14, 1794. December 8, 1765. earmuffs, March 13, 1773; genetic engineering, July 31, 1790. Kodak cameras, September 4, 1888. pencil with eraser, March 30, 1858. roller skates, April 22, 1823. safety pin, April 10, 1849. sewing machine, September 10, 1846. telephone, March 3, 1847; March 7, 1876. teletype printer, September 9, 1875. washing machine, March 28, 1797; April 18, 1934. windshield wipers, November 10, 1903
Peace Corps, March 1, 1961
"Peanuts" (cartoon), October 3, 1950

Pearl Harbor, September 1, 1939; December 7, 1941
Peary, Robert E., April 6, 1909; December 14, 1819
Peck, Annie Smith, October 19, 1850
pencils, March 30, 1858
Penn, William, October 14, 1644
Pennsylvania, December 12, 1787
Perkins, Frances, January 30, 1882
Perrault, Charles, January 12, 1628
Perry, Matthew, January 7, 1800
Picasso, Pablo, October 25, 1881
Pierce, Franklin, November 23, 1804
Pilgrims. *See Mayflower;* Thanksgiving Day.
Pinocchio, July 7, 1881; November 24, 1826
Pisces, February 19
Pitcher, Molly. *See* McCauley, Mary Ludwig.
Plimpton, James, April 22, 1823
Pluto, February 18, 1930
Plymouth Rock, September 6, 1620; December 21, 1620
polio, October 28, 1914
Polk, James K., November 2, 1795
postage stamps, January 2, 1893
presidential Inauguration Day. *See* Inauguration Day, presidential.
public libraries. *See* libraries, public.
Puerto Rico, July 25, 1952

Radio City Music Hall (New York City), December 22, 1932
radioactivity, April 20, 1898; October 20, 1891
Rankin, Jeannette, June 11, 1880
Reagan, Ronald, February 6, 1911; March 1, 1961
Red Cloud, December 10, 1909
Revels, Hiram Rhodes, September 27, 1822; October 26, 1919
Revere, Paul, January 1, 1735; February 27, 1807; April 18, 1775; April 19, 1775
Revolutionary War. *See* American Revolution.
Rhode Island, May 29, 1790

257
◆

Ride, Sally, January 16, 1978; May 26, 1951
Rillieux, Norbert, March 18, 1806
rocket launching, March 16, 1926
Rodin, Auguste, November 12, 1840
Roentgen, Wilhelm Konrad, March 27, 1845
roller skates, April 22, 1823
Roosevelt, Eleanor, January 30, 1882; October 11, 1884
Roosevelt, Franklin D., January 30, 1882; May 8, 1884; October 11, 1884
Roosevelt, Theodore, October 21, 1833; October 27, 1853; November 9, 1906
Roquefort cheese, June 1, 1070
Rosh Hashana, September/October
Ross, Betsy, January 1, 1753; June 14, 1777
Ross, Nellie Taylor, January 5, 1925
Rubens, Peter Paul, June 29, 1577
Ruth, George Herman (Babe), February 6, 1895

Sacagawea, November 17, 1805
safety pins, April 10, 1849
Sagittarius, November 22
Saint Patrick's Day, March 17
Saint Switin's Day, July 15
Salk, Jonas, October 28, 1914
Sandburg, Carl, January 6, 1878; June 7, 1917
Sandwich, Earl of, October 14, 1744
satellites, communication, December 19, 1958
Schubert, Franz, January 31, 1797
Schulz, Charles, October 3, 1950
Schweitzer, Albert, January 14, 1875
Scorpio, October 24
Seuss, Dr. See Geisel, Theodore Seuss.
Sewell, Anna, March 30, 1820
sewing machines, September 10, 1846
Shakespeare, William, April 23, 1564. See also Valentine's Day.
Sitting Bull, December 10, 1909
Sixteenth Amendment. See United States — Constitution.
Skylab 2, July 28, 1973
slavery, January 7, 1800; February 20,

1895; March 10, 1913; May 9, 1800; October 2, 1800; December 18, 1865. See also Emancipation Proclamation; United States — Constitution, Thirteenth Amendment
Smalls, Robert, April 5, 1839
Smith, Margaret Chase, September 13, 1948; December 14, 1897
Socrates, June 5, c. 469 B.C.
SOS, November 22, 1906
sound barrier, October 14, 1947
sound motion pictures, October 26, 1927
tures, sound.
Sousa, John Philip, November 6, 1854
South Carolina, May 23, 1788
South Dakota, November 2, 1889
South Pole, October 25, 1988; December 14, 1919
space. See Apollo II; Challenger space shuttle; Gagarin, Yuri; Glenn, John; Ride, Sally; Skylab 2; Sputnik; Tereshkova, Valentina; White, Edward.
space shuttle. See Challenger space shuttle.
space walk, June 4, 1965
Spitz, Mark, February 10, 1950
Spring, March 21
Sputnik, October 4, 1957; October 14, 1890
stamps. See postage stamps.
standard time, March 13, 1884
Stanton, Elizabeth Cady, November 12, 1815
"Star-Spangled Banner, The," September 14, 1814
Statue of Liberty, July 22, 1849
steamboats, January 12, 1812
Stevenson, Robert Louis, November 13, 1850
stock market crash, October 19, 1987; October 29, 1929
Summer, June 21
Sutter, John, January 24, 1848

Tabei, May 23, 1975
Taft, William Howard, September 15, 1857
Tallchief, Maria, January 24, 1925

Taurus, April 20
Taylor, Zachary, January 7, 1800; November 24, 1784
Tchaikovsky, Peter Ilich, May 7, 1840; December 18, 1892
telephone directories, February 21, 1878
telephones, March 3, 1847; March 7, 1876
teletype, September 9, 1875
Tennessee, June 1, 1796
Tereshkova, Valentina, June 16, 1963
Texas, December 29, 1845
Thanksgiving Day, October 24, 1788; November
Thayer, Frederick, April 12, 1877
thermometers, May 14, 1686
Thirteenth Amendment. *See* United States — Constitution.
Thorpe, Jim, May 28, 1886
Tilden, Samuel J., October 4, 1822
Titanic, April 15, 1912; September 1, 1985
Tolkein, J(ohn) R(onald) R(euel), January 3, 1892
Tombaugh, Clyde, February 18, 1930
Treaty of Paris, September 3, 1783
Truman, Harry S., May 8, 1884; July 16, 1945; October 11, 1884
Tubman, Harriet, March 10, 1913
Turner, Nat, October 2, 1800
Twain, Mark. *See* Clemens, Samuel Langhorne.
Tyler, John, March 29, 1790

United Nations, January 30, 1882; October 11, 1884; October 24, 1945
United Nations Day, January 30, 1882. *See also* Human Rights Day.
United States — Constitution, September 17–23; Bill of Rights, March 16, 1751. ratification, January 2, 1788; January 9, 1788; February 6, 1788; April 28, 1788; May 23, 1788; May 29, 1790; June 21, 1788; June 25, 1788; July 26, 1788; November 21, 1789; December 7, 1787; December 12, 1787; December 18, 1787. Thirteenth Amendment, December 18, 1965; January 1, 1863. Fourteenth Amendment,

February 15, 1820; May 17, 1954. Fifteenth Amendment, February 15, 1820; March 30, 1870; November 12, 1815. Sixteenth Amendment, February 25, 1913. Nineteenth Amendment, February 15, 1820; August 26, 1920; November 12, 1815
United States — Labor Dept., March 4, 1913
United States Weather Service, February 9, 1870
Uranus, September 23, 1846
Utah, January 4, 1896

Valentine's Day, February 14
Van Buren, Martin, December 5, 1782
Van Gogh, Vincent, March 30, 1853
Vermont, March 4, 1791
Verne, Jules, February 8, 1823; May 5, 1867; October 2, 1872
Vespucci, Amerigo, March 9, 1454
Veteran's Day, November 11
Virginia, June 25, 1788
Virgo, August 23

washing machines, March 28, 1797; public, April 18, 1934
Washington (state), November 11, 1889
Washington, Booker T., April 5, 1856
Washington, George, February 22, 1732; April 28, 1758; June 8, 1786
Watergate, January 9, 1913; June 17, 1972; July 14, 1913
Webster, Daniel, January 7, 1800
Webster, Noah, April 14, 1828; October 16, 1758
West Virginia, June 20, 1863
White, Edward, June 4, 1965
White, E(lwyn) B(rooks), July 11, 1899
White House, March 15, 1767; March 16, 1751; October 30, 1735; November 1, 1800
Whitman, Walt, May 31, 1819
Whitney, Eli, March 15, 1794; December 8, 1765
Wilder, Laura Ingalls, February 7, 1867
Wilson, Woodrow, May 29, 1914; October 21, 1833; December 28, 1856

windshield wipers, November 10, 1903
winter, December 21
Wisconsin, May 29, 1848
women's rights. *See* Anthony, Susan B.;
  Stanton, Elizabeth Cady; United
  States — Constitution, Nineteenth
  Amendment.
Woodhull, Victoria C., September 23,
  1838
Woodson, Carl. *See* Black History
  Month.
World War II, July 8, 1935; July 16, 1945;
  September 1, 1939; December 7, 1941.
  See also Holocaust, Jewish.

Wright, Frank Lloyd, June 8, 1869
Wright, Orville, August 19
Wright, Wilbur, May 14, 1908; August 19
Wyoming, July 10, 1890

X rays, March 27, 1845

Yeager, Chuck, October 14, 1947
Yellowstone National Park, March 1,
  1872
Yom Kippur, September/October
Yonge Street, February 16, 1796
Zodiac signs. *See* specific sign.